meet me at the Fudge Shop

praise for
Meet Me at the Fudge Shop

"I'm having a great time reading all about Jonathon Island and its people. This series is an amazing kickoff for summer and Lily and Declan's story is wonderful. Definitely a top contender for the top of your TBR list this summer."

—**Jesus Beach Girl Reads**

"Sweet as fudge, cheerful as sunshine, and as good as ice cream, this adorable story is definitely worth the read. Journey to Jonathon Island for a fun filled read."

—**Joni, GOODREADS**

"So sweet! Okay, but really it was a great book. I loved reading Lindsay and Rachel's book from beginning to end. This story made me want to yell at a couple characters and then cry and laugh alongside others. And it definitely left me craving a good chunk of fudge. Great job ladies! The third installment of Jonathon Island did not disappoint!"

—**Kate, GOODREADS**

"Loved this sweet story. *Meet Me at the Fudge Shop* has it all—bitter family feud, former high school sweethearts now rivals, close proximity, and a competition over a fudge shop. I enjoyed the sparks that flew between Declan and Lily, the faith elements woven into this story, and how Declan's and Lily's strengths and personality complement each other. Such a fun read."

—Allyson, GOODREADS

"Warning! This book will activate your sweet tooth! And it'll satisfy your craving for a sweet, second-chance romance between two great characters, Declan and Lily, who are easy to root for. Combine that with a multi-generational family feud with Declan and Lily caught in the middle, a unique contest peppered with suspicions of sabotage, the special charm of Jonathon Island, and the biblical wisdom I've come to expect from Sunrise books, and you have the recipe for a great read with "all manner of chaos and joy." (Awesome book quote!)"

—Natalie, GOODREADS

LINDSAY HARREL
& RACHEL D. RUSSELL

SUNRISE PUBLISHING

Meet Me at The Fudge Shop
Published by Sunrise Media Group LLC
Copyright © 2025 Sunrise Media Group LLC
Print ISBN: 978-1-963372-83-0
Ebook ISBN: 978-1-963372-84-7

This book is a work of fiction. Names, characters, places, and incidents are either products of the author's imagination or used fictitiously. Any similarity to actual people, organizations, and/or events is purely coincidental.

For more information about Lindsay Harrel and Rachel D. Russell, please access the authors' websites at the following addresses: www.lindsayharrel.com and www.racheldrussell.com.

Published in the United States of America.
Cover Design: Sunrise Media Group LLC

To everyone who has ever wondered if
their failures make them unlovable—the answer is a
resounding NO. This one is for you, beloved.

"The Lord does not look at the things people look at. People look at the outward appearance, but the Lord looks at the heart."

1 SAMUEL 16:7B NIV

Jonathon Island

Meet Me on Jonathon Island (prequel novella)
Meet Me at the Grand
Meet Me on Lilac Lane
Meet Me at the Fudge Shop
Meet Me on Blueberry Hill
Meet Me at Sunset Cove
Meet Me at the Christmas Cottage

JONATHON ISLAND
N
W E
S
Jonathon Family Home
Sullivan Pumpkin Farm
Lake Shore Drive
State Park
Sullivan Way
MacBride Resort
Airport
Jonathon Blvd
Sunset Cove
Quinn Ranch
Sugar Maple Ln
Blueberry Hills Neighborhood
LAKE HURON
Barrett House
Partridge Ln
Dahlia Dr
Lilac Ln
Zinnia Blvd
Poppy Place
Rose Rd
Blueberry Blvd
Pinnacle Dr
Blueberry Hills Park
GRAND HOTEL
Main Street
Downtown
Marina Way
Marina

One

GENIUS DIDN'T ALWAYS STRIKE AT three a.m. on a Friday in June, but when it did, it involved caramel, a decadent truffle center, and roasted cashews—all wrapped in a hand-dipped, dark chocolate shell with a zigzag of white chocolate garnish to make it pop.

Lily Hart's secret ingredient? Bergamot oil, just the right number of drops to create a citrusy, herby deliciousness.

Elusive. Mesmerizing. Sublime.

So what if she hadn't slept last night? Hadn't even gone home after working a grueling twelve-hour shift. But that's what was demanded if you wanted to be an apprentice to Master Chocolatier Oscar Granger at Palm Coast's Florida Sullivan Resort.

Who needed sleep, anyway?

This was brilliance. And yes, it had taken her all night,

but these candies were her ticket to having Oscar's ear at long last. To being more than a grunt worker.

To finally proving to herself—to everyone back home—that she *was* successful. Or at least was on her way.

She glanced past the gleaming commercial-grade, stainless steel prep station, where The Sullivan's kitchen staff would soon be cooking up one of the best breakfast spreads this side of Orlando, toward the gleaming glass clock set over the swinging double doors that led to an opulent dining room. Soon, Oscar and her fellow apprentices would walk into the kitchen and make their way toward the pastry section in the back corner, roll up their sleeves, and begin another day of creating the award-winning desserts worthy of The Sullivan's acclaim.

And she'd have one already prepared for Chef Oscar Granger, award-winning, albeit exacting, baker, head of the pastry kitchen.

He'd take one look—and then one taste and . . .

Well, her big sacrifice of moving thirteen hundred miles from home, hours and hours of training, and even the scrutiny of her resort boss, Daniel Sullivan, would be worth it.

Not an apprentice anymore, but a full-on bakery chef, in one of the best pastry kitchens in Orlando, with multiple convection and deck ovens and space for roll-in ovens when needed, plus a stove, a long wooden island for bread making, a marble one for tabling chocolate, three massive refrigerators, a proofing case, two mixers, and every other tool a pastry chef could desire.

Take that, Declan-the-Jerk Kelley.

Blinking away the exhaustion that kept sneaking up on her, Lily took a swig of her coffee, now cold, and leaned down to take one final look over her confections at eye level. Ten gorgeous chocolates seemed to wink back at her from their placement on a simple white plate with a golden caramel spiral. She inhaled the sweet, rich chocolate aroma.

Mmm. Yes. Genius.

Grabbing her pen, she added one final word to her recipe card.

Enjoy.

"Lily!"

She jumped, her pen clattering onto the island as she glanced up to find her coworker-slash-friend Kayleigh standing over her, hands on her hips.

Kayleigh sported a frown to go with her stark-white apron and brown hair pulled tight into a bun at the base of her neck. "How long have you been here?"

"Hi." Lily straightened, smiled. "All night. But look what beauty my efforts produced."

"All night? But why?"

"I couldn't exactly create on my wonky stovetop. I needed the chocolate tempering machine—"

"No," Kayleigh said. "Why?" She pointed to the dessert.

Oh. "I just told you. I was creating." Lily rotated the plate. "Oscar can't ignore my suggestions anymore once he tastes these. I've worked here five years, Kayleigh. *Five years* of making the same old boring chocolates."

"And I've been here three. What's your point?"

"It's time for a change."

Kayleigh gave her a look. "Oscar *hates* change."

"He only *thinks* he hates change. But when he tastes these, he'll change—his mind, that is."

"I highly doubt that." Kayleigh lifted an eyebrow and pushed Lily's cup of coffee toward her, as if to indicate she needed to drink more.

Fine, maybe she *was* getting punchy.

Lily drained her cup and tossed it into the garbage. "You'll see. These chocolates will wake him up from the boring dessert world he's been living in. He'll discover there are more ingredients than caramel, walnuts, and peanut butter—though I have nothing against any of them, if jazzed up a bit."

"Oscar likes classic desserts. That's the job, Lily. Besides, since when does the word dessert belong with *boring*?" Kayleigh glanced back at the door. "He's going to be here in ten minutes. And we're supposed to be prepping for the McAllen wedding." She'd donned her pastry hat. "What kind of bride doesn't want a cake?"

"I think it's fun—a dozen different desserts and chocolates for the dessert table instead. Which is why I made these."

Kayleigh shook her head. "You know Oscar's never going to accept one of your suggestions, right?"

"You don't know that. Last month, Carlos suggested we add sprinkles to the strawberry Pop-Tart fudge for that kid's birthday bash we catered, and Oscar agreed to try it."

"But that was *Carlos*."

"Yeah, the Golden Boy." She finger-quoted the words.

"The man has zero imagination. Sprinkles? For a ten-year-old boy? How about the sparklers I suggested?"

"Carlos is smarter than you think. He's already created a five-year plan to own his own shop. *He's* going places."

Lily blinked at her. "And what, I'm stuck in a vat of cooling chocolate hardening around my feet? Seriously. Did you not see these chocolates?" She held up the plate. "*Perfection.*"

But Kayleigh wasn't looking at her. In fact, she pushed past her and peered into the tempering machine. "Lily, you need to clean this. You know Oscar insists on a spotless kitchen at the start of the day."

Oh. "I guess I got too involved with finishing the chocolates." She hurried toward the tempering machine, grabbed a ten-pound mold, and flipped the switch to empty what was left of the chocolate from last night's batch into it. The chocolate pumped out steadily at first, then slower, filling the air with the sugar-laden smell of melted chocolate.

"I'll get these." Kayleigh walked Lily's spatula and a few other tools to the sink and began washing them.

"Thank you." The chocolate stream ended, and Lily moved the chocolate mold to the counter. Then she removed the auger from the machine and placed it in the right side of the sink. "I'll wash that in a minute."

"I don't mind."

Lily stopped at the exasperation in Kayleigh's tone. "Clearly you do."

Kayleigh picked up the mold, started scrubbing. "You just always do this."

"Do what?"

"Lose track of time, get your head stuck in the clouds, forget about what you're *supposed* to be doing."

Her words struck something deep inside Lily—and a memory surfaced from long ago. Another voice, much angrier, more masculine, saying similar things. She pushed the thought aside. No. She was different now.

But Kayleigh's words still stabbed at her. And maybe she hadn't changed that much because shoot, it ignited all her defenses.

"What I'm *supposed* to be doing here is becoming a better chocolatier. Learning from one of the greats. But how can we become great, how can we push ourselves to become better, if we aren't allowed to experiment, to create? That's the best part of this whole job."

Kayleigh dropped the clean mold into the rinse sink, looked at her, suds on her arms. "The best part of this job is keeping it. We've got an amazing opportunity here."

"I know that."

"Especially after the pandemic." Kayleigh dove again into the sudsy water, this time with the auger. "You're lucky you had a connection with Mr. Sullivan. I waited two years, and called every week, hoping they'd take my apprentice application."

No, she was lucky that her childhood friend Dani Sullivan had talked up Lily to her father, Daniel, who had grown up eating the Hart Family Fudge.

No, lucky might be her family's shop *not* dying after the pandemic.

Maybe she didn't believe in luck, really. Just . . . reality.

Tempered occasionally with a good dessert. Like Mr. Sullivan said, desserts brought people together.

She wanted to believe that with everything inside her.

"Listen, I'm grateful that Oscar hired me."

"Are you?" More suds went flying as Kayleigh dropped the auger into the rinse sink. "Because you seem intent on throwing that opportunity away."

Okay, ouch. "I just think this job should be, I don't know, fun. Creative." She scraped the remaining chocolate down the drain.

Kayleigh sighed. "I'm sorry, Lily. I shouldn't have said that. You've clearly got a lot of talent. I just think you should be careful. Stay focused. I won't always be here to clean up your messes."

Lily's head shot up. Never mind the *clean up your messes* part. "Are you *leaving*?"

Kayleigh grabbed a towel. Turned, her mouth tight.

Oh no.

Finally, "Oscar recommended me for a job as Assistant Master Chocolatier at a new hotel in Nashville."

A beat. Then, somehow, "Wow. Congratulations," emerged from her mouth. Nah, she could do better. Kayleigh was her *friend*. "That sounds like an amazing opportunity. But I'll miss you."

Kayleigh lifted a shoulder. "They wanted someone with a degree. Otherwise, I'm sure Oscar would have recommended you, since you've been here longer than me."

She didn't bother to argue that an associate's degree was a degree. But Lily knew what Kayleigh meant. They wanted a bachelor's degree, and Kayleigh had graduated top of her class with a bachelor's in Chocolates and Confectionery Arts Entrepreneurship from the Sunshine State Culinary Institute.

The same program Lily had failed out of five years ago. So yeah, there was that.

"Lily . . ." Kayleigh took a step toward her.

Lily held up her hand. "I'm fine. It's fine. And great for you. Seriously. You deserve it." She gave Kayleigh a quick hug. "And to celebrate—here." She moved to her plate of chocolates, pulling one off and holding it out to Kayleigh's hands. "You can be the first to try them."

"You haven't tried one yet?"

"Don't need to. I did several small batches that weren't right, but I just have a feeling about this batch."

"You and your feelings." Kayleigh huffed out a laugh. "Honestly, they're usually right. At least where chocolate's concerned."

"Thank you." Lily took a bow, then grinned and held up a second chocolate. "Here's to new beginnings."

Kayleigh's eyes shimmered with unshed tears, a rare sight. "That means a lot, Lily. And I know you'll get your big break someday."

The sentiment warmed Lily's heart. "If this chocolate is as amazing as I think it is, maybe sooner rather than later."

"I hope so." Then Kayleigh took a bite of the chocolate. Her eyes closed and she tilted her head toward the ceiling. Then groaned. "Okay, I think I just got seven cavities. That's delicious."

Lily pumped her fist and then took her own bite. Flavor exploded on her tongue—unique, immersive.

And yes, perfect.

The door slammed open behind her. "Good morning," a baritone rang out.

Carlos stood on the other side of the island, staring at the kitchen behind Lily, his bushy black eyebrows bunched together. He made a huffing noise and shook his head. Gave a small grin. "You are in so much trouble, Hart."

What—?

But behind him, through the door walked Oscar, a tall fifty-something with a handlebar mustache and piercing brown eyes.

His gaze landed on the tempering machine, still crusted with chocolate on the inside.

He looked at her. "Tell me." And then he pointed at the machine.

"I'm sorry, sir. I was just getting the machine cleaned."

"You mean the machine I assigned you to clean last night?"

Lily darted a glance at Kayleigh, whose eyes widened.

"Um, yes. Well, actually, I did clean it but then took the initiative to create some new chocolates for tonight. I worked all night on a new recipe for a bergamot chocolate crunch. That's not the name—I haven't come up with the name yet, actually, but—"

"Ms. Hart—"

Nope, she couldn't stop now. "Try one, sir. I think this could be our next big thing. I even wrote down the recipe so we could mass produce it for tonight's wedding if you like it."

"Tonight's menu is already set."

"Sir, if you'll just try one, I think—"

He held up a hand. "I don't pay you to think. I pay you to do what I assign you. And you clearly haven't done that."

"No, but if you'll just try—"

"This isn't the first time, either. You know what's holding you back? Discipline. You're impulsive and flighty. Not dependable."

She stilled, the words pinning her in place. No, that wasn't . . . she wasn't—

"If you could just taste—"

"I don't need to."

And then he walked over to her plate of chocolates, picked it up, and . . .

Dumped it in the trash.

She stared at the mess, then back at him. "Have you lost your mind? That—those took me all night!"

And maybe something just snapped inside her. "They were delicious. Artwork. Pomp and circumstance. It's a medley of flavors, a symphony for the mouth. And you just dumped them because of what? Pride? Just take a look at the recipe!"

He just stared at her, nostrils flaring.

Okay, so maybe . . . um. She cut her voice low. "I'm sorry, I'm not trying to insult you or your work, but—"

"That's enough, Ms. Hart." He snatched the recipe card from her hand, glancing at it, then back to her. "The thing you don't seem to understand is that this is *my* kitchen. My kitchen, my rules, my recipes. When you have your own kitchen—and honestly, Ms. Hart, I *very much doubt* you'll ever reach that level of success—*you* can decide what to make. Until then . . ."

He ripped the recipe in half, then again, and again. Then he added the papers to the chocolate, spilled in with the other debris from last night's dinner.

She barely had a voice. "Why did you do that?" She took a breath, found more of it. "I've given you five years of my life. I've catered to your every stupid whim, spent countless hours doing tedious work, cleaning and sanitizing, and—this is how you treat me?"

She might be shouting now, so she schooled her voice. Hated the tears that rimmed her eyes. "That was mine. You had no right."

"Correction," he snapped, stepping up to her. "You used company resources to create it, so it was actually *mine*. And I decided I didn't want it." Oscar slid the garbage receptacle back into place. "Just like you, Ms. Hart. I don't want you."

She blinked. "What?"

"I don't want you here anymore. As of this moment, you are no longer an employee of The Sullivan."

Lily just stared at him, the words not quite landing. The silence buzzed loudly in her ears.

What—?

No, no, no. This is not how things were supposed to go. Lily pressed her lips together and blinked her eyes rapidly. She would *not* cry. Crying hadn't stopped her grandpa's disappointment in her. Hadn't stopped the Kelleys from accusing her, or Declan from turning away from her. Hadn't stopped Professor Hamilton from failing her.

Oscar folded his arms over his chest. "Did you not hear me? You're fired, Ms. Hart. And I won't be giving you a reference, so don't even ask." He pointed toward the door. "Your chocolate-making days are over."

Declan Kelley stepped off the Chicago "L" train—and straight into his new life.

Adjusting his tie, he made his way down the platform, relishing the tug of the crowd flowing around him. Everyone had somewhere to be, something to do.

Including, finally, him.

At seven thirty, the July humidity lay on his skin, his shirt sticky under his three-piece suit. But not even the oppressive heat could steal the pep in Declan's step as he approached the skyscraper on The Loop where McGentry Food Company occupied the top four stories. Was his corner office visible from way down here? His neck craned upward, taking in the building's seemingly endless rows of windows glinting off the rising sun—a gorgeous sight, given how cloudy the summer had been so far.

If Declan believed in omens of good luck, he might think the appearance of the sun on his first day as McGentry's business operations manager portended good things.

But Declan just believed in the value of hard work. And goodness knew he'd worked his tail off—both in his career so far, and all throughout his MBA program—to get to this place. Add to that six months of job searching . . .

But that was then, this was now, and hello to a perfect future.

Cold air blasted him as he stepped inside, blowing so hard he smoothed his hand along his hair, but his new gel had seemed to hold things steady up top. Being inside muted the din of honking taxis but enveloped him into a sea of people in suits, many talking on their Bluetooth devices, dressy shoes echoing against the travertine and through the stories-tall lobby. Declan flashed his shiny new-as-of-yesterday badge at a security guard, who waved him in, and headed toward the bank of six elevators.

His phone vibrated. He pulled it out—Brandon, his cousin. Probably just calling to wish him good luck, but the doors to the elevator opened, so he declined the call and got on with a handful of others.

He'd text him back later.

Scanning his badge, Declan hit the button for the eighty-first floor.

Eighty-first. Which meant a view of the Windy City. *Looks like we made it.* A tune sang in his head as he flashed a grin at the pretty brunette in a pencil skirt across from him. She smiled back.

Oh—he didn't want to get too friendly. He pulled out his phone, swiping open his email as an excuse to look somewhere else. Not that he wanted to be rude, but after Kim, the last thing on his mind was dating.

His phone vibrated in his hand. Brandon again. Weird. His cousin wasn't the type to call twice.

Not unless something was wrong.

He glanced up at the numbers. Only at floor eighteen, with clearly five more to go.

Declan answered, pitched his voice low. "What's up,

Brandon?" He put a hand to his other ear, bent his head to capture his voice.

"Did I catch you at a bad time?"

"I'm on an elevator—"

"Right. Sorry." Wind blew across Brandon's receiver. Probably his tour-guide cousin was standing on a cliff somewhere in Arizona, overlooking a different kind of view. "And now you're the jerk talking in the lift."

"Yep."

The elevator stopped and opened. Two of the businessmen stepped out, one glancing over his shoulder at Declan with a frown. Yeah, yeah, he knew it was rude. Declan raised his hand in apology but the guy was already walking down the thick-carpeted hallway.

A sigh came over the phone, and he forgot about the men. "What's going on?"

"It's Grandma."

Sweet Grandma Kelley, who had been frailer and frailer every time Declan had visited home. Who never had a cross word to say to anyone, even though the Kelleys (except for maybe his Aunt Jill) weren't generally known for their ability to win friends.

"What about Grandma?"

"She had a small . . . episode last night."

"What do you mean, *episode*? Like a heart attack? A stroke?" He glanced at the brunette. She'd turned, staring at the numbers, as if trying not to listen.

"She fainted and they're still running tests to verify what happened. But she's stable now."

"Good. Stable's good." He blew out a breath. "Is she

at the Jonathon Island clinic or did they take her to the mainland?"

"She's at the Port Joseph Hospital, but they said given the fact she's eighty-three, they'll keep her overnight for observation. Sorry I didn't call you sooner. We didn't want to call until we had good news. I know how much she means to you—to all of us—and didn't want you to worry."

Oops, he hadn't realized he was pacing until the door opened and another man got out, and the woman took another step away from him.

He retreated to the corner, facing the wall, and fought to keep his voice low. "I appreciate the call, but you definitely should have told me sooner."

He'd never be ready to lose Grandma, but especially not now—before he'd figured out some way to restore his family's faith in him.

But this job . . . maybe it was a start.

"So she's okay?"

"She's okay. Physically, at least."

Declan stilled. "What do you mean?"

"Apparently the reason she had the episode in the first place is because the county is foreclosing on her home."

Foreclosing—it took a second. "What?" Declan schooled his voice as the elevator stopped again. He glanced, and the woman got out, leaving him, blessedly, alone. "Why would they do that? The house has been in the family for more than a hundred years. It's on the same road as all of us. All the kids. Aw, we should have never let her live alone."

"We? Dude, you haven't lived here for ten years—since graduation."

"I know, I know—sorry, it's just . . ."

Brandon's voice softened. "I get it. You never really leave the island."

Huh. But he was trying to, wasn't he?

"Apparently, she owes ten years' worth of back taxes . . . ever since Grandpa died," Brandon said. "And she didn't tell anyone, despite multiple warnings from the county. Now, it's too late."

Declan swore under his breath just as the elevator opened again. Oops, his floor.

He stood there, not moving.

This was his fault, wasn't it?

The doors started to close, but he stuck his foot into them. "Why didn't she ask Dad for help figuring out her taxes?" Frank Kelley, Grandma's oldest son, was a CPA and handled all of the accounting and marketing for the three family businesses.

"He asked the same thing. Apparently she didn't want to be a bother."

"Aw, Grandma."

A female receptionist greeted visitors from behind a sleek black desk, the logo of the McGentry Food Company behind her. She sent Declan a friendly smile, wiggling her fingers at him while she spoke into her fancy headset.

Shoot. He took his foot out of the door. It closed.

Declan leaned against the back wall. "Surely someone in the family has the money to bail her out of this."

"It's a lot of money, Dec."

"I get it—I'd do it myself, but most of my savings went to paying down my student loans and living while trying to land this job."

"I get it too. We all want to help. It's Grandma. But everyone's strapped—money is tied up in businesses and home and debt. They don't have enough pooled between them. And you know what the pandemic did to us. Every restaurant is leveraged, just trying to stay afloat. Mom with Good Day Coffee, and Uncle Patrick with Kelley's Bar & Grill, and your mom with Martha's on Main. And it doesn't help that the competition has rolled into town with the one-dollar houses—"

"The what?"

"It's a marketing thing—the town has been giving away houses for a buck for businesses that move to the island."

"Seriously?"

Someone had called the elevator, and it began to move.

"You do know they're restoring the Grand Sullivan Hotel, right?"

"I feel like Mom mentioned that, but kind of zoned out when she was talking. Shoot. I have to go, bro." The doors opened on the floor below, and Declan got out into a hallway of law offices. He followed the signs to the stairs. "Thanks for letting me know about Grandma, and please keep me posted. Are you on island right now?"

"I'm at the hospital in Port Joseph at the moment, but yeah, visiting my mom for a while. But Dec—"

"Declan, is that you?"

Oh, great. He opened the door to the stairwell. "Hi,

Mom." Clearly she'd stolen Brandon's phone from his hands. "I heard about Grandma. I'll be praying for her, all right?"

"Yes, it's just awful." But Martha Kelley's voice didn't sound tearful or weepy. It sounded . . . well, the same it always did. No nonsense. Commanding. There was a reason she'd assimilated so well into the Kelley restaurant dynasty on the island, running the café herself after she and Dad had gotten married, changing its name from Kelley's Diner to Martha's on Main. Nobody could say no to her. "You need to come home right away."

He stood in the cold hallway and rubbed the vein between his eyes—the one that always throbbed when he spoke with Mom. "I'm starting my new job today, remember?"

"Right." She sighed. "If they're a good company, they'll understand that family comes first."

Ha. And the words were right there, on his lips—then why didn't she get along with her own brother-in-law? Then again, if anyone outside the family ever spoke ill of Patrick, she chewed that person out. Apparently, only a Kelley could insult a Kelley and get away with it.

"Listen, Mom. Brandon said Grandma's doing okay. Maybe I can come visit this weekend, once she's out of the hospital." He did the mental math—he'd have to leave early on Friday to beat the traffic out of town for the Fourth of July weekend. Six hours to the ferry in Port Joseph, and then another hour to the island.

"You should be here. Now."

He sighed. "Mom, I appreciate your desire for our family to be together at a time like this—"

"What I *appreciate* is that shrewd brain of yours. You've got financial savvy, and we need that now to save Grandma's house."

"Me? What about Dad? He's the accountant."

"And he's good at what he does, but I need someone who can think outside the box."

Voices lifted in the hallway. Declan caught sight of several businessmen and women stepping off the elevators. He glanced at his watch, frowned. People were starting to arrive for work, and he was going to be late for his eight a.m. with his new boss. What kind of impression would *that* make?

"Send me all the information and documents, and I'll work on a solution from here." He started up the stairs.

"Declan James Kelley, this needs to be your main focus. Put that big MBA brain of yours to use."

"I'm trying," he muttered.

"What's that?"

"Nothing." Another glance at his watch. "Mom, seriously, I'll call you back in a bit. I promise, I'll think of something."

"It's so sad. Grandpa never forgot to pay his mortgage. Grandma's been lost without Grandpa."

And there it was. The reason he'd mostly stayed off island for the last decade except for holidays and a few weeks in the summers between classes.

Because the guilt would always be there, would always be a part of him, something he'd never forget. And if he did, his family was right there, more than happy to remind him of what he owed them.

What he owed Grandma.

Blowing out a frustrated breath, he squeezed his eyes shut for a moment. "I'll do my best to come."

Another sigh. "The family needs you, Declan. We can't lose that house."

She made it sound like they were in the mafia. Sheesh.

"Mom. I can't request a leave of absence on my *first day of work*."

"I know." Her voice shook.

"No, I don't think you do. If I do this—there's no guarantee my job will be here waiting for me when I return. And it took me six months to find *this* one."

"I know." A big sob. "It's fine. I just . . . we need you, Declan."

Oh, shoot, those were the words, weren't they? He closed his eyes, pinching the bridge of his nose. "Calm down, Mom." He sighed, and the words just spilled out. "I won't let you down."

Because it had only taken one selfish decision to let down the entire family ten years ago. One mistake that had changed everything. That had made him the family pariah.

And the consequences of that error in judgment had been fatal.

"I'll be there as soon as I can."

He barely heard her thank him as he hung up.

Then he sighed and stared up. So much for his first day of triumph.

Two

HER CHOCOLATE-MAKING DAYS MIGHT be over, but Oscar Granger had absolutely no say over how much ice cream Lily Hart could produce. And it was a lot.

Apparently, rage ice cream making was a thing.

"Our freezer is going to overflow soon." Lily's roommate and best friend Sadie Hudson breezed through the kitchen in her slacks and button-down blouse, setting her purse on the Formica countertop.

"Not if I eat it all first." Lily stuck a spoon into the top of her two-gallon ice cream maker, sampling the pistachio raisin flavor she'd just finished. Hmm. Not enough sugar in this batch. Grrr. She unhooked the base and carried the ice cream to the sink.

"Are you seriously going to throw that entire batch away?" Sadie reached for the base and grabbed a fresh spoon. Dipped it in and took a bite.

She groaned. "This is amazing. Lily! What's wrong with you? It would be a crime against humanity to throw this away."

"It's not amazing *enough*."

The glow of a western sun cast golden light through the window. Was it seriously already early evening? Sadie was home from her copywriting job, so it must be. And what had Lily done with her entire day? Made a lousy batch of ice cream that was either going to melt into oblivion or find its way into her mouth, adding another five pounds onto her hips like the ones she'd gained in the last twelve days.

Since being fired. Losing her career.

Epically failing at the only thing she'd ever wanted.

No wonder she was consuming ice cream at an alarming, just-a-taste rate.

"Hey." Sadie hip checked her. "Don't let Oscar get into your head. You'll find something else."

"I've already exhausted all of my old culinary school contacts. Nobody is hiring. Or maybe it's just that nobody is hiring *me*."

"You've got to give it longer than a week and a half, friend. Be patient."

"Patience is not a virtue I naturally possess." Lily worked her fingers through her pale blonde hair, now streaked with a little, I-lost-my-job-depression lavender. "Maybe my look is the problem. I could dye my hair brown and serious like yours. It worked for Kayleigh."

Kayleigh, who had already left for Nashville and texted

Lily a picture of her gorgeous new kitchen at her gorgeous new resort job.

Meanwhile, Lily was sweating it out in her tiny apartment kitchen day in and day out. She'd tried making chocolates, but her stovetop kept giving her fits. Thus, the ice cream. Besides, something about the whirring machine—watching the vanilla and cream swirl together to create something beautiful and rich, something surprising—comforted her.

As much as one could be comforted when one's whole world had fallen apart, of course.

Sadie tugged on one of Lily's waves. "You'd never make it as a brunette. We're *too* serious."

Her playful comment twisted something in Lily's gut. "And that's my problem, isn't it? It's always been my problem." Turning, she pulled two bowls from the cabinet and scooped pistachio ice cream into each one. "I'm not serious enough."

"That's not what I meant." Sadie gathered two fresh spoons from the rickety drawer that needed fixing. "You're creative and fun and spontaneous. That's why we're such a good pair. You make my life far more interesting. Think about how boring the last ten years would have been if you hadn't moved out here to live with me."

"That's true. You *are* pretty boring."

"I didn't say *I* was boring." Sadie made a face and stuck the spoons into the ice cream, then stole one of the bowls and headed for the worn red couch in the den. She gestured around the room, with its bright green accent wall, yellow side tables Lily had rescued from the apartment dumpsters and refinished, and a giant painting of the beach done in retro pinks and blues. "Remember how this place looked when you first moved in?"

Uh, yes, she did. Drab browns and grays. "I thought you hated all the color." Ice cream bowl in hand, Lily joined her friend on the couch, sinking into the soft deep cushions and propping her feet up on the dazzling blue coffee table. "You said it looked like a paint palette threw up in here."

Sadie laughed and pushed against Lily's knee. "You know I just like to tease you. The point is, you bring life and color to all you do, and that's something I deeply admire about you. So don't let stupid Oscar try to take away what makes you special. He's one man with one opinion. Listen to someone who really knows you."

"And see, that's why you're my best friend."

"Only because you were nice to me whenever I came to visit Gramps and Gran every summer." She dug into her ice cream. "By the way, have you talked with Dani lately?"

"Not since I visited the island last month. She's busy with the Tourism Bureau. I told you about her crazy idea about rebuilding the Grand."

"The Sullivan Hotel? Wow." Sadie took another bite. "Too bad your family didn't own an ice cream shop. You could go back to the island and open that."

"Right. Can you see the scandal?" Her hand ran through the air, like a headline. "Hart Family Fudge gets frozen makeover. My grandparents would roll in their graves." She finished her ice cream. "No. Florida is where I belong."

"Please."

"Seriously. The farthest state away from Declan Kelley."

"He's not even in Michigan anymore."

"Illinois is close enough," Lily said.

"You're going to have to forgive him sometime."

"Eat your ice cream."

Sadie laughed.

"Unfortunately, ice cream won't solve my problem." She set her bowl on the coffee table. "Oscar might be a jerk, but he's a jerk with a good reputation. Any potential employer will see that I spent the last five years working for him, and they'll want a reference. Besides, there's the pesky little thing about not finishing culinary school. Why would an employer even give me a chance when there are a slew of perfectly qualified candidates graduating with honors every year? I'm just a washed-up has-been."

"Are you tasting what I'm tasting?" Sadie shoved another bite of ice cream into her mouth. A little dribbled onto her white blouse and she wiped it with her finger, licking it off. "You are not washed-up. No matter what kind of dessert you're making, you're talented and experienced." She also set her bowl on the coffee table and turned to face Lily. "And okay, so say you're right and nobody in Orlando will hire you. There's still a possibility you aren't considering."

"And what's that?"

"I'm not enthusiastic about this option, mind you. But maybe it would make you the happiest."

"Spit it out, girl."

"Well." Sadie absently smoothed her finger along a crease at the top of her black pants. "When you got home from visiting your family, didn't you say your brother and his girlfriend asked you to reopen Hart Family Fudge?"

"I mentioned why I like Florida, right?"

"Seriously. From what I heard, Declan Kelley hasn't been back on the island for nearly a decade. I think you can set your defenses at Defcon 3."

"Maybe." Lily got up, picked up the bowls. "But yes, Mia asked me to reopen the shop. She was trying to fill the vacancies on Main Street with viable businesses to bring people back to the island. Jonathon Island is famous for its fudge. Or used to be. Plus, they had this crazy scheme to give every new business owner an abandoned downtown home for just one dollar—an enticement to draw people there."

"That's really smart. So you'd even get a place to live out of the deal."

"True. But I told them no." Because she'd already been *this close* to getting her own kitchen, to impressing Oscar. Or so she'd thought.

"It's still your family's shop though, right? Even though your parents had to close it, they still have the lease for it."

"True."

"Which means you could reopen it any time."

"Also true." Huh. She set the bowls in the sink, ran water in them. "As long as Mia hasn't opened another fudge shop. I'm guessing they would only want one, at least in the beginning."

"One." Sadie smiled. "Wasn't the whole reason you decided to move here and go to school was so that someday you could, and I quote, 'eventually move back to the island and beat the pants off the Kelley family fudge shop'?"

"Also true." Man, Sadie was on fire. "But then the shop closed, and I stayed."

"And the only reason it hasn't reopened since the pandemic ended is your mom's arthritis. But you could do it. You could move home and bring your family's legacy back to life."

The words reverberated in Lily's chest. A family legacy. Cody was reopening the family fishing business. Why shouldn't she also have a piece of history? Why couldn't she make her family just as proud as Cody made them?

Show them she could be serious and practical and successful.

Maybe this was how she did it.

"You sure you're not trying to get rid of me?" She came back over, plopped down beside Sadie. "You'd rather have a roommate who will let you get away with your ugly colored furniture?"

"Absolutely. That's my evil plan." Sadie nudged her. "I want you to be happy. Imagine it. You could experiment to your heart's content, no dull Oscar holding you back. You could put out all the best flavors. Elevate Hart Family Fudge higher than it's ever been, even when your Grandpa Hart ran the shop."

It sounded amazing. Better than amazing. To be back on the island, with her family . . .

To finally live up to Grandpa's legacy.

Still. "I really hate leaving you." And now her eyes burned. "Maybe . . ." She grabbed her friend's hand. "If I did this, you could come with me. You can do copywriting from anywhere. Your Grandma Henrietta would love it. *I* would love it."

Sadie squeezed, a sad smile taking over her face. "You know why I can't do that."

Lily sighed. It had been worth a shot. "I know. But maybe it's time to visit again?"

"Maybe. But we're not talking about me right now. We're talking about *you*, starting over. Taking control of your life and becoming the girl boss you were meant to be."

Girl boss. Rather than giving inspiration, the words made Lily freeze. "Only one problem with that picture. I failed out of my program because of the business classes, remember? Econ, accounting, marketing. I don't know the first thing about being a successful businesswoman."

"Sure you do. The only reason you failed is because you were so focused on the creative part and got distracted from finishing your business assignments. But that doesn't mean you didn't absorb what you need to know."

Hmm.

"And what you don't know, you ask for help. Your mom ran that business by herself for years after your dad's parents retired. Ask her for advice. Invest in a solid computer accounting program. I can even help with marketing when you're ready. The business stuff, you can get help with that. You've already got the most necessary ingredient for success."

"Chocolate?" Lily grinned in spite of herself.

"No, silly. You—and that creative brain of yours. You

can do this. And if not, then what's the worst that can happen?"

"Oh, I don't know. I go home, make a fool of myself and fail miserably, becoming the laughingstock of the island? Again?"

Sadie rolled her eyes. "First of all, that's not going to happen. But even if so, then at least you'd have tried."

"Yeah." Yeah. Hmm. That was true. If she could figure out some of the details—and if Mia hadn't already chosen someone else to open a fudge shop on the island—then maybe. "It's an open door, right?"

"Absolutely. The least you can do is peek your head through and see if it's dark and scary or bright and sparkly on the other side."

"You and your metaphors."

"Can't help it. It's the writer in me."

But she was right. This wasn't just *an* open door. At the moment, it was the only one.

Lily laughed. "Okay, then. Guess I've got a phone call to make." Standing, she walked toward her phone on the counter. "And afterward, whatever Mia says, we celebrate."

"Awesome. But can we celebrate with salads? Because all of this ice cream is gonna put me in a sugar coma."

Declan had stepped back in time to the island of his childhood. Hello, what had happened to Jonathon Island?

He stopped at the corner of Ferry and Main, a pack on his back and a suitcase at his side. Behind him, the familiar ferry horn cried out, a last call for passengers before the ferryboat turned around and headed back to the mainland.

The sun glinted off the shop windows down Main Street. Squinting, he read the sign to the shop on the corner, which had received a fresh coat of paint—Glass Treasures. Hmmm. That must be one of the new storefronts brought in by the town council, a revitalization effort to beautify the town and get the economy back on track.

A quick glance down Main Street said that they might be winning that fight. New shops mixed with old—Aunt Jill's coffee shop, with patrons coming and going despite the late afternoon hour. A new antiques store. The bank and the bar and grill, both boasting flowerpots overflowing with impatiens and begonias.

If they kept going like this, maybe tourists would find their way back to the once-vibrant island.

He turned left. Across the street, Declan could make out an actual flower shop—that was new too—along with a sophisticated storefront beside it labeled *Beautiful Homes Art and Realty.* Just beyond that lay the shuttered windows of the Hudson Bakery.

His mother's place still occupied her space, even farther down, with the public library bringing up the end of Main Street.

The Center for the Arts and the massive shell of the Grand Hotel—with scaffolding surrounding it—took up the view along the southwestern shoreline.

"Hey, cuz!"

Declan looked for the voice, realizing he'd stopped at the corner of Main and Jonathon Boulevard. Brandon waved to him from across the street. His muscled cousin looked like he was headed to a gym, wearing basketball shorts and a tight moisture-wicking shirt. He leaned against one of the four white posts standing sentinel outside the old two-story Hart fudge shop.

The wooden paneling of the old building had received a fresh coat of paint like the rest of the Main Street buildings. But the building appeared vacant, thanks to the grime on the inside of the windows and the faded crooked sign dangling from the green roof.

Declan crossed the street—currently free of cyclists and foot traffic, the only kind allowed on the island, since all motor vehicles, including golf carts, were banned now that the snow had gone. The horse-and-carriage combos that used to frequent the island hadn't been a thing since the pandemic, when all but a few horses had been taken to the mainland and the carriages put in livery storage.

Declan came up to Brandon. "You didn't have to walk all this way to pick me up."

"Oh yeah, I'm winded." He winked and they both laughed. The Kelley clan only lived up Jonathon Boulevard a few blocks away on Poppy Place. "But I'm a good guy like that." Brandon pulled Declan into a quick hug, nearly squeezing the life out of him. Declan wasn't out of shape himself, but Brandon was a beast. The hazards of his job, maybe.

Declan grabbed for his rolling suitcase, but his cousin—older than Declan's twenty-eight years by five—snatched it instead. Brandon headed up the boulevard.

"Didn't want me facing the firing squad alone, huh?"

"Oh, you won't be alone. The entire family is gathered to witness—I mean celebrate—your homecoming."

Right. His neck ached from his white-knuckled drive in bumper to bumper traffic, and the thought of facing all twelve members of the Kelley family was enough to make him want to turn around and climb aboard the next ferry.

"You sure they aren't just there to celebrate Fourth of July a day early?" Since almost the whole family worked in the restaurant industry, they typically celebrated holidays at different times than the rest of the town.

"Oh, yeah. That too." Brandon chuckled.

"Glad you think this is amusing." A seagull cawed as it flew overhead toward the water. "Besides, what's there to celebrate? I've left behind the perfect job to try to solve a problem of my own making."

"Come on, man. Grandma losing her house isn't your fault, no matter what your mom implied."

"Okay." Sure.

The road turned slightly uphill as it headed toward the older residential area just north of downtown. On either side of the road loomed seven of the largest homes on the island—gorgeous old Victorians with wraparound porches and turrets—along with a Greek Revival-style home with the Queen Anne cottage that used to house Kelley's Classic Fudge. Most of these homes were owned by rich people who liked to summer here.

Or had, before the downturn in the economy.

Maybe, if the town council's plans were actually successful, they'd return.

Brandon cleared his throat. "So what did your boss say, anyway?"

A breeze blew through the stately trees in the residential front lawns as they passed Rose Road, rustling the leaves and creating a cadence he always forgot when he returned to Chicago. Out here, a man could think—both a good and a bad thing, depending on the circumstances.

"Exactly what I expected. That he'd see if the guy I'm replacing can put off his retirement for a few extra weeks, but if I stay longer than four or five weeks, he can't guarantee he will hold my job. He wouldn't guarantee it either way, said that if a new prospect comes up and he could get them in sooner . . ."

"Sorry, man. That stinks. I know how hard you worked to land it."

Declan shrugged as they turned down Poppy Place. "It's what you do for family, right?"

"Your mom's guilt worked, huh?"

He shook his head. "Let's just say that I do this and maybe I fix . . . well, maybe things get better."

Silence. Then, "You're a good man, cuz. The family knows that."

"Whatever. You're a better man than me." A former adventure guide at the MacBride Resort, Brandon had only left the island out of sheer necessity, taking a job leading hiking tours at the Grand Canyon and surrounding northern Arizona trails. But Declan knew he worried constantly about his mom, Jill, who had always taken good care of Brandon, despite having him alone at the age of twenty. He'd move back here in a heartbeat if a viable job ever opened up.

"How's your vacation going?" Declan glanced toward Grandma's house as they walked by. The white paint of the three-bedroom bungalow with a small porch popped against the lavender trim.

"Not bad. I've gotten in some good hiking, helped Mom out a bit in the coffee shop." He glanced at him. "By the way, I moved my stuff to Grandma's. Figured it would be good to have someone with her right now."

"You beat me to it. I was going to volunteer." It would have been so much better than staying with his parents.

"No need."

"Her yard looks good."

"Yeah, Isaac and I did some work on Grandma's lawn today. We mowed, trimmed the trees, that kind of thing. Got it cleaned up since Frank and Patrick have been busy with the town revitalization stuff."

"Wait. Isaac? As in, *my younger brother*, Isaac?"

Brandon laughed. "The very one."

"How'd you get him to do more than sit around and play video games?"

"Aw, he's not the kid you left behind. Besides, I threatened to beat him up."

Declan snorted. "No you didn't. No one threatens Mom's baby—even when he's twenty-two years old with a beard."

"You know your mom made him start taking some shifts at the café, right?"

"Seriously? Good."

"She might be regretting it, though. The other day I stopped in and he was just standing there watching a sports game on the TV, moving his rag around an already clean table. For like five minutes. Lost in thought."

"He was always a dreamer. Used to take apart radios and try and create gadgets with them. Never put them back together." They passed Uncle Patrick and Aunt Whitney's house and approached the well-lit, two-story house where Declan had grown up. The lawn was perfectly manicured, the weeds all pulled, the garden blooming full and brilliant under the front window, and though many houses in this older neighborhood looked weatherworn—a common occurrence given their proximity to constant wind coming off the lake shore—there wasn't an inch of peeling paint to be seen.

Perfect. Just the way Mom liked it.

Brandon grabbed the suitcase handle and took it up the front porch stairs. "Ready?"

"As I'll ever be."

As his cousin opened the front door, waves of sound rushed out. The television, broadcasting the evening news. A triumphant shout of "I won!" mingled with groans.

And then there was the all-familiar bickering of his parents.

He followed his cousin into the foyer of the home and the smell rushed over him—the garlic and basil of his mother's lasagna, the scent of pasta boiling, and maybe the deep comfort of baked chocolate cookies. His mom's diner wasn't the most popular eating establishment on the island for nothing.

Declan peeled off his backpack and dropped it on the bench in the entryway. His leather jacket still hung on the hook there—funny Mom had never moved it. He touched it a second, and just like that, a memory rose—the scent of summer, laughter, a feeling of freedom.

Lily.

Stop. That wasn't him—was never really him.

"Declan? Is that you?" Mom popped her head into the hallway from the kitchen, a big black serving spoon in her hand. A dark green apron draped her heavyset figure, and a true smile graced her face. "My boy! You made it."

"Hey, Mom." He walked down the hallway, past the wall of historic family portraits, and leaned down to kiss her on the cheek. "Good to see you."

Declan glanced back into the kitchen, where his aunts Jill and Whitney were chopping vegetables. They waved, knives in hand, before returning to their conversation. At the four-person kitchen table, Patrick's kids—including Declan's eighteen-year-old cousin, Olive, and her two younger brothers, Scott and Donovan—played a round of UNO.

Brandon inched past Declan, giving his mom a squeeze on the shoulders before settling into the seat beside Olive and tapping the spot in front of him. They dealt him in.

Meanwhile, in the great room, Isaac and Patrick watched the Tigers baseball game, cans of soda in hand. Patrick, at least, offered a grunt and wave to Declan before turning back to the game.

His brother glanced at him, raised a chin, as if to say hey.

He raised his back. Hey.

But his gaze landed on the frail figure in the large, fraying recliner.

Grandma.

Even from here, he could sense the weariness in her—and not just because her eyes were closed, her mouth open in a clear indication she was dozing. But also, her graying hair, once a source of such pride, was unkempt, the curls too long for her perm. She wore a sweatsuit, so different from the slacks and blouse she used to wear even when cleaning her house—*Because you never know who will stop by, dear*—and her cheeks were sunken, the same pale color as her lips.

She looked, in a word, defeated.

"She's been excited to see you, but is still tired out from her stay at the hospital," Mom said in a low voice as she tucked a lock of her graying, dark hair back up into her messy bun. "Speaking of that, I think I've got a solution to her housing dilemma."

He blinked at her. "Already? We just talked yesterday."

"And I was just sitting around a hospital all day considering solutions. Nearly drove me batty."

Maybe Mom didn't need him at all. Which would be great, actually. "Do you want to talk now or wait until after dinner?"

Mom peeked inside the oven. "The lasagna still has about fifteen minutes. Let's go in the front room and chat. Ladies, can you watch the pasta on the stove for me?"

"Of course." Aunt Jill's bright red hair stood out in the muted colors of the room as she sliced another tomato.

She winked at Declan. "You two just go solve the world's problems."

"One of us has to," Mom muttered as she ushered Declan back down the hallway and into the small sitting room at the front of the house.

Despite the seventy-degree weather outside, the fireplace flickered, a blaze fighting for life. Two bookshelves flanked the mantel, holding an assortment of tomes and crystal figurines that held some sort of special meaning for his mom. As a kid, he'd never been allowed to sit in this room—the "fancy room"—and it felt all kinds of wrong as he sank into the white couch with a white crocheted blanket folded along the back. "So what's the idea?"

Mom sat, swinging her legs to the side so she faced him, hands folded in her lap. "As you know, I'm on the town council, and our plan to bring new businesses to town has been threefold: rebuild the Grand Hotel by the end of next year so our seasonal workers have housing and tourists have more options for where to stay. Number two, promise low rent on Main Street storefront leases for the first two years, and three, offer town-owned homes in this very neighborhood to new business owners for one dollar."

"Yes, it's quite the plan."

Behind Mom, Dad appeared in the doorway. He leaned against the frame, hands in his pockets. Bald, with pale blue eyes, he glanced at Declan, no smile. Declan didn't expect one.

"So, while I was pacing in the hospital waiting room, I had the thought—what if we could convince the county to release Edna's house to the town of Jonathon Island?"

"Why would they do that?"

Mom waved her hand. "It means nothing to them. I know for a fact—my old friend Sandy works at the bank and told me so herself—that they're overrun with fore-closed homes. Right now, they can barely give homes away here, let alone resell them. The house is more trouble than it's worth. Of course, they can't just give it back to Grandma, because they don't get a tax break doing that, but this way, they will."

Declan did the math, came out at net zero. "But that doesn't benefit us at all. So when the town owns the prop-erty—it's still out of Kelley hands."

"It does if the town ties Edna's home to the revitaliza-tion program. If the council attaches it to a storefront."

"I thought the council already filled all of the available storefronts."

"All but a few, most of which still are under lease by their previous owners or owned outright by someone other than Seb Jonathon."

The mayor, Seb Jonathon, also was the landlord to most of the buildings on Main Street, with a few exceptions. "Like the old Hudson bakery."

"Exactly." Mom tapped the side of her nose, and her blue eyes gleamed. "But there is one property whose lease has recently expired. Just three days ago, in fact."

The picture was getting clearer. "So you're thinking that if we can get the county to release the property to the town—"

"It's all but done. Sandy is pushing the paperwork through tonight."

Declan arched a brow at Mom. "Tonight? The day before the Fourth of July?"

"Time is of the essence. Besides, she owes me."

Dad grunted.

"Okay, so once you can get the property released to the town, you get the council to attach Grandma's house to the final storefront available for leasing . . ."

"Right."

"And"—he grinned—"you apply to run a business out of the storefront, thereby granting us ownership of Grandma's house for one dollar." He sat back. "Mom. You may have your crazy moments, but this . . . this is a brilliant business move. Problem solved."

Mom rubbed her hands together. "Not me. You."

Wait. "What? *Me*?"

"Yes, you. The rest of us are busy running our own businesses. You're the only one old enough and responsible enough—with the right experience—to open a shop and make a success out of things."

"Mom—"

"The contracts the council has been giving out state that home ownership reverts to the town if the business ceases operations within three years. It has to be you."

His mouth opened. Closed. He took a breath. "I'll admit, it's a great plan. But I've already got a job, remember? Back in Chicago."

She took his hand. "I know. And I'm sure it's a great job, but you're needed here, Declan. At least to help start it. Once you've got it going, if you need to return to your job, we can hire Olive or someone else to work there and report back to you. She just graduated and would probably like to branch out beyond working at the coffee shop."

"Mom. I have to be back within a month if I want to keep this job. You can't start a business then abandon it a month later."

"She's not really asking, son." Dad spoke up, eyes flashing. "And you know how Grandma feels about that house."

Declan stared at him. He did know, but—"Dad, I want to help, but . . ."

"Let's not beat around. You owe her, son. So, just man up and do it."

It was always so cut-and-dried with Dad, wasn't it?

Declan's mouth tightened, and maybe he should just grab his suitcase and . . . and leave.

Never look back.

Which had been Plan A all along.

Mom placed a hand on his arm. "I know this isn't your first choice, but it's a way to help."

A way to make amends, she meant.

He looked away, at the pictures in the hallway, the legacy of the Kelleys. Shoot.

"Fine. I'll do it."

"Oh, Declan, thank you. I've already called an emergency meeting of the council on Monday. Seb is out of town, but that will just make it easier."

"Easier? Why?"

"Oh." She made a face and Declan stiffened in his seat. "The lease you'll be taking over, it's a bit complicated. A bit of history there, and I'm afraid Seb might not give us a fair shake."

"What's complicated about the lease, Mom?"

But somehow, he knew.

"It's for The Fudge Shop on Main."

He finally let loose the groan he'd been holding in. "Seriously, Mom?" How was he supposed to take over the space that had once been occupied by the family—by the woman—who had changed his life, and not for the better? "That space belongs to the *Hart* Family Fudge shop."

"Not anymore. Because the lease expired. And they've had it shut down for years."

"Still. You really want to reopen that old wound? You might start that stupid feud up all over again."

"Calm down. Randy Hart retired from his fishing business. Nancy Hart retired from fudge making. And that shop is just sitting there, perfectly good real estate rotting away. It's just begging for a new resident, and Kelley's Classic Fudge needs a rebirth." She stood up.

"Does it, though?"

Mom's eyes flashed. "For Grandma's sake, yes."

Right. It came down to that, didn't it? And that was why Declan was here.

Apparently, if he had to make fudge, he'd make fudge.

Anything to save Grandma's house.

Anything to show how sorry he was for his role in Grandpa's death.

So, he'd open a fudge shop, and maybe then he'd finally be free of this weight he just couldn't shake.

"Fine." He stood up. "But for the record, I hate fudge."

Three

"CREEPIN' COBWEBS, MOM. WHEN WAS the last time you used this place?" Lily entered the front door of Hart Family Fudge shop ahead of her mother and dodged a trailing diaphanous web. "It looks like you've decorated for Halloween. You're only three months too early."

"Oh, stop." Mom closed the door behind them and turned the latch. "It isn't that bad—and it hasn't been that long." She wore her salt-and-pepper hair piled in a messy bun, her faded jeans and green T-shirt reflecting her casual island life.

Lily shivered. "You sure about that?" She swatted several more sticky tangles away and took in the shop. Cloths draped the marble fudge tables in front of each of the pop-out windows, and a layer of dust covered the black-and-white checkered floor.

Along with everything else.

This open door of Lily's was looking a little less sparkly in the light of day than it had seemed five days ago in her Florida apartment.

"I was in here at the beginning of May when I made a dessert spread for our ladies' book club," Mom said. "You know I've slowed down on catering orders."

Aw, Mom. At fifty-five, she was far too young to be plagued by debilitating joint pain when her arthritis flared up, but Lily was glad she hadn't given up her catering altogether. "Maybe you should have hired a housekeeping service in between."

"You're here now." Mom elbowed her playfully.

"I am." She was. "And I still can't believe it."

After spending the last several days packing up her room, helping Sadie find a new roommate, and spending way too much time on Pinterest creating a fudge shop mood board, Lily had finally arrived on Jonathon Island yesterday on the last Sunday evening ferry. She, Mom, Dad, and Cody—along with Mia Jonathon Franklin and her two young kids—had spent the night eating burgers, laughing, and reminiscing about old times.

It had been a strange kind of wonderful to be back, knowing this time it was for good.

After a night sleeping in her old bedroom, she'd bounced into her parents' kitchen and declared it was time—time for Mom to take her to the fudge shop.

Lily's fudge shop, if all went well.

Which it totally, one-hundred-percent would.

"I can't believe it either. But you're exactly what the place has needed." Mom rubbed the joints of her hand, her eyes a little wistful as she looked over the shop. "This is so exciting."

"And a little bit terrifying." Okay, *a lot* bit terrifying. Here, there was so much history—over seventy years of it, since Great-Grandma and Great-Grandpa Hart had driven their Volkswagen van over on the ferry (before the vehicle ban) and decided that Jonathon Island would be the perfect place to start a business and raise a family.

It caused a little ache in Lily's chest. How had her career brought her full circle, back to this tiny island and the fudge shop where she'd spent her entire childhood? She'd followed the legacy home, just like she'd always intended to do.

She only hoped she didn't grind that legacy to dust.

"It's good to be a little terrified. But you're going to do great. You're a Hart. This fudge shop is in your blood."

"Thanks, Mom." She rounded the long wooden counter—which ran parallel to the front door and was flanked by display cases on either side, creating a long U-shape that separated the workers from the lobby—and headed through the swinging door that led to the kitchen.

And here . . . here was where the real magic happened. It wasn't large, by any means, but it was just right, with three more marble tables taking center stage. On the other side sat the dinged-up door of the walk-in refrigerator, the storage pantry to its right, the doorway leading to the back alley to its left. And along the right wall were the perfectly arranged kettles, thermometers, and everything else she'd need to create fudge day in and day out—dusty too, but brimming with history. Finally, on the left side of the kitchen sat the sink, dishwasher, and stovetop, followed by another door that led out to the shop's small hallway, where hidden away from customers she'd find a small office, the storage room, and a bathroom.

This was going to be her home away from home once again.

"It's like I never left."

Mom squeezed her shoulder. "It will be—once it's clean."

"Subtle, Mom." Squatting, Lily opened the cabinet under the sink and found a pair of bright pink cleaning gloves, still in the wrapper, two rolls of paper towels, and disinfecting spray. She hoisted her treasure to the old tiled countertop. "But cleaning is the least of my worries. For the rest, you're here to help guide me if I need it, right?"

"Of course, though I don't know what I could teach you that you didn't learn in that fancy school of yours. I'll bet you're thrilled to finally put that important degree to great use."

Lily froze.

Nearly groaned out loud.

Who knew that the little white lie she'd told about actually graduating with her bachelor's—instead of failing out—would come back to bite her now?

Probably she should come clean. She eyed the cleaning supplies in front of her. The irony. "Mom . . ."

"Hold that thought." Her mother approached the bulletin board hung on the wall beside the door and pointed to the calendar hanging there. She flipped it from May to July. "I meant to tell you, the second weekend of August,

Dani Sullivan is planning a Main Street Festival. It's a way to get tourists back and introduce all the new restaurant and shop owners—and what they have to offer—to the town. Do you think you can be up and running by then?"

Lily glanced at the calendar. "What's that? Just under five weeks away?"

Mom nodded. "The festival is sort of a little teaser of what's to come next season, when part of the Grand Hotel is reopened, and of course the season after that, when the hotel renovation and repair will be complete. We don't know how long it will take for tourism to build back to the previous levels. So many moving parts—businesses, housing, employees. But if we can start small, build, if we can get people coming here for day trips, that's a start."

Restarting up the fudge shop didn't feel like starting small. "Right." Deep breath. Maybe a week of hard work and she'd have the place in order. "I think I should be operational well before then, so long as I can figure out financing for the start-up costs. I've got a little in savings, but I need to be smart with how much I spend right away."

Probably she should have made an appointment with Mr. Michaelson at Great Lakes National Bank, but she'd been so busy.

Mom took up a cloth and indicated that Lily should follow her through the door to the front of the shop. "That's something I've been meaning to talk with you about." She started wiping down the counter and register that must be twenty years old. It might take ten cloths just to get through the dust, but Mom didn't seem to mind.

Still. With her hands, she didn't need to be doing the

cleaning. Lily came up beside her and gently took the rag from her. "Oh yeah?"

Mom lifted her shoulders in a shrug and moved aside without a fuss. "Yes. Your father and I have been talking about it, and we want to contribute."

"What? No. You guys basically just retired. You're saving for a trip to Arizona in the fall. I'm not letting you—"

"Letting us? Well, someone's gotten a little big for her britches." Mom's eyes twinkled as she laughed.

"It's not a pride thing at all."

"I know, honey. I'm just teasing." Mom drew a figure eight in the dust, then blew it off her finger onto the floor, which would need a good vacuum and scrubbing anyway. "We gave Cody the fishing company license and sold him equipment at a discount. That was our way of helping him get started, and this is our way of helping you. It's not a whole lot, but enough for you to operate for two months, maybe three."

"Are you sure?"

"Of course I'm sure. We're proud to see you guys carry on both of the family businesses, and we want to do all we can to make that happen. In fact, after book club today I'll head over to Seb's to pay your first month's rent."

It was so incredibly sweet that they believed in her. But how much of that confidence was based on the lie that they thought she'd graduated with the knowledge of running a business? "But what if I fail?"

"You won't."

Lily opened her mouth to say that she already had. But

before she could confess, Mom hoisted a box of fudge gift cartons and carried it toward the back storeroom.

She hurried after her. "Mom, you shouldn't be carrying that."

"Nonsense. I'm having a good day." Mom had already set the gift cartons down by the time Lily reached the room.

Her eyes landed on a boxy metal appliance that took up a nearly two-foot by two-foot space on the shelf and stood almost three feet high. A latched door with a metal chute stuck out of the front. "Is this an ice cream maker?" She eyed the digital buttons at the top of the unit.

Mom dusted off her hands. "Cool, right? I got it at an auction. They were closing an ice cream shop in Saginaw and no one else had bid on it—it was a steal. Thought it would come in handy for summer parties or weddings, plus I know how much you love to experiment with different flavors as a stress relief. Unfortunately, I've been struggling to get it to work. I've tried three batches, and it shuts off too soon."

"Did you have Dad take a look?"

"No." Flipping off the lights, Mom headed back to the front. "He knows his way around a boat, but ask him to fix a small appliance and he gets grumbly."

Ha. So much truth in that statement. "What about Cody?"

"When would he have time? He's the town's only handyman, plus he's fixing that boat so he can get the fishing company up and running again." Mom took a broom leaning against the back wall and started sweeping up dust mites. Some swirled in the air. "Besides, with all the time he's been spending with Mia, he's too busy to be fixing an ice cream maker."

Lily sprayed down the countertop and scrubbed it to a sterile sheen. "They do seem really happy."

"I agree." Mom paused. "Who knows. With all the new people moving to Jonathon Island, maybe you'll find someone to make *you* happy."

Lily rolled her eyes. "Mom."

"What? A mother can dream." Looking up from the broom, she winked at Lily. "And pray."

"Don't waste your prayers on me—at least as far as love's concerned." After Declan, even after Tony, yeah. Romance was not at the top of her list of priorities. "Instead, pray I can make this fudge shop a success."

She sensed Mom's eyes on her. Lily turned. Mom's lips were drawn into an uncharacteristic frown. "You're okay with this? Reopening the fudge shop? Living on the island again? I hope you don't feel like we're pressuring you."

"Not at all. It was my idea, remember?"

"Good." She resumed her sweeping. "Because your dad and I made peace a long time ago about letting the fudge shop go. We had to. The economy had tanked, nobody was buying fudge—or anything but the essentials, for that matter. And then once we might have considered it, I got my diagnosis. But I'll admit. This is exciting, to see your grandparents' shop come back to life. To see my legacy living on, in you."

"It's what I always intended to do. The reason I went away to learn about candy making in the first place. I'm glad I have the chance to keep it going." Even if it scared the pants off her. "This is a special place."

"It really is. I remember the first time I stepped inside as a college student on vacation. The smell of the chocolate, the mesmerizing way your dad's parents and aunt threw the fudge onto the marble slabs and used nothing but a wooden paddle and their brawn to make something spectacular out of so few ingredients. Well, I knew I had to get a job here."

Lily could picture it—Grandpa William and Grandma Karen working alongside William's sister, Felicia. The two older women had taken Mom under their wings and shown her everything they knew about fudge making. "And then you met Dad."

"Rough and tough fisherman Randy Hart. He'd breeze in here after a day's haul, looking for something sweet. His mom would yell at him to get out of her fudge shop stinking of fish, and I'd take pity on him and sneak him a bite of fudge from the back alley." Mom leaned against the broom handle and sighed. "Pretty soon, that wasn't all I snuck him."

"Gross, Mom!" Lily pretended to gag, though the idea of her parents kissing actually brought a smile to her heart. "But see? It really is a special place. It's literally my origin story. How could I not want to be here?" She lifted her rag and revealed a trail of clean white against the thick dust borders.

"You always did like it here. My little shadow, helping make batch after batch of fudge."

"I made myself sick more than once when I ate every last drop of residue from the copper kettles."

Mom laughed. "Then there was the time you convinced me to make peppermint fudge."

"It was a good idea." The memory warmed Lily's heart. She'd been seven, maybe?

"It was a *great* idea—became our hottest holiday seller. Far better than your idea to make cranberry fudge. That did not go over well."

"Creativity always has risks." She should revisit that recipe, though. Experiment with an improved version.

"You're definitely the risk taker in the family. I've always admired that about you. That and your free spirit, your impulsivity."

"Thanks, Mom." A memory surfaced, pinching the air from Lily's lungs. Grandpa Hart's voice. Scolding. Not everyone enjoyed that particular facet of her personality. "I'll have to see how that pairs with running a business."

"You'll find your way. I have faith." Mom checked her watch. "Oh! It's almost time for book club at Constance's house. Are you okay if I take off for a few hours? I can come back and help later." She set the broom back against the wall.

"No, no, I've got this. Really. Have fun."

"Oh, I will. We just finished reading a new romantic adventure by Susan May Warren and I can't wait to discuss all the ins and outs." Mom pulled a key ring from her purse and removed a key, holding it out to Lily. "You'll have to take my key for now. I'm not sure what happened to the other one, but I'll look for it tonight. Or we can get a copy from Seb when he returns from his cruise."

With a kiss and a hug, Mom was gone, and Lily continued cleaning until her back ached and her arms felt like noodles. There was still a lot to do, but she washed up and headed into the back of the shop to take inventory of the equipment. Hopefully everything just needed a good cleaning, but if she had to order parts, that would take a chunk of time she didn't have to waste.

From the back room, a sound caught Lily's attention. She palmed the single key, still in her pocket.

Not Mom. In fact, no one else had access. Maybe Seb Jonathon, who had leased them the property, but he wouldn't enter without warning. And like Mom said, he was out of town. She turned her head to listen. Tried to talk sense to herself. This was Jonathon Island. They didn't have crime—did they?

Of course, she'd been gone awhile. The world had changed. Newcomers had come from who knew where to set up shop here. Maybe one of them was a murderer who broke into other people's places of business and—

"Seriously, Lily?" she hissed. Great, now she was talking to herself.

Then the grunt of a very, most definitely male, voice lifted every hair on her body.

She had to get out of here. But she didn't want to leave the shop unattended. Maybe she could call for help . . . except, shoot, her phone was inside her purse in the kitchen.

The unmistakable sound of footsteps resounded down the hallway. Getting closer.

Maybe it was her brother.

Or maybe not.

A weapon—she needed a weapon, just in case it was, what? A burglar?

Maybe. Still. She felt around on the nearest high shelf, and her fingers slipped around the cold steel of something. Bringing it down, her heart sank. A metal ladle. Too bad they didn't run a meat shop. There wasn't a cleaver or blade to be found, at least back here.

This would have to do. Maybe if she employed the element of surprise . . .

Lily tightened her grip on the ladle and tucked herself behind the ice cream maker. Her throat had dried to thick paste, and she stifled her reflex to cough.

The door opened and a large form stepped inside.

Lily screamed and jumped out in front of him, the ladle held over her head. "Gotcha!"

His first reflex was to grab the weapon out of his attacker's hand.

His hand closed on it, and she kicked at him, hitting his shin.

"Knock it off!"

Declan ducked as the metal object flew past his face. What—?

He turned back and just barely dodged a metal bowl flying at him like a frisbee. "Stop!" His aviators went flying.

She stepped up to him, now holding a rolling pin and

this was just—enough! He snagged her wrist. "Calm down!"

"Let go of me—" The woman tugged at him. "Help!" she screamed. "Help!"

Screaming? "Come on. I'm not going to hurt you!"

But apparently she might hurt him. She'd managed to pick up a wooden fudge paddle—

Now *that* would hurt. He grabbed her hard to himself, trying to wrench it free. In the struggle, she'd tangled herself against him, between the door and the storage rack.

"Seriously!" he said. "Listen, you're the intruder here—!"

"Let me go!"

That voice—he stilled, and she wrenched herself away. Rounded on him, breathing hard. Their eyes met.

Oh no.

She may as well have whacked him in the head with the fudge paddle.

"Lily." Her name, foreign on his lips, rushed out in a whisper.

Lily Hart. She wore her pale blonde hair down, lavender streaks framing her face.

Ten years older and still pretty, despite the fury in her electric blue eyes. She wore a slate blue T-shirt that nearly matched her eyes and leather leggings, and he definitely did not notice that, um, his high school flame had *grown up.*

Maybe she thought the same thing because her mouth opened. Closed. Then, "What are *you* doing here?"

That was a loaded question, since she was in *his* fudge

shop. He'd come straight over from the emergency meeting Mom had called, where the town council—all save the mayor, Seb Jonathon, who was on an anniversary cruise with his wife—voted unanimously to let him lease the fudge shop property.

In all his years of business, a transaction had never gone more smoothly. And it had lit a fire in him that, yes, maybe this wouldn't take as long as he'd thought. He'd get in, set up a profitable fudge shop model, hire a team to run it, and be back in Chicago in a week, maybe two tops.

He'd signed the paperwork Patrick had drawn up and paid his dollar to secure Grandma's house, which Mom had indeed convinced the county to gift to the town, with the express agreement in writing that it be used as incentive for whoever operated the fudge shop on Main Street.

Declan held up his hands and pasted what he hoped was a friendly smile on his face. "I'm here because I drove back to the island yesterday."

"Doesn't explain why you're in this shop, Slick." Her gaze went to the sunglasses he'd scooped off the floor. "How did you even get in?" Lily squeezed past him and walked down the hallway and toward the front door. She tested the handle and muttered to herself when it opened. What, did she think he'd broken in or something?

"It wasn't locked." Which was a good thing, because otherwise he'd have had to wait until Seb returned from his vacation so he could make him a copy. "And wait a minute." Declan's brain, finally, started firing on all synapses. He moved to the door, shut it, and whirled on Lily, who backed up against the display case. "Why are *you* here? Aren't you supposed to be in Florida? Far away from here?"

She cocked her head at him. "Aw, are you keeping track of me now, Decky?"

He scowled. She knew he hated to be called that. "It's a small island. Everyone knows everyone else's business."

She tapped her chin. "And yet, I know nothing about where *you've* been and what *you've* been doing."

He might have opened his mouth to tell her, but she held up her hand. "Nope. Don't wanna know. Just leave." She pointed to the door, then headed toward the swinging kitchen door.

"I . . . wait."

His voice stopped her at the door.

"Listen." She held the door open. "I don't want to hear about your *big life*. Because guess what? I. Don't. Care. The only thing I care about is getting my fudge shop back up and running, which means getting back to cleaning and organizing it. So bye, Slick."

Then she banged through the door before he could say another word.

Wait—what? *Her* fudge shop?

Mom had said the Harts weren't planning to reopen their fudge shop because of Nancy's arthritis. That their lease had expired last week.

But now, Lily was here.

Uh-oh.

Before he could follow her and get some answers, the fudge shop's front door opened, and Uncle Patrick walked in with a folder of papers.

"Oh, good, you were able to get inside. I just brought you the paperwork. You forgot it at the meeting." Patrick set the folder on the counter beside the register, then looked around. "A bit musty, a lot dirty, but I think you can whip it into shape." His eyes gleamed and he absently rubbed his thumb along the edge of the antique watch Great-Grandpa Casey Kelley had left to him. "My granddad would be proud. He always envisioned us having the premier fudge shop on the island. Now, we'll have the only one. And in the best location too."

The door to the kitchen banged back open and Lily charged through. "I thought I told you to—" At the sight of Patrick, she stopped short. "Why is my fudge shop being overrun by Kelleys today? I'm not open yet, sir, so if you want fudge, you're just going to have to wait a week."

Patrick's smile faded at the sight of Lily. "What—what are you doing here?" He took a step back.

"I don't mean to be rude, but I think it's best that you both go. I have a lot of work to do."

They simply stood there. Then Uncle Patrick said, "I'm not sure what you're doing here, Ms. Hart, but the town council has officially leased this Main Street storefront to Declan."

A moment of silence and then she laughed.

Laughed.

"Don't be ridiculous. This is my family's fudge shop. We've had a lease from the Jonathons for seventy-four years that says it belongs to the Hart family. So . . ." She shrugged.

Ouch. He couldn't really blame her for being defensive. The Kelley name convicted him as much as their own past.

Uncle Patrick shook his head. "Sorry, sweetheart, but several months ago, your mother indicated to Seb that she wouldn't be renewing her lease for the next five-year term, and it expired last month." He picked up the folder.

Lily stared at him, then swiped it out of his hand, wrenching the top flap back. "That's a lie. She's the one who brought me here this morning." Her eyes scanned the top document, then she flipped to the next. "This isn't right—"

"Perhaps she doesn't remember having the conversation with Seb, but Martha overheard it."

"Oh yes, let's break a seventy-four-year promise on your mother's *word*." She slapped the folder back onto the counter. "How convenient."

"Hey," Declan snapped. "My mom doesn't lie." She might be a lot of things, including a gossip queen, but a straight-up liar wasn't one of them.

Lily held up a hand. "The point is, she's wrong. My mother had no intention of giving up the lease. And from the paperwork, it's only *lapsed*. Which isn't a thing anymore because I'm back, my mother is headed over to pay the rent today, and I'm reopening the shop. Case closed."

Uncle Patrick's expression tightened. "Ms. Hart, regardless of your mother's intentions, the bottom line is that the lease did indeed lapse, leaving it open for a viable business to use—and let's face it, your mother hasn't been using it for viable business for years."

"Not true. She's been using it to cater."

"Yes, but she can do that out of her own home. She doesn't need prime downtown real estate to do so. And given that it's the town council's job to ensure such locations are used well, and the fact the lease was up, we exercised that right to vote in the first applicant we received."

"Whatever. Aren't there like two Kelleys on the council, including Declan's own mother? Seems a bit unfair to me. Besides, this is *my* family's fudge shop. You can't just steal it away."

"No one is stealing anything," Declan said, glancing at Uncle Patrick with an *I'll handle this, thanks* look. Last thing he wanted was new shots fired on the old feud that had managed to stay mostly dormant, at least for the last decade.

Since he left town.

Now, he schooled his voice. "But the fact is that the lease did lapse. By all accounts, your mother was ready to let it go. We obtained the lease legally, Lily."

She raised an eyebrow. "Please. You know that business around here is pretty lax. I'm sure my mom intended to re-sign the lease once Seb returned from his trip. It's only July seventh. According to your paperwork, it expired on June thirtieth. That's a week out from it being renewed. What's the big deal?"

Declan swallowed. Problem was, she was right. Even if it wasn't signed, he'd have to evict her. And that could take months.

So much for his short turnaround.

He looked at Uncle Patrick, who wore the past in his

eyes—the feud, the hurt, the years of fracture on the is-land.

Not to mention that this was their only hope of saving Grandma's house.

Besides, Lily would probably give up and go back to Florida after a month when business turned out to be harder than she thought. Because that's what she did—ran away when things got hard. And he wasn't going to let her steal the only chance he had at saving Grandma's house.

"Does Mia Franklin know about this?" Lily said, her hands on her hips. "She's the one who originally told me to come back and reopen the shop. Why would she do that if it wasn't available to us?"

"She must not have known the lease expired." Patrick shrugged as if to say *too bad, so sad.*

"But I called her last week to confirm. She set this up."

"While Ms. Franklin was tasked over the last few months with vetting and selecting candidates, she presented them all to the council—which she is not on—and we ultimately decided who would be a good fit for the Jonathon Island culture. She isn't necessarily privy to all the other lease agreements her father has with current tenants," Patrick said. "And until this morning, this shop was empty."

"You're splitting hairs here. It seems to me that you're taking advantage of a situation to get the thing you've always wanted—my family's fudge shop. We always beat you out because of our Main Street location, and now you're making a grab for it. It was bad enough your father tried to steal my grandpa's recipes—"

"Lily—" Declan started.

Too late. Uncle Patrick had ignited. "Those were lies, and the Hart family knows it!"

This whole thing was going off the rails, and fast. Once upon a time, Lily had respected Declan. Maybe he could reason with her. "Lil—"

Her eyes flashed at him. "Save it, Slick."

"I'm just trying to get us talking, so we can hear each other's sides without all of the emotion—"

"That's pointless. We all know whose side you're on."

Oh.

She stared at him, her eyes glossy, her jaw tight.

He sighed. Yes. Yes they did. Still, "Lily, let's not—"

"What's going on in here?" Tara Chamberlain, the pastor's wife and another member of the town council, stepped inside. Though most women on the island dressed in casual jeans and T-shirts, Tara looked professional and put together in her slacks, red blouse, and heels, her silver-blonde hair twisted back in a clip. "I could hear the screaming from Martha's across the way."

Then her gaze landed on Lily. "Lily!" Her face brightened. "I didn't know you were back visiting. When . . ." Tara's voice trailed off and her eyebrows drew together before her gaze swung to Patrick's. "Patrick, what's going on here?"

"Just a simple misunderstanding, I assure you."

"There's nothing simple about it." Lily rounded the counter and approached Tara. For a moment, her angry mask melted, and she smiled softly at the pastor's wife.

"It's good to see you, though. I was sad you were away last month when I came for a visit."

"It's always great to see you." Tara embraced her, then pulled back, hands on Lily's shoulders. "But what's going on? Why are you inside your family's old shop?"

"That's the thing. It's not our 'old shop,' Tara. My mom didn't know the lease lapsed, or if so, she's in the process of renewing it. She brought me here this morning, excited that I've decided to reopen the shop."

"You have? That's amazing!"

Patrick cleared his throat. "It would be amazing, indeed, if this shop had not already been leased to *another fudge company* just this morning."

"Oh dear. Hmm." Tara pinched her lips together. She'd lived on the island long enough to know the long-standing feud between the two families that had started fifty-five years ago when Declan's Grandpa Barry had decided to open Kelley's Classic Fudge in direct competition with his best friend William Hart's shop.

Boom.

Declan had always found the feud immature. He understood the hurt on both sides, and he and Lily had tried once upon a time to forget that it existed.

And look how well that had turned out.

But maybe he should concede now. Be the bigger man. Walk away. Figure out another way to save Grandma's house.

Except there was no other way. The contract had already been drawn up. Whoever owned the fudge shop owned the house. And there was no way—with the fury flashing in her eyes—that Lily Hart would ever concede either. She'd battle him to the death.

A battle.

That was it. The answer to how he was going to best Lily Hart and save Grandma's house—and to be honest, he wasn't sure which would feel better.

"I've got an idea." He waited until all eyes were on him. "What about a contest?"

Four

A CONTEST?" AS A SLIGHT WIND BLEW off Lake Huron, Mia scooped up a handful of her brown curls and pulled them back into a messy ponytail. "What kind of contest?"

They walked along the boardwalk, the sky clear, blue, summer in the breeze.

"Yes, I'm intrigued too." Dani Sullivan, Mia's cousin, sipped her hot chocolate in a to-go cup. "What's the big SOS you called tonight? I had to cancel a date with Liam." But she winked, a teasing glint in her blue eyes. She'd lived on the island longer than either of them, since birth, and she'd never left.

Someone whizzed by on a bicycle, their bell dinging. Jack, the town terrier, trotted along beside them, tongue lolling. More crowded than usual tonight, half the town seemed to be out enjoying the beautiful summer weather. She'd forgotten how the sun wouldn't set until later.

"I'm just glad Cody was able to watch my kids." Mia was a bit younger than both of their twenty-eight years, and despite the fact her family had founded the island over two hundred years ago, she hadn't moved here until she was in grade school.

"Seems like he's bonding well with them," Dani said. Then she grabbed Mia's left hand and sighed. "Feels like there should be a little hardware here soon."

Mia laughed and pulled her hand away.

Sweet. At least her friends had their lives figured out, and not completely derailed. "I called in the SOS to help me sort out this mess."

"The Declan Kelley mess? Oh, honey, that's way above our pay grade," Dani said.

"No—I didn't mean *that*. Listen, Declan and the Kelleys are trying to push the Harts out of the fudge shop—"

"Here we go again." Dani sipped her coffee.

"Yeah, well, the Kelleys are starting it again. Apparently, they say our lease lapsed. And your dad is out of town, so he's not here to sort it out." She directed the statement to Mia. "And in the meantime, the council voted in their fudge shop to take the place of ours!"

"What do you want us to do?" Dani asked.

"I'm hoping you can exercise your power as tourism director and mastermind of this dollar-house scheme and get the council to rescind the approval."

Dani made a face. "I am so sorry, Lily. Yes, I thought up the dollar-house plan, and got the Grand Hotel project going, but you know the council. They make their own decisions."

Mia tucked her arm through Lily's. "I'm just sorry I didn't know about the lease situation before you packed up your life and moved back. I wish there were something more I could do, but until Dad gets somewhere with service—and chooses to check in—I think it might be a sit-and-wait situation. Even then, I don't know if he has the power to undo it since he basically agreed to give the town council the right to select tenants for all unleased property on Main Street as part of the revitalization project."

"Well, Mom had already emailed him. Apparently, she knew about the lease issue, and when I told her I was coming home, she shot off a note. But he was probably boarding his cruise about then, so . . ." She sighed. "Let's hope that counts for a renewal notice."

"Maybe. The law is a bit gray," Mia said. "I looked over the paperwork, and even with my realtor's license, I'm having a hard time knowing what's technically right."

Lily pulled away from Mia's grasp, stopping in the middle of the boardwalk, the pebbled public beach behind her. "But you don't think it's right that they get the shop, do you? It's been in my family for decades." She looked past Mia to Dani. "This isn't okay. They can't just steal my shop from me."

Dani squatted to pet Jack. "Maybe they have a reason."

"Like wanting to own the entire town, not to mention win the Great Fudge Wars, finally." She also bent to pet Jack, who rolled over to expose his belly. "I mean, when they open Kelley's Classic Fudge, they already owned five restaurants on the island. Talk about greedy. And never mind that their fudge recipe tasted just a *liiiitttle* too much like ours."

Dani stood up. "Come on, Lily. You never believed that. You were always the one in high school talking about how stupid the feud was. I mean, you and Declan were even friends."

Try more than friends.

Lily stepped off the boardwalk onto the beach, where a few families with young kids skipped rocks off the gently lapping lake. She crossed her arms over her chest and looked out across the expanse of sparkling blue. "That was before I knew better."

Before she knew not to trust a Kelley.

And so what if he'd looked surprised to see her today. *Yeah, that's right, Slick.* He might have shattered her heart and sent her running, but hello, she was back, heart intact and stronger this time.

Still pinched, just a little, that he'd sided with his family. Especially after knowing her plans for the shop. But she should have known he hadn't changed, even after a decade and his fancy education. Rules versus renegade, that's what her mom had always said about the two of them.

Oil and water and flames. Talk about reigniting the family feud.

Her friends joined her on the beach, Jack sitting at her feet. Sweet. She ran her hands over his ears.

"So, how was it?" Dani asked. "Seeing Declan again?"

Oh. Clearly they could still read her thoughts. "Perfect. I don't know why he's even here—he wore a suit. Who wears a suit on Jonathon Island?"

"Liam wore a suit when he got here—" Dani said.

Lily shot her a look. "Yeah, but Liam wasn't from JI. You know what I mean. And he was wearing these stupid aviator sunglasses, and . . ."

"I thought he looked pretty good when I saw him in town," Mia said.

Lily looked at her. "Seriously."

"Aw, c'mon, Lily. Declan was never hard on the eyes. Dark hair, deep blue eyes, and it looked like he still works out. And once upon a time, you called him charming—"

"Well, now he's arrogant and sneaky." She picked at the pebbles on the beach, found one and threw it into the water. "I can't believe he suggested a contest."

"Okay, what are the terms of this contest?" Dani said. "You make it sound like he stabbed you in the back. Unless it's sheep herding, or a horse race, you can bake circles around Mr. Windy City—"

"Slick."

Dani laughed. "Right. Slick. Against Ms. Orlando cooking school graduate, and master chocolatier. I don't see the issue."

Lily winced at the mention of her supposed graduation. "He wants to share my shop."

Mia raised an eyebrow. "Wait. Work in the same space?"

"Until the Main Street Festival. And whoever sells the most fudge during that time gets to keep the shop. Permanently."

Mia and Dani eyed each other over Lily's head. Smiled.

"Stop. I can see where you're going with this. No way,

no how are Declan and I going to be friends again. He's the enemy."

"Come on, Lily. It sounds like he's trying to make the most of a difficult situation," Mia said.

"Wouldn't it be worse if Uncle Seb got back and decided that the council actually had the *right* to give the shop's lease to the Kelleys? Then you'd have no shot at all."

Lily sat up. "You really think that might happen?"

"You know the Kelleys. Especially Martha and Patrick. They'll go to the mattresses for this shop." Mia tugged her sweater close against the breeze off the lake. "I wouldn't be surprised if they tried to get my dad to recuse himself."

"Why would he—"

"Because his daughter is going to marry a Hart." She winked. "Hopefully."

Dani bumped her shoulder, and Mia grinned.

Lily stared at her. "You're saying it's a conflict of interest for Seb to side with us."

Mia shrugged. "You know they'd try it."

"That's hardly fair, given the fact they're on the council."

"True," Dani said. "So if all the involved parties recused themselves—Uncle Seb and the Kelleys—that would just leave Tara Chamberlain and Janine Dirks. And wasn't Tara there when Declan mentioned the contest?" She took another sip of her cocoa. "What did she say about it?"

"She was all for the idea." And that had hurt, given Tara's knowledge of the past. "I know she was trying to be fair, but still."

"Listen. You got this," Mia said. "You can totally whip

Declan at making fudge. I mean, did you ever see him in his family's shop growing up?"

Hmmm. "Not really. He was more interested in school and helping his dad with the financial parts of the business. Probably why he got his MBA."

She looked away from her friends. Yes, Lily was completely aware of exactly where Declan had been and what he'd been doing. You couldn't live on a small island—even go home and visit that island—without hearing all the gossip about former and current residents.

And shoot, but she'd listened, her broken heart just a little too curious.

"Whereas you worked in that shop basically since you were born," Dani said, reaching for her hand. "Plus, you're no business slouch. I know they taught you how to run a business in that fancy culinary college."

She sighed.

Silence, just the wash of water on the shoreline, a few kids shouting, rocks spilling as they ran up the beach.

"Right?" Dani said.

She looked at her friends. "I may have failed out of the last year of school. The part that focused on running a business."

Dani raised an eyebrow.

Mia made a face, scrunching up her nose. "Oh boy."

"I know."

"Do your parents know that?" Mia said. "Does Cody?"

"No, and you can't tell them. They think I can do this—"

"You can, Lil," Mia said. "You're an amazing candy

maker. Creative. Great instincts. And, you were in the fudge shop every day, working with your grandparents and then your mom. You know how to run a store—with or without a degree."

Um . . . and even as she looked at Mia, her grandfather's voice raked through her head. *Get your head out of the clouds, girl. You won't get anywhere in life if you can't focus for more than a minute. There's no room here for such impulsiveness.*

But—well, he wasn't here anymore, and maybe she'd changed. Not a renegade anymore, but a businesswoman. A fudge shop owner. She pushed out a tight breath. "I don't know. But I do know one thing: I'm not letting the Kelleys run me out of town again."

She got up, stared out across the blue, the sky pale and clear, the sun just starting to drop. "I'm going to win that stupid contest. And Declan Kelley isn't going to know what hit him."

"Just what exactly were you thinking giving Lily Hart the chance to own that fudge shop again?"

Declan sighed at his mom's voice, coming from behind him. He stood at his parents' living room window drinking his morning coffee—in peace, until now.

Fog twined through the trees in the front yard, despite the sun's valiant attempts to cut through. The golden sphere was a blurred orb of light.

He turned from the window. "Good morning to you too, Mom. I figured you'd be at work already." Had been counting on it, actually. After a full afternoon and evening spent scrubbing every inch of the fudge shop, he'd timed his arrival home perfectly—his parents in bed, and Isaac busy in his room with his computer, headset, and video game controller in hand.

"Trying to avoid me?" Mom pulled the coffee pot off the warmer where Declan had left it. She wore her standard uniform of soft linen pants and black shirt. "I heard you come in late last night."

"Spent all day and late into the evening cleaning the shop." And tried to tell himself that he hadn't just set himself and his family up for disaster. Because the Harts knew their fudge.

And he wasn't entirely sure that the rumor about his own family and the "stolen recipe" wasn't true. At least, that's what he'd thought years ago. Now, maybe it didn't matter.

But cleaning had sort of helped him get Lily's expression—and her fury—out of his head.

Oh, she was going to be trouble, he knew it in his bones.

"Well, your Uncle Patrick called. Told us about your contest idea." She filled her coffee mug. "I almost had a heart attack. Honestly, Declan, don't you know that girl has a college degree in chocolate entrepreneurship?"

Huh. No. No, he did not. Still. "I have an MBA."

"Yes, and you're brilliant at business. That plus our classic family fudge recipe is a sure win. But we don't really know what *she's* capable of." She raised an eyebrow. "You don't still have feelings for her, do you?"

His mouth opened. "C'mon, Mom. Please. That was a high school . . ."

Did he still think Lily Hart was gorgeous in that raw and real way she'd always had about her? Sure. But she was like a Cat-5 hurricane. Unpredictable. Destructive in her realness. "No," he said finally. "I do not."

His mother capped her mug. "You can't blame me for asking. That girl, well, she did a number on our family. I don't want it happening again."

Right. "Me either."

Sighing, Mom nodded, then stepped up to him and patted Declan's cheek. "You're a good boy, Declan, and normally you're so levelheaded. I just want to make sure you know what you're doing here."

She wasn't the only one.

But he didn't want to fight. "I spent the day cleaning the shop from top to bottom yesterday. Today, I'm going to start working on a business plan. Then I'm going to figure out how to execute it. The goal is to have production underway next week."

"What is this contest, anyway?" His mom picked up her thermos.

"To sell more fudge than the Harts during the upcoming festival."

His mother took a sip.

"Once we have the shop, and Grandma's house, secured, I will turn over the shop to another capable Kelley or hire full-time help, and I'll manage from Chicago for as long as you need me to. Just like we talked about."

Her lips pursed, his mom considered him. Finally nodded. "It's a good plan. And I have faith you've got what it takes. But are you sure about the contest? Maybe I should speak with the other council members again—"

"Tara was there yesterday and yes, she did suggest that we could wait until Seb gets back to settle the matter. But I don't have time to do that. My boss only gave me a month. As it is, I'm already risking my job."

"I know, I know. Though you could always stay here and manage the shop if you *were* to lose that job."

"Mom." He rolled his eyes. "I didn't get my MBA to stay on JI and make fudge. No offense—I know you love it here. But it holds a lot of memories." Ones he didn't especially want to be confronted with every day. "I'm here for Grandma, and for you. But I don't intend to stay."

Her mouth tightened, and what looked like hurt flashed in her eyes.

Great. Declan drained his mug and eyed the coffee pot. He probably needed another entire pot to survive this day.

Even this conversation.

Would another cup be enough to get him through this conversation? This day?

"Fine. Well, I guess it's on now." She reached for her satchel, tucked the thermos in. "Just make sure you win."

"I don't know, Mom." The voice came from his brother, Isaac, who came into the room freshly showered. He pulled down a mug and snatched the coffee pot off the warmer just as Declan decided to reach for it. He drained the pot and stuck it back. Looked at his big brother. "Decky here hasn't made fudge in how long?"

Decky? "Listen. I know it's been a while since I was in the shop."

"Oh, stop. He was a big help when Grandpa first got dementia," Mom said. "Kept the books while Brandon made the fudge. Who knows, but if the Grand Hotel hadn't burned down, maybe he'd still be here—"

"Doubtful, Mom, but we can't go back in time. I'm here now—" He looked at his brother. "And it's *fudge*. Not rocket science. I'll follow the recipes." He lifted a shoulder. "What this shop really needs is a good business plan." He pulled out the bag of coffee beans and filled the grinder.

His mother picked up her bag. "I'm off to the diner." She turned to Isaac. "I'll see you in an hour, yes? You're on the breakfast shift."

Isaac leaned a hip against the sink. "Can't wait."

His mother walked out.

"So you're working at the diner? Are you cooking?" Declan asked.

"Bussing tables." Isaac tore open a cellophane package and pulled out a brown sugar Pop-Tart. "I'm not the family savior, you are."

He frowned. "I—"

Isaac held up a hand. "Listen, bro. Not everyone wants to go to school and change the world."

"You like living at home, spending all your days playing video games?"

"Yep." He glanced at the toaster, his mouth tight.

Declan shook his head. Turned on the grinder.

The Pop-Tart finished cooking, and Isaac grabbed it out as Declan filled the coffee maker.

Isaac headed for the door, but stopped and turned. "Just watch your back. That Hart girl's gonna get her claws into you again, then she's going to smoke you. And poor Grandma's gonna suffer for it."

"Thanks for all the support, bro."

"Just here to keep you humble." His brother lifted his Pop-Tart in a salute. "But don't say I didn't warn you."

Declan didn't need a warning. He needed a plan. A plan not to let Lily Hart derail his life again.

Five

T HE REOPENING OF HART FAMILY FUDGE would be an epic comeback—because epic was Lily's style. Go big. Be innovative. Create unexpected surprises to enhance the customer experience.

Win this thing.

She inhaled the morning air, letting the sunlight—and her friends' encouraging words from their conversation last night—infuse her with hope as she rode her old pink Schwinn cruiser down Lake Shore Drive. Her parents lived in the upscale Driftwood Hills neighborhood on the west side of the island, so while she could have walked the mile and a half to the fudge shop—*her* fudge shop, whatever the Kelleys said—the bike allowed her quicker access. Hopefully, she'd beat Declan there.

And given his lack of a key, if she just so happened to get busy in the back storeroom, unable to hear him knocking on the front door, well.

That would just be so *unfortunate*.

Lily couldn't help but grin as she rounded the island's southwestern curve and came upon the Grand Hotel, in full renovation mode with its specially permitted cranes and construction vehicles beeping through the early-morning haze. She waved to Liam Stone, Dani's boyfriend, who was talking on a phone in a yellow hard hat near the side of the road.

Dressed in jeans and a T-shirt, the handsome California businessman looked like he'd relaxed a lot since arriving. She'd met him last night when he'd swooped in and stolen Dani away mid-walk, unable to keep himself away from her for a second longer despite their canceled date.

Lily was happy for her friend, but there had been something of a pinch in her chest. Because the only guy who had ever really looked at *her* like that had ended up tearing her world apart.

And now he was trying to do it again.

Lily's grip tightened on the handlebars as the asphalt of Lake Shore Drive turned into the cobblestones of Main Street, where there were more pedestrians and other bicyclists. As she bumped along, Lily smiled and nodded at forty-something Allean Meyer, who was on the public library's steps flipping the sign from Closed to Open. Just beyond that, Martha's on Main was crawling with customers, the line out the door.

It was good to see the town returning to life in a way it hadn't for a decade—even if it did benefit the Kelleys too. Lily missed the clomp of hooves from the dray wagons hauling goods or the carriages toting tourists. Hopefully, someday, they'd return too.

She'd have much preferred their presence to Declan's.

Unfortunately, *that* she couldn't escape. Because there he stood across from Martha's, leaning against the wall of the fudge shop. Waiting with those stupid aviator sunglasses, sunlight turning the highlights of his hair copper.

Every girl's dream come true.

Well. Every girl but her.

For a brief moment, she considered passing him and heading for the back alley door that led into the kitchen. But knowing Declan, he'd anticipate what she was up to and follow her.

There was nothing for it. Guess she had to let him in.

She pulled her bike to a stop and swung her leg over, taking a moment to adjust her leather leggings where they pinched at her thighs. Then she fished her key out of her backpack and popped it into the metal lock of the wooden door. She felt his eyes on her the whole time. Turning to him, her gaze narrowed. "What?"

"Nothing, Widow. Nothing at all."

"Widow?" She glanced down at her pants, rolled her eyes. "As in Black Widow? Really?"

He shrugged, hands still in his pockets like he didn't have a care in the world. Like his very presence here wasn't completely upending her world.

"Whatever." The key clicked in the lock. She pulled on the door handle, but then faced him again. "Are you really going to do this? Fight me for my family's fudge shop?"

She made herself as tall as her five-foot-four frame

could be. Like a sparrow against an eagle while Declan stood over her, somewhere near six-foot-two. Maybe she could just make him stand here, never letting him inside. Of course, that would mean never going inside herself, and that would hardly lend itself to a profitable shop.

"I really don't have a choice, Lily."

"Sure you do. You can head on back to the airstrip and fly on out of here, back to Chicago. Out of my life." Where he should have stayed.

"Can we just go inside?" He held out his arm, glanced behind him. "You're making a scene."

She peeked around him. Across the street outside of the diner stood Mia's mother-in-law, Constance Franklin, and a frail-looking older woman along with retired nurse Peggy Martinez. They were looking their direction with raised eyebrows before turning with grins and slipping inside Martha's. A pair of older gentlemen also watched them from one of the café's large picture windows.

"Argh. Fine." She opened the door and forced herself to hold it for him. A whiff of his annoying, expensive aftershave settled over her when he passed by. "But this isn't because you told me to. It's because I'm being generous, *Slick*. Don't get comfortable, because you won't be here long."

"Whatever you have to tell yourself." He had the nerve to walk straight through, taking a position behind the main counter. Like he already owned the place. His fingers glanced across the left-most display case as he slipped his briefcase from his shoulder and pulled a laptop from inside. "Now, how do we want to approach this?"

Lily opened her mouth to respond that there was no *we* here, but shock stole her words. Because the entire lobby—from the counter and display cases to the two marble demonstration tables that sat in front of the large front windows, to the supplies and copper pots lining the left side of the shop and even the counter-height table and barstools along the right window overlooking Jonathon Boulevard—was spotless.

Lily turned a circle. The floors gleamed. The windows exhibited nary a spiderweb or crusted section of grime. Even the light fixtures hanging over the counter had been scrubbed clean.

"Did you do this?" It must have taken him hours. All afternoon and late into the evening. When Lily had been busy trying to find a way out of the contest, Declan had been dirtying his hands.

As if it were already his shop. Her hands flexed at her sides. He was seriously so . . .

"You're welcome." Flipping open the laptop, he clicked around on the keyboard. "Ah. Okay, here it is. I think—"

"You had no right."

His left eyebrow lifted. "Excuse me?"

"To do all of this." She flicked her finger around the room. Then she walked over and shut his laptop lid, leaning forward. "This isn't your shop—and it never will be."

"I'm sorry, are you actually *mad* at me for cleaning up the shop that *your* family left in disrepair?"

What—? "My mother has arthritis, you jerk. She can't exactly keep everything spotless on her own."

The hard planes of his face eased just a bit. "I am sorry

about that. But I didn't clean this place so I could stake some sort of claim over it."

"Right." She pulled back, slipped her own backpack to the floor, and crossed her arms over her chest. "Seems everything you've done since arriving here has been calculated. But that's your way, isn't it?"

"Better than just improvising, hoping it all just works out." He finger-quoted the last words. For a second, too, his stony expression seemed to falter. Emotion flashed through his eyes, then vanished. His hard gaze returned. "Because that's not how the world works. And for your information, I cleaned the shop because you were nowhere to be found, and it needed to be done. Now." He reopened the laptop lid and looked at her with those cool blue eyes. "I think it would be easier if we could work together when need be. Like ordering supplies. It'll be a lot cheaper if we bulk order and split it up when it—"

"Work *together*? Are you serious? I'd rather shave fifty pounds of chocolate by hand than work with you." She didn't need his Kelley ego, sucking the oxygen out of her airspace.

He cocked his head. "I don't like this any more than you do."

"Really? You're not enjoying the opportunity to stick it to a Hart?" To *her*.

"Grow up, Lily. We're adults now. This childish feud is a thing of the past."

She didn't know why his words felt like a slap.

Shoot. She wanted—*needed*—to be away from him.

Before she could reply, he set both hands on either side

of the computer. Blew out a breath, maybe of exasperation. As if she were a *child*. Oh, heavens, save her from arrogant Kelleys, especially the one she used to date.

"This is an unfortunate situation we find ourselves in, and while yes, we are competitors, we're going to have to tolerate being around each other, at least for the next five weeks. I'd rather we keep things civil. Professional."

Oh, she'd give him civil. Professional. It was only July in Michigan, but the arctic freeze was beginning early this year. She mustered a fake smile. "If it's so difficult and unfortunate, I've got a solution: you can just give up now."

He scowled. "Is this a game to you?"

She scowled right back. "Of course not. I gave up my whole life to be here." And sure, her whole life back in Florida hadn't amounted to much, but still. She'd moved here for this shop—not to lose everything to a Kelley.

Again.

"Are you sure it isn't a game to *you*? You could do a thousand other things, Declan. Why would you want to come back here and run this fudge shop? Is it just to spite me?"

And maybe her words had landed hard because his mouth opened. Then something sparked in his blue eyes. "Not everything is about you, Lily. This isn't personal. It's business." He paused, glanced up at her before flicking his gaze back to the counter. "Family business."

"Guess I shouldn't be surprised." Because it always came back to that, didn't it? Family loyalty over everything else.

Not that she was against family loyalty. It was a big reason she was here too, the reason she'd left Jonathon Island in the first place . . . eager to go away so she could learn all there was to learn about making fudge, so she could one day return and make Hart Family Fudge the best on the island.

And she had learned. She'd learned so many little techniques to improve her candy making, tricks that expanded her knowledge, gave her a wider perspective on best practices.

There was just the pesky part about running an actual business that had managed to escape her. But she was older now. Wiser. Knew that she couldn't totally ignore the business side of things.

Especially if Declan—Mr. CEO himself—was her competitor.

Huffing, Lily rounded her shoulders and stalked to the supply shelf in the corner of the lobby, lined with boxes, ribbons, sea salt, caramel, sugar, and several other ingredients for easy grabbing by employees who would cook in the copper kettles and use the marble tables to demonstrate fudge making for passersby. The kitchen was also lined with pots and extra tables for those times when they wanted privacy for their creations.

She ran her fingers along the rim of one of the copper kettles, one her mom had used countless times. So many memories.

And if she had to play nice in order to hold on to them, then so be it.

"Fine," she ground out between her teeth.

"What's that?"

She turned, found him watching her. "I said fine. We can order supplies together. Or whatever."

Declan nodded, no indication of what he was thinking as he pulled a notebook and pen from his briefcase. "Have you already placed your order for baking supplies?"

She didn't want to answer him. It felt like sharing insider knowledge. How would she keep her recipes secret if he knew what she was ordering?

He tapped his pen. "You have to order supplies."

"Seriously? Give me a whole second to make a list." Which probably started with a plan of what she might be making, right? "My mom has some supplies left from her catering. I was going to start with those and then see what I needed."

"I'm guessing it'll go quickly, yeah? What with the way you like to experiment." He froze, frowned, cleared his throat. "I mean, the way you used to."

Oh, look who was flustered. But before she could come up with a reply, he shook his head and added, "Anyway, with the drop in tourism right now, I think we should target about one-third of full weekly production, so I'll adjust the order accordingly." He punched something into his phone and turned it to face her. "Here's my estimate of what you'll save if you're buying the same basic ingredients I am for about eight to ten batches of fudge per day."

She had to walk closer to read the screen. His calculator app was open and revealed a number higher than she'd expected. "Fine."

"Fine, you'll give me your order?"

Dropping into a squat, Lily fished in her backpack and pulled out several loose pieces of paper. To-do list. Grocery list. A sort of fudge shop supply list.

"Here." She stood and thrust the list in his direction. "Wait—" She pulled it back and tore off the bottom section. The part that had her next-level, top-secret, epicurean delight ingredients. She shoved the torn end into the small pocket on her leather leggings and handed the rest of the list back to him.

He took it, a quirk to his brow. Oh, yes. He wanted to ask. She could tell.

"It's need-to-know." She crossed her arms. "And you don't need to know." She'd get that stuff on her own, thank you very much.

"Whatever you say."

Declan went back to his computer and typed something in. Lily rounded the counter and stood behind him.

"Do you need something?" he asked.

"Just making sure you aren't resorting to sabotage."

"I don't need to resort to sabotage to beat you."

"Mm-hmm. I'll just watch what you order." She leaned against the counter while he pulled up several websites, entering their supply order and making notes on the page beside his computer.

Shoot. He smelled good. A little too good.

She'd have to bring a nose plug to work tomorrow.

Finally, he turned the screen toward her. "See? Whatever you think, I'm not out to destroy you. At least by cheating." He whispered that last part. "Does everything look okay?"

She reviewed the list. Of course, it was all perfect. Precise. So very Declan. "Yes. Thank—" But nope. She wouldn't thank him.

"What was that?" He cupped a hand to his ear. "I believe the words you are looking for are *thank you*."

Was he teasing her? Or just being a downright jerk?

It didn't matter. She refused to let him get to her.

Lily smiled. Kept her voice sweet. "I will say thank you when you hand over the keys to my fudge shop."

"I don't have a key—"

"Which you will. Because I can fudge circles around you, Slick, and you know it." She added a wink, picked up her backpack, and walked into the back kitchen.

And refused to acknowledge that maybe, just a little, she was shaking.

Declan refused to let Isaac be right.

Lily was *not* going to get her claws back into him. She wasn't.

He wouldn't allow it.

Setting his head back against the exterior wall of the fudge shop, Declan groaned as he waited for the ferry freight delivery that was supposed to arrive any moment. He'd spent the last half a week drafting his business plan, strategizing a marketing plan, and pulling all the original Kelley's Classic Fudge recipes together. Now it was late Saturday afternoon, and this was the first time he'd been still in days.

And of course, where did his thoughts automatically land?

On Lily Hart. And the fact that she'd barely said a word

to him, which had only made him, stupidly, uber-aware of whenever she walked into the room.

Felt a little like a game, who would look up first.

Clearly not her. Oh, the woman was cold. But he knew that, didn't he?

Shoot. Probably he couldn't blame her because *he'd* been the one to tell her to grow up. Which she should, thanks, but . . . yeah, that hadn't come out quite like he'd meant it.

And then he'd actually *teased* her. Like, what? They might be friends? Sheesh, even he wanted to bang his head against the wall because it was like a red flag to a bull.

Lily Hart would use everything in her arsenal to destroy him.

Thankfully, they'd mostly avoided each other since then—him staying holed up in the small fudge shop office beside the storeroom, her experimenting in the kitchen. He assumed so, anyway. The few times he'd trudged through to grab a cup of coffee or his lunch from the fridge, it had looked like a vat of chocolate had exploded all over the counters and kettles.

And then there was the time they'd passed in the tiny hallway, outside the restroom, and he'd had to hold his hands at his sides instead of reaching up to swipe away the chocolate smeared on her cheek.

Muscle memory. That's all it was.

Don't get crazy.

The rumble of an ATV emerged from the east, where Ferry Street joined Main, and Declan pushed himself off the wall as Luke Harris—one of the ferry company's delivery men—puttered toward Declan, toting this weekend's supply load. His was one of the few permitted vehicles on the island during the season, though Declan had heard that the horse-drawn drays of the past would be back once the horses returned to the island next year.

Declan waved and stepped off the sidewalk onto the cobblestones. "Hey, Luke."

The guy had been several years ahead of Declan in school, and now lived in Port Joseph working for the ferry company along with his brother Martin. "Welcome back, Declan. Looks like someone's opening shop." Luke, a former basketball player with his tall, lanky frame, hopped from the ATV and walked to the back of the utility trailer.

"We sure are." *We.* He cringed.

Luke lowered the gate of the trailer. "Mind if I run over to your mom's place real quick and grab a chicken salad sandwich?" He patted his stomach. "It's been a while since breakfast, and Martha's got the best sandwiches in Michigan."

"Sure. I'll unload."

"Thanks, buddy. The packages at the very back are yours. The rest are going to the hotel."

"No problem. Enjoy the grub."

Luke hurried across the street, and Declan loosened the cargo straps, glancing at his watch. Hopefully Lily would get here soon so the supplies wouldn't melt in the heat of the day. He was definitely over this not-having-his-own-key situation. The sooner Seb got back, the better. How long did a cruise last, anyway? Hopefully it wasn't one of those around the world in a year ventures.

Now that the supplies were here, he could open the shop this week. Once he got his first batches of fudge made, of course.

Of course. He'd taken a look at the family recipe so many times he had it memorized. But the entire idea twisted his gut. He didn't know the first thing about *fudge*.

Lily, however, made it look easy.

The few times he'd snuck into Hart Family Fudge when they'd been together for those two short months—after hours, so no one from either of their families would see them—he'd been positively captivated watching her heat and swirl ingredients together in a large copper kettle. Then, when it had reached the right temperature, he'd lean against the counter and follow her every movement as she lined up the framing on a marble slab, poured the liquid gold inside, and paddled it all into something edible.

No, more than edible. Something delectable.

Aaaaand there he went again. Thinking about Lily. About them, together. Once upon a disastrous time. No happy ending there—and probably he needed to focus on that, thank you so much, if he wanted to win this thing.

Declan hoisted a large box of butter, turned and spotted Lily walking down the sidewalk from the direction of the hotel and lifting her sunglasses onto the top of her head. Her hair pulled back in a loose ponytail, today she wore cutoff jean shorts and a T-shirt that accentuated her curvy, feminine figure.

How annoying that he noticed.

"You're late, and the butter is melting."

"Calm down, Slick. I saw Luke and I hustled over." She unlocked the door and propped it open. "Happy?"

His reply was a grunt as he headed inside and on through the door that led to the kitchen, stacking the boxes on the counter. He'd move them into the refrigerator once he'd brought everything else inside.

When he returned to the road, Lily was reading the box labels. She shot him a narrow-eyed look. "You addressed them to Kelley's Classic Fudge? Really, Declan?"

"I had to create an account with the supply company, so of course I used the name of our LLC." He sighed. "Do you have to make everything a battle?"

"You're the one who suggested the battle—I mean competition—in the first place. Not me." She walked toward the door, and in her wake he caught a strong whiff of disdain woven with the annoying notes of an alluring floral.

Focus.

"It was the only fair thing I could think of at the time. But believe me, I am deeply regretting not just waiting for Seb to return so he could give me the shop outright."

"Ha! You're assuming a lot there, buster."

"Come on, Lily." He pinched the bridge of his nose. This woman. Seriously. "Can we please pretend to get along? This is exhausting."

"Pretend? Sure, I can pretend to not despise you for trying to steal my family's company. Let's get this stuff moved." Lily heaved a large box from the trailer.

"You're going to hurt yourself. Let me take that one."

"Nope." And there she went, carrying it through the door she'd propped open and into the kitchen, bypassing the counter where he'd stacked his boxes, and headed straight for the walk-in refrigerator.

He jogged ahead of her and opened the fridge door. Blinked at what he saw inside. "Is that tape?" Blue painter's tape had been placed down the wall and across the floor of the cooler, splitting the space in half.

She dropped her load on the line. "It is. That's Kelley-land." She pointed to the far side. "You keep all your cold ingredients over there. Don't touch mine."

"Drawing the literal battle lines, are we?"

She shrugged. "Gotta protect my stuff."

Did she really think he would mess with her ingredients? Sure, he wanted to beat her, but he wasn't a cheater. "Let me guess—the dry goods storage is similarly delineated?"

She folded her arms. "Of course."

"Fine. If that's how you want to play it. Maybe we should divide the front of shop too."

"That's my plan. I just ran out of tape."

"That's going to look really professional. Nice." Shaking his head, Declan followed her out of the cooler, back to the street, where they continued hauling in their order of butter, sugar, cream, chocolate, nuts, and the rest of their raw materials, placing cold things into the fridge and everything else on the open counters surrounding the edges of the kitchen.

By the time he carried in the last box, waved to Luke as he pulled away, and closed the door, Lily had grabbed a utility knife and was already opening up the boxes. "I'm going to start sorting the order."

"I'll help. We should start with those bags of sugar, though." They had a stack of fifty-pound bags. He grabbed his clipboard while she sliced open the various boxes. "Just tag them with an H or K and I'll move them later."

"I can carry them too."

"I know you can. I just don't want you using the excuse that you injured yourself as the reason you lost."

"Not gonna happen, because I'm not going to lose."

"Can we just get this done? Preferably in silence? I'm starting to get a headache."

She pursed her lips. "Fine by me."

"Good."

"Great."

And now they were back to the arctic freeze, and maybe he deserved that. In silence, Lily worked through all the boxes and bags, dividing, labeling, and moving them.

After an hour or two, he glanced over at Lily as she yawned. Flexed her hand before lifting the knife to the tape on the box that was poised on the edge of the counter. Her fingers trembled a bit.

And he shouldn't have taken pity on her, he knew. But still. Declan stood and stretched, holding out a hand. "Here. I'll take a turn with the knife."

"So you can stab me in the back?" Lily stayed focused on the box, not even bothering to look his way. "No thanks."

"Don't be so stubborn."

"Not being stubborn. I'm fine." She sliced through the box just like she'd done several times already.

Except this time, the knife skidded down the cardboard and kept going, cutting right across the top of her knee.

Lily yelped and dropped the box cutter. Bright crimson pooled and dripped from her leg onto the floor.

And she just stood there, staring at it, blinking.

"Lily!" Declan grabbed a freshly laundered cleaning rag and rushed over, lifting her onto the counter without thinking about it. He then knelt, pressing the rag to her wound and holding it snug to stop the bleeding.

She grimaced. "Stop. I don't need your help." Except her words didn't match her actions, because she just leaned back on her elbows and lay perfectly still while Declan cradled her leg.

"Clearly, you do." He held tight. "Are you going to faint at the sight of blood?"

"You'd like that, wouldn't you? Then you'd probably just leave me here to bleed out."

Really? "Tempting as that is, it wouldn't be good for business."

"You're only half joking." She let out another groan when he shifted the pressure.

"Am I hurting you?"

She closed her eyes. "It isn't you. I mean, it hurts, but not from the pressure." A grunt. "Ugh. I can't believe I did that." She swiped away a stray tear from her cheek with her other hand.

He lifted the rag away for a moment. Yikes. "It's definitely going to need stitches."

"You think?" She smeared another tear across her face, this time taking a smudge of black mascara with it.

"We need to get you to the clinic."

"And how do you propose we do that?"

Hmm. "Good point." The clinic was northeast of here. All the way down Main Street and then a little ways up Blueberry Boulevard, past Blueberry Hill Park, near the police and fire station and the public school.

In other words, too far for her to walk with this injury. A bike was probably out of the question too.

"I have an idea. Don't go anywhere." Tying the rag around her knee, he started toward the back alley door.

"Where exactly am I gonna go?" Then, with less bravado, "Dec?"

The old nickname, said with such timidity—even, dare he say, softness?—did something to his heart. He paused, turned. "Yeah, Lil?"

"Hurry, please."

He chuckled. "That hurt to say, didn't it?"

Her face paled as she opened her eyes and looked at him, and man, he felt bad for teasing her.

"It's going to be okay," he said. "And yes, I'll hurry. Because as much as it would help my odds exponentially to have you stuck in ICU with some sort of gangrenous infection—which might even be some sort of poetic justice—I am too much of a gentleman to allow that."

"Ha. You. A gentleman."

He lifted a shoulder. "Believe what you like. Now I'm going to go save the day, if you don't mind." Declan stepped into the alleyway and headed for Jonathon Boulevard, jogging up the road until he reached his parents' house.

Thankfully, nobody was home as he snatched the keys off the rack in the foyer and headed out to the western side of the house where Mom and Dad's golf cart sat covered. He pulled back the covering, praying there was enough gas left from the winter months when they'd last used it.

Declan inserted the key and breathed a sigh of relief when the engine sputtered and finally rumbled to life.

Now to just drive this thing without getting caught.

He eased off the gravel path and onto Poppy Place, eyes scanning this way and that for anyone who might scold him for illegal use of a golf cart during the season. Thankfully, the coast was clear—a sheer miracle given that it was a Saturday afternoon and plenty of people were likely home.

The drive to the alley behind the fudge shop took thirty seconds. Declan kept the engine running and headed inside to grab Lily.

She still lay there, eyes closed, and her lips were moving. Perhaps in prayer?

"Widow? You still with me?"

Her eyes opened. "Unfortunately for you, yes." She sat up, groaning, and he rushed over to help her.

"Do you think you can put any pressure on it?"

She just looked at him.

"Right. Okay, then." He shook out his hands and bent to scoop her up.

"Um, excuse me. What are you doing?"

"Carrying you."

"I can hop on one leg if I have to." She started to slide to the edge of the counter and gingerly placed all of her weight on her good leg. Hissed between her teeth.

Hopped. Stopped. Tried again. Hissed again. "Come on, Lily. You've got this," she muttered to herself.

"Okay, there, Grandma." Declan tapped his watch. "I think I just turned one hundred waiting for you."

She glared at him. "I stabbed myself with a knife, if you hadn't noticed!"

"And you were worried *I* was going to be the one doing the stabbing." At her further narrowed eyes, he bit back a smile. "All right, well, if you're going to insist on doing everything yourself . . ." He started to turn.

She snatched his shirt and tugged him back around. "Wait." Lily looked up at him with those luminous eyes. "Fine. Help me."

He stepped closer. Too close, but he couldn't move away. "What's the magic word?"

She gritted her teeth—maybe not, this time, from the pain. "Please."

"Good girl." Then he scooped her up as gingerly as he could and tried not to think about how soft her curves felt against him. How well she fit in the crook of his arms.

How familiar this felt—

How right.

Nope. How *wrong*.

He cradled her as he walked her right out into the alley toward the idling golf cart. "Your chariot awaits."

"Wait, seriously? You—Declan Kelley—are breaking the law?" Her wide eyes flitted back to him.

Something thumped in his chest, and it took all his willpower to look away from her. "Extenuating circumstances." He settled her ever-so-gently onto the soft tan passenger seat. "It was the only viable option."

"Mm-hmm."

He popped around to the driver's side and glanced carefully about, taking the back roads toward the clinic. Hopefully Police Chief John York or one of his deputies wouldn't be waiting around the corner.

Lily was quiet for a few moments when Declan looked over to make sure she hadn't fainted. But she sat there watching him, gnawing on her bottom lip. "I'll find a way to pay you back for this, you know."

"Is that a threat?" And why couldn't he help but smile as they bumped along the road? "You don't owe me for helping you, Lily. It's called basic human kindness. I'd hope if *I* was lying helpless and afraid—"

"Hey!"

"—that you'd help me too."

"Hmm. Maybe." She leaned back against the seat, grimacing. Must be hurting pretty bad now that the adrenaline was wearing off.

"Hang tight. We're almost there."

She grunted, nodded. And said nothing more as he drove her to the clinic.

Several hours later, after a longer-than-usual wait at the clinic, Lily had been stitched up, medicated, and given an overdue tetanus shot. In the dim evening light, Declan pulled up on her street. Somehow, they'd managed to evade the Jonathon Island police. He'd become a criminal for her.

Lily Hart struck again.

He cut the engine, drummed his fingers along the steering wheel. "It feels like I should drop you off around the corner. You know, so nobody sees."

She glanced at him sideways. "We're not kids anymore, Declan. Or . . ."

She didn't have to finish. *Or a couple, sneaking around.*

Declan swallowed against his dry throat. "No. We're not."

Instead, they were competitors. Enemies.

Except tonight, under the stars, with the moon illuminating her eyes, it didn't exactly feel that way.

She'll get her claws in you, Decky.

Nope. "Goodnight, Lil." Oops, the nickname just slid out. He held his breath.

Her mouth tightened, and she drew in a breath. Then, "See you tomorrow, Slick."

She got out and hobbled to her house.

And he drove away without looking back.

Six

ND NOW, SHE OWED HIM.

The annoying fact of it only upped Lily's speed as she headed south toward downtown from her parents' house along Lake Shore Drive, her three-days-old stitches still pulling a bit in her knee. A bike was out of the question for the next ten days, but Dr. Lake had said she could walk—and good thing, since Dani had requested her presence at tonight's Jonathon Island Business Association mixer.

"Please. All he did was take you to the ER," Sadie piped up in her earpiece, having just heard the entire wretched story.

She'd left out the strange look he'd given her Saturday night, with the moonlight in his eyes, as if . . .

No. No *as ifs*. "And did I mention he called me Lil? How dare he!"

"Oh my. Pistols at dawn."

"The point is, he spent hours helping me, and now I feel like I can't beat him fair and square."

"Your logic escapes me." Sadie's wry voice felt eons away. Nine years since they'd been together, instead of nine days.

"It makes perfect sense." Lily slowed her pace at a twinge in her knee. Her eyes wandered across the lake, where the lowering sun cast a long ray of light across the water. "I don't want him holding this over me. And I know God doesn't work this way, but what if God chooses sides and He blesses Declan for helping me? And wins?"

"Please. Didn't you text me just yesterday that the man can't even make fudge? He's literally trying to run a fudge shop."

"Is it terrible that I did a little happy dance when I peeked into the kitchen and saw the disaster he had on his hands yesterday? He overheated the fudge, so it got all separated and oily on top. And the look on his face..."

"His handsome face?"

A beat. "What—no. He's...sure, he's still hot. All that sweat turned his hair slightly curly, and—" She stopped. "I see what you did there."

Sadie laughed. "Sorry. I was just wondering if being with him had stirred up any old feelings."

"Not. A. Chance. He's annoying and arrogant, and I did mention he's trying to torpedo my entire future, right? And now he's being *nice*."

"I know. What a jerk."

"Exactly! And now I feel guilty that he had to spend hours helping me on Saturday night. Now we've got an unbalanced score. He's one ahead of me. And believe me, I need all the advantages I can get."

She sighed as she rounded the southern bend of the island, trees flanking her on one side, the water on the other. A bicyclist passed—Pastor Arnie, Tara's husband, still dressed in slacks and a short-sleeved button-down. Maybe he was headed to visit a parishioner in her parents' neighborhood.

"You have plenty of advantage—like a lifetime of experience."

Lily waved and continued her jaunt. "I don't know. Declan's really good at business stuff. He's got an MBA. He's spent most of the last week tucked away in the fudge shop office, clacking away on his laptop. Whereas I . . ."

"Have been making fudge?"

"That is going to waste. I thought about opening shop today, but the day got away from me."

"I'm sure it'll fly off the shelves once you're open."

The Grand Hotel came into view. Just beyond it, nestled in a grove of trees, stood the island's famous gazebo, originally built for a movie set. A group of thirty or more people gathered there, mingling—the business association.

Lily sighed. "Or I could fail at this, Sadie. Big fail. And then what?"

"Then you just come back to Florida. Find another dead-end job you hate without an ounce of creativity and see how it sucks away your soul little by little," Sadie said, her tone full of sarcasm. "Oh wait, I'm talking to you, not me, huh?"

"Haha, I'm being serious here."

"I kind of am too." Sadie sighed. "Look, Lil, we talked about this. You need to ask those around you for help. In fact, what about asking Declan for advice on the business stuff? He's certainly qualified."

"Girl, have you heard nothing I've said about the scales of justice already being tilted in his favor?"

"It's ridiculous to think you owe him anything for being a decent human being."

Funny. Declan had said the same thing. Still. "I just don't want to be in his debt."

"Then do something for him. Show him how to make fudge."

"And lose the only advantage I have over him?"

"I give up, Lily. You say you want to repay him for his kindness, but it doesn't sound like he needs anything else from you."

Ouch. "I guess that's true." As Lily approached the business owners' gathering, soft classical music and chatter met her ears. A breeze lifted the ends of her skirt—the one she'd put on just for this occasion—and she inhaled a deep breath.

"Just because you show him the process doesn't mean his fudge will beat yours. You're a creative genius. You don't have to share any of your secrets with him. Just the basics." Her friend paused. "You *can* stick to just the basics, right?"

"Stop. Of course. But I'm not falling for him again. Ever."

"And why not? I know he hurt you in the past, Lily, and

it was absolutely wrong of him and his family to blame you for his grandfather's death—"

"It *was* wrong." How was Lily supposed to have known that Barry Kelley—recently diagnosed with Alzheimer's and asleep in his bed—would wander out alone that night? That he'd somehow find his way onto the ferry, cross to the mainland, and be involved in a fatal pedestrian hit-and-run?

Except it *had* been her fault that Declan had been with her when he was supposed to be watching Grandpa. "It was wrong of them to blame me, but I was wrong too."

"You were young. And in love—"

"Crush. I had a crush. Nothing more."

Silence. "Never mind that you fled the island, your entire life and everything afterward—"

"So did he."

And she hadn't really let that settle until now. That night had derailed both of them.

And now they were back.

"Listen, a whole decade has passed, and you're a different person now."

Was she, though? Yes. No.

She walked closer to the gazebo now. It was even more beautiful than Lily remembered, with softly lit bulbs wrapped around the posts and hanging from the ceiling. A spread of drinks and appetizers topped two six-foot tables lining the edges of the brick pathway that led to the three steps of the octagonal structure.

Dani stood on the steps with Liam and another man

whose back was to Lily. She glanced at her watch and placed her hand on Liam's broad shoulder.

"I've gotta go," Lily said. "The meeting is going to start soon."

"Lil?"

"Yeah?"

"You *can* do this. I believe it. Your parents believe it. But all of that means nothing if you don't believe it."

Aw, Sadie. "Thanks," she managed to eke out past her clogged throat. "Love you."

"Love you back."

Lily hung up and stuffed her phone into her cross-body purse. Her eyes scanned the crowd, and wow. There were a lot of new faces. A lot of serious faces, belonging to people who held drinks and clear plates with cute bite-sized appetizers. A few wore fancy dresses, a couple men in suits. Clearly the newbies.

She did recognize several people, though. Fifty-something widower Doug Manning—of Doug's Market fame—adjusted his thick glasses and perused the veggie tray, maybe avoiding the dessert table to keep his athletic figure strong. And she spotted Island House Inn owner Caleb Kennedy, who had been a few years ahead of Lily in school.

She spotted Mia and Cody holding hands, talking with someone she didn't know, and then her gaze landed on . . . oh no. There, by the hors d'oeuvres, stood the Kelley clan. Jill and Patrick and Martha and Frank.

Somehow, Lily had managed to avoid them all since that first day in the fudge shop with Patrick. But right now, they were all—save Jill, whose eyes held some sort of pity—glaring at her. Especially Martha.

Lily's stomach turned over on itself. If tonight's gathering wasn't a Main Street Festival information session in addition to a get-to-know-you and welcome for new business owners, she'd be fleeing to the shop kitchen about now to see if she could get Mom's old ice cream maker working and whip up a pint of raspberry chip.

"Lily! Over here!" Dani, waving her over.

Lily's gut loosened as she hurried toward her friend—but tightened again when the mystery man in front of Dani turned.

Declan.

He wore a suit, of course, unlike the other flannel-clad locals, and that only made him—shoot—stunningly handsome. His dark suit cut perfectly across his shoulders, and the silvery-blue of his tie electrified his eyes. He held some sort of sparkling drink in a flute, looking every bit like the fancy, la-de-da businessman from Chicago.

As if he owned the air on the entire island.

Run.

Lily pressed her hands against her many-colored skirt, the fabric of which was much more wrinkled than she'd remembered. That's what happened when you grabbed something at the last minute from the back of the closet.

Dani took the steps down to hug Lily. "I'm so glad you made it. How's your knee?"

"Doing fine." Lily glanced around. "Um, I didn't know it was going to be such a formal event tonight. I feel way underdressed."

"Girl, look at me." Waving her hands up and down her body—where she wore a red blouse and black slacks that looked more comfortable than stylish—Dani cocked an eyebrow. "I think these newbies don't yet understand how casual we are here."

Liam laughed. "You'll whip them into shape soon enough, babe." Indeed, Liam wore khakis, a golf shirt, and Dockers. So, still preppy, but he'd lost the New York vibe.

Dani grinned. "It worked on you."

Somehow the four of them had ended up in a circle. Lily's bare arm brushed against the soft fabric of Declan's jacket, and of course, the man smelled good too. Cardamom, she thought, and, hmm. Cardamom. That would made a lovely addition to her holiday fudge menu.

What—no. She absolutely would *not* be adding anything to the menu inspired by Declan Kelley.

"I want to grab something to eat before the meeting starts," Dani said, her gaze flitting quickly to Lily and Declan.

"I'll go with you," Lily said. Anything for some cardamom-free air.

"Great. I'll introduce you to some of the new shop owners. Be back in a bit, boys." Dani looped her arm through Lily's and dragged her toward the food table. "I'm guessing you've been so busy getting your own store ready to open that you haven't had a chance to meet everyone else yet."

"How did you know?"

"Because I think that's the case for the others here too. But I wanted everyone to feel like part of Jonathon Island."

"So they'll feel invested in the community and want to stay?"

"Exactly." She squeezed Lily's arm, then released it once they'd reached the table. "Though whatever happens with the shop, I hope you find a reason to stay here. Now that you're back, this town might get fun again."

Lily laughed. "C'mon, I wasn't that much of a troublemaker."

Dani waggled her eyebrows. "I do remember some late-night golf cart shenanigans."

"What?" She laughed. "What happens on the island stays on the island."

"Exactly," Dani said, winking. They'd reached the table.

Lily piled her plate with mini meatballs, fruit kebabs, tiny quiches, and some carrots to round out the food groups.

Then Dani led her to a group of people talking in the grass. "Hey, guys. This is Lily Hart, one of the business owners at the fudge shop."

An older gentleman with oversized glasses and a comb-over licked barbecue sauce off his thumb. "That's the shop with the competition, yes?"

Dani nodded. "Sure is, Fred. Lily, this is Fred Miller and his wife, Ginny. They run Miller Antiques just up the road from you, between Jemma Swanson's glassblowing shop—she's around here somewhere—and Good Day Coffee."

"Nice to meet you."

"You too, honey." His wife, a sweet-looking older woman with powder-blue hair and wrinkled cheeks, leaned in closer. "So, just how do you plan on beating your competition?"

"By making the best fudge on the island." Lily winked— because honestly, what else could she say?

"That's not enough, though, is it?" A dark-haired man in his fifties with a shrewd brow handed the woman beside him his plate and unbuttoned his jacket over his girth. "We've all competed for these spots, so we know that it's not just about what you're offering, but how you're offering it."

"So true, so true." Dani flashed a smile, but Lily could tell it was strained. "Lil, this is Mickey and Jocelyn Harper. They are running Island Souvenirs next door to Doug's Market."

"Welcome to Jonathon Island." Lily couldn't keep the shaking out of her voice. Because as much as Dani had glossed over Mickey's statement, he was right.

After another round of introductions in a separate group—this one much younger, including the owners of Holly's Flowers (Holly Joseph), Maritime Dreams (Grace Marconi), Bella Island Boutique (Britta O'Keefe), and Hair Haven Salon (Ivy Dawson)—Lily's head was spinning. The buzz of conversation grated on her nerves. And yes, there was a general excitement in the air as the new business owners spoke about the possibilities, all the ways they would capitalize on the hotel's reopening in stages, how amazing this business opportunity was, how they planned to attract clientele.

But Lily didn't want to talk bottom lines and brokers and business plans. Her fingers itched to move, to create.

She didn't see a single woman wearing a tie-dyed skirt. Mostly pants, blouses, no one in heels, but no one wearing tennis shoes, either.

Business people.

As opposed to the neighborhood fudge maker. Sheesh, she might be lucky she didn't have chocolate in her hair.

Dani could fill her in later about the details of the festival and what was required of the business owners, but right now, Lily needed to get out of here. Go somewhere she actually belonged.

For now.

This was a mistake. *More* than a mistake.

It just bugged him that Lily had left the event.

No, what bothered him had been the strange, almost defeated expression on her face.

He shouldn't have noticed. But she was hard to miss in that crazy floral skirt and bright blue tank top. Of course it made her blue eyes only that much bluer.

And all evening, as he'd chatted with new business owners, Declan had watched her shoulders get lower and lower.

Aw, he definitely shouldn't have left the business association mixer.

Now he stood outside the closed fudge shop, leaning his forehead against the front door—hand hovering over the doorknob.

He'd expected her to come back when Dani's meeting had started. But she never did.

And he knew where she'd go, of course.

When Lily was upset, she created.

When Lily was happy, she created too.

At least, the old Lily had. And while they'd both grown up, Declan hoped that was something about her that would never change.

So he'd slipped out of his chair beside Dad, claiming a stomachache. Not exactly a lie, since the fact he was here, about to check on the one person who could destroy him, was indeed causing him great intestinal distress.

Okay. Get in, check on her, get out.

Declan twisted the knob and it gave way. *Come on, Lil. At least lock it behind you.*

Grunts, thumps, and exclamations spilled out from the kitchen.

Closing the door behind him, he popped the deadbolt in place and headed for the kitchen. What state would he find it in? To his knowledge, he'd been the last one to use it—after his latest failed attempt at making fudge—but Hurricane Lily never took long to leave a mess in her wake.

When he eased open the kitchen door, his eyebrows rose at the sight of Lily, her back to him, leaning over the counter, nose deep in a manual while a large, unfamiliar stainless steel appliance sat on the counter beside her.

As he approached, the door squeaked and Lily jumped, whirling, hand to her chest. "Wha—?"

"It's just me." He held up his hands. "But I do see you're unarmed."

"Haha. Funny man." Lily rubbed her nose, which was slightly red. Had she been crying? Yep, her eyes were puffy.

He stifled the crazy urge to reach out—

Stop.

If he knew what was good for him, he'd turn around. Sprint out of the shop.

Instead, he loosened his tie and tugged off his jacket. "So, you do know there's a party going on up the road."

She shrugged. Then turned back to her manual.

Ho-kay. Clearly she wasn't going to let him in on whatever made her flee the event.

And now that he knew she was okay, he should go back to the mixer. Hear all the details about the upcoming festival, all the ways he could use it to his advantage as a business owner.

His eyes caught on a few dirty bowls and utensils in the sink, traveling to some dripped cream or milk on the counter beside it. And then they snagged on the top header of the page where Lily ran her finger along some words, gaze intense. "You're making ice cream?"

She sighed. "Trying. But this thing isn't working."

"You do know this is a *fudge* shop, right?" Declan looked over her shoulder at the manual.

Wrong move, because she smelled sweet—vanilla, maybe? And some sort of floral scent.

Seriously. Stop.

She glanced at him. "News flash: I can make more than fudge." Lily waved her hand up and down to indicate the dusty appliance. "Mom bought this commercial ice cream maker at an auction, but it's not working."

"And you thought, hey, now's a good time to fix it?

When you're in the middle of getting a fudge shop up and running?"

She stepped away from him, sighed. "I just . . . I just don't want to think about fudge right now." Her voice was quiet, and something about it sounded so lost.

Aw, and now again, he nearly reached out to her. She had a sort of terrible power over him—always had, really.

Nope. "What's wrong with it?"

"It keeps shutting off too early."

He rolled up his sleeves. "Can I take a look?"

"I really don't need your help."

He raised an eyebrow.

She sighed. "Fine. But I definitely can't let you fix this without repaying you somehow."

"Just what did you have in mind?" Oh—wait. No, that came out wrong.

Her eyes widened.

Aw. "Forget I said that. Really, let me help."

Her lips pursed.

He held up his hands. "All right, all right. Look, if it makes you uncomfortable, I'll just step aside and let you figure this one out yourself. Even though I know what's probably wrong with it."

She considered him for a long moment. Finally, "Fine. But in exchange, I'll show you how to *actually* make fudge."

"What are you talking about? I know how to make fudge. It's simple. I have the family recipes. All I have to do is follow the directions."

Except, inside he heard his own voice calling him a liar.

He'd spent hours over the last two days, and thrown out more batches than he wanted to admit.

Lily studied him. "Some things in life don't follow exactness and precision."

She *was* talking about fudge, right?

"Isn't that the point of the recipes? To recreate them again and again?"

"There are other factors you have to consider. Every batch of fudge is slightly different, and you kind of have to feel your way through the making of it. Do you think you can do that, Slick?" She added a smile, and his heart suddenly woke up and slammed against his chest.

He hadn't actually forgotten how pretty she was. Just wanted to.

"So, can you?" Now, she cocked her head, raised an eyebrow, hands on her hips. "*Feel* it instead of think it to death? Or have you lost all sense of emotion?"

She must not have heard the way his heart beat wildly in his throat at her nearness or she'd never question his ability to *feel*.

He swallowed, ignored her words. "So, you'll really give me some fudge-making lessons if I fix your machine here?"

"Yes." She stepped aside and flourished her arms toward the machine. "Have at it."

He stepped past her, ignored the sense of her, standing too close, and ran his fingers across the control panel, his fingers searching its edge. "Do you have a screwdriver? I want to pop the control panel face off."

"Hang on." Lily opened a lower cabinet and rummaged around, emerging with a pink Tupperware toolbox. Opening it, she plucked a flathead from inside and handed it over.

"Thanks." Declan found the lip of the panel and popped it off. "Hmm."

"You're just pretending to know what you're doing, aren't you?"

He flashed her a look. "Do you want my help or not?"

"Fine."

"What's wrong with it, again?"

"Shutting off before the cycle's done. I'm getting slightly colder mush. Not ice cream."

"Sounds like it isn't running long enough, cold enough, or both. Could be the sensor."

She'd stepped up, next to him, peering into the wiring. "So, how do you know so much about ice cream machines?"

He'd found the sensor, and unattached it with the flathead. "During my freshman year of college, I worked in an ice cream shop." He handed the screwdriver back.

"I'm having a hard time imagining you serving up scoops in the Windy City." Lily placed the flathead screwdriver back into the plastic tub. "Did you have one of those cute retro paper hats?"

"Yes. And an apron too."

"Bet that was a real chick magnet."

Declan pulled the sensor out of the machine, studied it. Looked like the sensor plate had dulled. "As a matter of fact, yes. My first college date came after I served a group of ladies their cones."

He glanced at her, grinning. And was it just his imagination, or was there a flash of something—maybe even jealousy—in Lily's eyes?

Oh? Declan cleared his throat. "Your thermostat sensor is rusty. Do you have a small scrub brush?"

"Maybe." Lily fished around and grabbed an old toothbrush. "Will this work? If not, I think there's some steel wool under the sink."

"We can try it." He gently scrubbed the end of it until the dull end had some shine. He set it back in place. "Let's try that. I recommend ordering a new sensor, though."

Replacing the panel cover, he plugged the machine back in. "Did you save your mixture?"

"The last one, yeah."

"Okay." He plugged the machine back in. "Give it a go."

Lily grabbed the cream mixture from the refrigerator and poured it back in. Turned on the machine. "Now we wait." She turned to him. A beat. Finally, "Thank you."

"You're welcome. See, that wasn't so terrible, right?"

She looked away, and maybe it had been. Ouch. Then she sighed and met his eyes. "I don't understand, Declan. Why are you trying to run me out of my family's fudge shop? Your family already owns enough restaurants on this island. They don't need this shop. And besides, their legacy of fudge isn't nearly as long as my family's."

She held so much pleading in her eyes he wanted to hold up his hands, to agree.

Except, "I'm doing this for my grandma."

Lily frowned. "What does any of this have to do with your grandma?"

Oh. "I guess I thought you knew."

"Knew what?"

Huh. "My grandma's house is being foreclosed on. The whole ordeal was so stressful for her that she had a small episode—not quite a heart attack, but close."

"Oh, Dec, I didn't know." And just like that, in the softness of her tone, he saw her. The Lily he once knew.

Once loved.

She made it worse by adding compassion into her blue eyes. "Is she all right?"

"She's okay. Back home and resting. I visited her yesterday, and she's looking stronger. But ever since Grandpa died, she's been . . ." He sighed. "Well, just a shell of her former self, you know?"

She nodded then, as if she *did* know. Huh.

"Anyway, don't ask me how she did it, but Mom worked it out so that her house could be part of the whole revitalization program. The one that promises a house for a dollar to new business owners."

Lily's mouth opened. "And so the house that's tied to this business . . ."

"Is Grandma's. Yes." His eyes searched Lily's. The hard edges had melted, softened. "The whole reason I'm here is to save her house." He swallowed. "And because it's my fault that she's in this mess in the first place."

She frowned. "How do you figure?"

"Grandpa took care of paying the bills, the property taxes."

She drew in a breath. "Right. And because he died that night . . ." She folded her arms across her chest, drew in a breath. Nodded. But the softness had hardened again.

"Funny, all this time I thought it was *my* fault. You blamed me."

And it was back—the terrible words, her hurt. "I never really blamed you—it wasn't your fault that . . . well, that I got caught up in the idea of us."

She flinched. "Sure seemed like it when you said you should have listened to your family and never gotten involved with 'someone like me.' When you shut the door in my face and left me crying in the rain outside your house."

"Grandpa was missing—I needed to help find him. But you're right, it wasn't your fault. It was mine." His voice softened. "I owe you an apology, Lil. I was grieving and my family blamed me. Still blames me." He reached out for her, but she took a step back.

He dropped his hand. "After you left, I did call to apologize, but you ghosted me."

She said nothing but her eyes misted. "You destroyed my reputation."

He hadn't thought about that, how she'd lost her home, her legacy. "I'm sorry. But there *were* consequences to our actions. I shouldn't have left Grandpa."

She said nothing.

He sighed. "And it's the same now. We both have responsibilities, things we are trying to do here. I recognize your position and respect your reason for doing this. Hopefully now, you can respect mine. So, what do you say? Can we call a truce?"

She considered him, and a tear dropped onto her cheek.

Shoot, and once again he wanted to reach out, pull her to himself . . .

He reached for his jacket instead.

"Fine," she said quietly. "A truce. For now. But that's all, Declan. Don't start thinking we're going to be friends—or anything else—again." She said it without softness, void of emotion.

Right. "Of course not, Lily. I wouldn't dream of it." Then he pulled on his jacket, straightened his tie, and headed for the door.

Seven

TODAY, HER FUTURE WOULD GO DOWN in flames.

Lily flipped on the lights and removed the heating blanket from the first of the three marble tables in the middle of the kitchen. Hart Family Fudge had always used them to keep the tables at just the right temperature for the first morning run. She'd helped make thousands of batches of fudge in this very shop—and there was no way she'd relinquish it to the Kelleys.

What had Lily been thinking, offering to help Declan make fudge?

Guilt, that's what. But today, she'd repay her debt—and then, hopefully, be free of Declan Kelley.

At least, metaphorically speaking.

Sunlight burned at the eastern horizon, glazing the sky in orange, pre-dawn light casting through the front windows. She loved the early-morning quiet of the shop kitchen.

Not today. Today she just kept hearing his words from last night. *I got caught up in the idea of us.*

Whatever.

He'd only made it worse then by looking like he'd wanted to . . .

What? Hug her? More.

Nope.

But the whole thing had her head spinning, and when he'd asked for a truce . . .

Oh, the man was good at his game of manipulation. First, a deal for her to teach him the family secrets—nope, not happening. She could teach a man the basics of fudge making without sharing their secret sauce.

And then he'd asked for the truce. And looked so earnest.

She should have run after him and taken it back, but frankly, the fact that he'd left the business meeting to check on her had sunk in, never mind his help with the ice cream maker. And then of course he had to tell her why he wanted the fudge shop. And despite the wounds of the past, it felt, okay, a little heroic to give up his life in Chicago to save Grandma's house.

Heroic and maybe manipulative—probably something they taught him in business school.

Lily folded the blanket, stowed it in the bin under the table, and took stock of the shop. In her haste last night—after a quick round of ice cream making to ensure Declan's fixes had worked—she'd left bowls and utensils dirty in the sink. But now they sat clean and sparkling on the drying mat beside the sink.

He'd returned to the shop after she left and cleaned up. Great. He probably thought her a mess. Note to self—maybe Oscar wasn't so wrong about leaving behind a pristine kitchen.

But never mind that. Where had she placed her recipe cards? She'd had them out last night, hoping to spark some ideas for new ice cream flavors based on some of her favorite fudge recipes, but now they were nowhere to be found. Hmm. Probably Declan had placed them somewhere as well. She'd ask him later.

Lily opened the refrigerator, humming, forcing her mind away from the subject of Declan Kelley while she placed chocolate, cream, vanilla, sugar onto the counter. Then she pulled a clean copper pot—her mother's favorite kettle—from its home on the storage rack and onto the cooking base. Gathered the wooden paddle, measuring cup, and a few other tools.

Even from back here, she could hear a key jiggle in the front door lock.

Her heart gave a quick pit-pat at the sound. *Aw, c'mon.*

Apparently Declan had rustled up a spare key somehow. Maybe Mia had searched Seb's office since he was still away.

A few seconds later, Declan walked through the swinging kitchen door wearing those sunglasses . . .

Lily looked away, hating her rampant heartbeat.

"Good morning, Lily."

Lily. Not Lil. Not even Widow.

So, no nicknames today, then. Good. Good. He was keeping things professional, just like she needed to do. "Good morning. Ready to make fudge?"

"Hopping right in. I like it."

"I figured the sooner we both have some batches made, the sooner we can get this competition officially under way." She walked toward the peg where a pair of aprons hung. Her mouth quirked. She shouldn't. But she couldn't help herself. Reaching for the navy blue apron, she looped it over her neck and around her back.

He eyed her, but walked over and picked up the other. Pink polka dot, Lily's favorite—except not today.

Aw, she was being childish.

He said nothing as he wrapped it around his torso. It barely fit, the pink apron ending around the same place as his white shirt.

"Cute," she said.

He smiled. "Real men can wear pink."

Yeah they could, because it only outlined his in-shape form, and the joke was on her.

Worse, now she really felt petty as she moved past Declan and partially unwrapped a slab of butter. She moved it slowly back and forth across the first marble table.

"What are you doing?"

"The first step in making fudge is to pull the warming blanket off the marble table—which I've already done—and butter it so the fudge doesn't stick."

"So that was my problem."

"One of many."

"Har har." Declan came alongside her, studying her

hand movements. A pad of paper and pen had magically appeared in his hands. "And why do we use the blankets again?"

"We use marble tables in particular because they help cool the fudge more quickly so the whole process doesn't take too long. But with our climate here, they get too cold overnight and would make the fudge set up too quickly if left uncovered overnight."

"Ah." He scribbled on his paper.

She set the unused butter back on the counter. "I'm curious—how many batches did you try that didn't turn out?"

"I'm not gonna answer that." He tapped the pen against the paper. "What's next?"

"We add water and liquid glucose to the kettle, then light the burner. For the first one of the day, it takes a minute or two to heat up." Lily followed her own instructions in real time as she explained. "Then you add the chocolate and let it all melt." She grabbed a paddle and stirred the mixture in the pot counterclockwise. "Now comes the sugar."

"That's a lot of sugar."

"It's fudge. Basically chocolate-y sugar."

"Is that an official recipe name?"

"Maybe for your boring recipes." A rich, sweet smell filled the shop.

"I believe the word you're searching for is *classic*." But he wore a smile when he said it.

And oh no, she smiled back. *What?*

She pointed to the kettle. "Okay, now we're gonna add

butter and evaporated milk. Let that melt. You want to try?"

"Sure." He set down the pen and paper, got the ingredients, dumped them in, then took the paddle. Stirred. "Like this?" His arms easily worked the mixture, muscles flexing with each go-round.

He glanced up at her. "Lily?"

"What?" Yikes. He'd caught her staring. "Oh, yep. Looking great." She winced at her choice of words. "I mean, you're doing a great job."

His brow furrowed as he focused on letting it all melt together. "Now what?"

"Now it's important to wash the residual sugar off the top insides of the kettle with some water on a pastry brush so it doesn't burn."

"Ah."

"Yet another ruined batch story?" she teased.

"No comment," he grumbled, and Lily couldn't hold back a smile as he worked the sugar down with the brush. When he was finished, he looked up at her. "Now we heat the fudge to two-forty, right? That's what my research said."

"Yeah, but the exact temperature changes based on different factors. Things like air temperature, humidity, the softness of your butter, the speed of heat application. Typically, I heat it to two-thirty-four and then slowly allow it to increase until it feels right."

"Feels right? Can't you give me some exact measurements?"

She shrugged. "Sorry." Then she shooed him aside and

reached for the wooden paddle he held. "Here, I'll stir while you set up the metal framing on the table. We'll pour the fudge from the kettle onto the slab and let it cool for five or ten minutes. I'll show you how to know when it's cool enough to cream up."

"You got it, boss."

Well, that was a new one. She stirred while he assembled the metal framing.

"Wait," he said. "I figured you'd have something funky and uber creative to add to the recipe."

She said nothing, just glanced at him.

"Oh, I see. Not sharing your secrets, huh?"

She raised an eyebrow.

He held up his hands. "I get it."

"Well, most of the time you don't add those things until after the base has cooked."

His silence made her laugh.

"Let me guess . . ."

Declan sighed as he finished the framing. "Yes, okay? Another mistake made by yours truly."

"Don't feel bad. I remember some doozy errors in my early days."

"Like what?"

"Oh, just basic stuff."

"Like what I'm doing."

She sighed. "Yes, and more." And suddenly, the past rose up, tied a knot inside her.

"Lily? What's that face for?"

She looked up, and he stood closer than before, brow furrowed. Almost like he cared.

"It's nothing."

"I know you. That's not *nothing*."

He knew her? She refused to let those words land while she turned the fudge round and round in the pot while it heated. "When I was ten or eleven, I completely ruined a batch of fudge. It went rock hard because I overbeat it."

"Doesn't seem like such a big deal to me." Declan took the candy thermometer off the wall, stuck it into the fudge.

Two-seventeen. Still a bit to go.

"Yeah, well, I was . . . I was daydreaming. Conjuring up a new recipe in my head. My grandpa was furious."

"I did hear he was a bit of a hot temper."

She gave him the side eye. "You've heard, huh?"

He held up his hands. "Yes, and it has nothing to do with the names he may or may not have called my grandpa when he accused him of theft."

"Oh." She could imagine that. "Well, he probably had his reasons." Oops. She wasn't trying to reignite the war.

Apparently, he wasn't either. "Sorry." The thermometer beeped upward. Closer to being ready. "So, what happened with your grandpa?"

"He basically told me to stop being an airhead." She shouldn't be telling him this—but frankly, talking to him felt . . .

Stupidly easy.

Oh boy. "He said I'd never amount to anything if I couldn't focus."

"Over *one* ruined batch of fudge?"

She shrugged. "Like you said, hot temper. I think he hoped that he might pass the fudge shop down to Cody, but Cody was a little fisherman through and through and had no real interest in fudge making. My grandpa was stuck with me, and he was *not* thrilled about it." Lily stopped paddling as the fudge reached two-thirty-six. "All right, it's done."

He peeked over her shoulder—too close for comfort, and of course his cologne swept over her. "How do you know?"

"Here." She handed him the paddle. "Stir it. Feel the viscosity? Not too hard, not too soft."

"Okay, Goldilocks." He took the paddle from her and swished it around once, twice, three times. Nodded. "Got it. Now we pour it out, yeah?"

"Yep."

Without saying a word, Declan hoisted the pot and carried it to the table, where Lily took one handle, and they tipped it over the table. The chocolate spilled out, a waterfall of sweet, gooey heaven.

"Wow—that smells good," Declan said as he held the kettle handles so she could scrape out the remains with the paddle.

"It does. Now, if you were going to add peanut butter, you'd spread it out on the table before pouring this out. Nuts and candies you add later, before it cools." Lily smoothed the liquid fudge across the table, filling the framing completely.

"Cool. Can you show me how to make that one next? The peanut butter one, I mean."

"If you've got a recipe for it, sure."

He raised an eyebrow. "What, you think I'm going to steal yours?"

She narrowed her eyes at him.

"Okay. I'll see if my mother has something."

"Speaking of recipes, where did you put my recipe cards from last night?"

"I didn't touch them."

She glanced up at him, and strangely, believed him. "Huh. Guess I misplaced them, then." With how she'd been feeling last night, it wouldn't be too far out of the realm of possibilities.

"I'll keep an eye out for them."

"Not too close an eye, I hope."

Shaking his head, the hint of a smile on his lips, Declan took the pot to clean. After a few minutes, Lily grabbed a metal scraper and sliced from the corner to the center, testing the fudge for thickening. It held, so she removed the framing bars and began the process of scraping and piling the fudge toward the center of the table, turning the fudge creamy.

Meanwhile, Declan leaned against the counter, arms folded.

"Yes?" She glanced at him.

"Just watching," he said, and now heat pressed into her chest.

Ten minutes later, the creaming process was complete, and Lily began to shape it. The motion of shaping it with a wooden paddle had always been relaxing to her. Like she might be a sculptor. With every flip of her paddle, the fudge held its shape more and more until it resembled a large loaf of chocolate bread.

"Very impressive, Ms. Hart."

She looked over. "Thank you, Mr. Kelley. Now, we'll finish letting this set and then can cut it into half- to one-pound slices—some smaller for samples." Pointing to the clean pots along the wall, she smiled. "The next batch is all you."

He rubbed his hands together, got another kettle, and started the process all over again. He flipped in his notebook to a page and started adding measurements according to his recipe.

"What kind of fudge are you planning to make first, once you've got the process down? A little pistachio? Pecan-maple?"

"Think I'll stick with chocolate for now."

"Chocolate." Her brow quirked.

"You can't go wrong with chocolate fudge. It's a classic."

"You're right. That's exactly right." She pressed her lips together to smother a smile, then waved her hands toward the kettle. "Please proceed."

He stared at her for a long moment before grunting and getting back to work. She watched at his side, speaking up if he needed a reminder, but for the most part, he took her advice to heart.

The first sign of trouble occurred when he removed the metal framing and the fudge started to run every direction. "Shoot." He ran around the table trying to catch it, but his frantic movements only scattered the warm chocolate faster. It ran over the edges of the marble table and dripped onto the floor.

What was the saying? Like a chicken with its head cut off? That was Declan—if the chicken were really fit and wore a frilly pink polka dot apron.

And Lily couldn't help it. Giggles just erupted from her. And oh, it felt good after so much tension over the last month.

She glanced up at Declan again. He'd abandoned the paddle at the center of the table and just stood there, arms crossed over his chest, clear amusement on his features despite the mess behind him. "You done?"

Lily pressed a hand to her mouth. "Mm-hmm." But then she bent in half, laughing some more.

"I'll give you something to laugh about, Lil."

Unfolding, she glanced up at him, at the way his eyes glinted with something dangerous as he rushed toward her.

What—? "Stop, Dec!" She raced around the dirty marble table, nearly slipping in the pooling—and now cooling—chocolate on the floor. Her sneakers squeaked as she tried to outrun him, but then he caught her around the waist, pinning her back against the table.

His laughter was deep and warm and full of…delight? The sound of it settled over her as warmth soaked the back of her shirt.

And then his laughing stopped. And her heart thundered against the quiet intensity of his stare.

Both of their breathing turned ragged, and time suspended in that moment. It was almost like she was transported back to that day at Disney World, when they'd been paired together on their senior trip scavenger hunt—the day that had changed everything in Lily's world.

Even though they'd been in second place, she'd convinced him to skip the rest of the list. To make their own adventure. After all, they were only there for one day.

And what a day it had been.

The rides. The cotton candy. The coy smiles. The laughter.

And their first kiss, as they snuggled on a bench under the fireworks.

He hadn't been a Kelley, and she hadn't been a Hart. And they'd returned to Jonathon Island, decided to try. To continue the adventure at home. To see if it was possible to undo the last fifty-five years of family feuding.

It hadn't worked then, and it wouldn't work now.

But for some reason, the thought didn't move her. She was frozen, wondering. What if . . .

"Lil." The whispered word was like a caress against her cheeks. But no, that was Declan's actual thumb, stroking softly upward until he tucked a loose piece of her hair behind her ear.

Just what was she supposed to do with that? Her entire body heated at his nearness, and slowly her hands—which had somehow gotten pressed to his chest—worked their way up and around his neck. "Dec."

His Adam's apple bobbed, his jaw tightened, and then he was moving closer.

"What's going on here?"

They both turned their heads to find Declan's younger brother, Isaac, standing just inside the kitchen.

Declan jerked away from her so fast, she might be made of flames. Lily's elbows slumped backward in a pile of mostly cooled fudge. Ugh.

Grabbing a towel, Declan tossed it her way. "Nothing's going on," he said, his attention on Isaac. "Lily just fell, and I was helping her up."

"Is that what the kids are calling it these days?" Isaac shook his head, tsked. "I warned you, brother. But did you listen? Nope."

Warned him? About what?

Whatever it was, it lit something in Declan. "Shut up, Isaac. What are you doing here, anyway?"

"Mom sent me over to make sure things were going well for you." Isaac pulled a stick of gum from his hoodie pocket, unwrapped it, and stuck the gum in his mouth. "Apparently, yes." He gave a wink.

Oh, now she felt gross. She walked to the sink to finish wiping off the chocolate. What in the world had just happened . . . or almost happened? What would Declan have done if Isaac hadn't shown up?

What would *Lily* have done?

Maybe she should be grateful his kid brother showed up.

Declan grabbed Isaac by the shoulders and started to push him through the door. "Let's go."

"But—"

"Now."

"Sheesh, big brother. Fine. Just remember what I said.

Don't let her get her claws into you." The door swung open, and Declan hauled Isaac through—but not before Lily heard the rest of what he had to say. "You made that mistake once before, and Grandma paid the price."

Grandma paid the price.

She shook her head, refusing to listen. But shoot, Isaac was right.

And then Declan's retort rose, angry, from outside, through the open window. "I know, bro. I know."

Yeah, they both knew.

Declan stuck his head back in, taking off the apron. "I'm just going to take care of this little pest problem, all right? Be right back to finish our lesson."

She gave him a thin smile.

But nope. They'd had enough lessons. She'd learned all she needed to.

She'd put a blue line of tape down the middle of the shop.

He'd spotted it yesterday when he'd returned after his short visit to the diner to tell his mother that really, he didn't need a babysitter.

But maybe she did deserve an update, rather than what Isaac might tell her.

Yeah, that would be great—the entire Kelley clan rallying to reignite the Hart-Kelley war. And he and Lily caught in the middle again.

Except, no worries there—she wasn't talking to him. Again.

"Thank you so much for coming in." Declan wrapped up yet another order of Kelley's Classic Fudge—yes, *plain* chocolate—and handed it to a forty-something woman and her two preteen daughters, who were showing each other something on their phones, glancing up at Declan, and giggling. "I highly recommend enjoying that with a cup of coffee or some hot chocolate. Because you can never have too much chocolate, am I right?"

The woman's eyes brightened. "We'll definitely do that. Can't wait to try it. The sample was delicious."

Yes, making fudge had been anything but simple. But selling it? That was where he shined.

"That recipe's been in the family for generations. When you're ready for your coffee fix, hit up Good Day Coffee just down the road. My Aunt Jill runs the place, and if you tell her I sent you over, she'll give you a discount."

"Oh, perfect." The woman shifted a shopping bag from one arm to the other. "We'll head over there now. Come on, girls." She waved at Declan and, with a final look and smile behind her, ushered her daughters out the front with a merry jingle of the bell Lily had put up last week.

A cough barked from Declan's left. His eyes skated across the counter—to the other side of the blue tape—and found Lily arranging her platter of full-size samples, not for the first time. Lips pursed, she refused to make eye contact with him.

Funny, that hadn't been her response yesterday when—

Nope. He wasn't going back to that moment where he'd almost, nearly, yes wanted to abandon all his clear thinking.

"So that's your brilliant marketing move. Flirting." She tied back her hair in some sort of quick knot that bared the soft curve of her jawline. Not that he was noticing.

"I hardly think smiling at her constitutes flirting. She came in, tried samples from both of us, and chose mine."

"Really. That's what you're going with." She shook her head.

He gave her a smile. "Do I detect jealousy?"

Her mouth opened. "I'm not jealous. But really—there's no other reason someone would choose plain chocolate over this sticky toffee pudding masterpiece." Lily pulled a piece of white fudge with chopped pecans from her sample plate and waved it in the air.

"Someone who likes the classics would."

"Wrong. Someone who was hypnotized by the man behind the counter."

"Really. So now I have hypnotic powers?"

"Oh brother." She shook her head. "I suppose *some* women might find the Top Gun look you have going on attractive."

Her gaze flitted down him—today he wore dark wash jeans, Amberjack leather boots, a white T-shirt, and his aviators hanging from the collar.

"Top Gun?"

"Whatever." She lifted a shoulder, but what looked like a blush stole across her cheeks.

Interesting. Maybe it was time to address what had happened yesterday, again. They were both adults. And yes, he hadn't handled things well after Isaac had left, but she'd been the one with the deep freeze. The tape down the room.

And maybe he'd gotten a little annoyed with his attempts at asking what was wrong—and her not answering him.

"Lily—"

The bell jingled again, and in walked two twenty-something women.

"Welcome in!" Lily called, turning away from him.

The women, one blonde and one a redhead, looked back and forth between Declan and Lily, at the two registers, the blue tape, the two platters of samples, Lily's significantly larger than his. "Do y'all have the same fudge?" the redhead asked in a Southern accent. "Why are there two registers?"

"Oh, just a little friendly competition we've got going on." Lily waved them over.

The women exchanged a look and a shrug before approaching Lily's side. Declan tried to busy himself with pulling more chocolate fudge from his display case and chopping it for the sample platter, but couldn't help watching from the sidelines.

"We're looking for some fudge for our mama," the blonde said.

"Fabulous. I've got at least fifteen different flavors." Lily's voice was bright, vivacious. Okay, she did have a way with people—other people, not him—that seemed genuinely warm. "What does your mama like best?"

"Oh, well, I'm not sure." The blonde peeked at her sister. "Kerry, what do you think?"

Kerry pushed at the roots of her already large hair. "Can we try a few to see what we think would strike her fancy?"

"Of course." Lily pushed the sample platter forward. Each sample was about four ounces compared to Declan's half-ounce samples. "Feel free to try whichever ones you'd like. I've got your classics, of course—peanut butter, almond sea salt, white chocolate—and then some that are more unique, like bergamot, lavender, and chocolate-cherry. Oh, and for the truly adventurous among us, I've got some lemon blueberry mascarpone fudge in the back."

"Oh my, those all sound amazing," Blondie said. "Would you mind if we tried one of each?"

Now it was Declan's turn to cough. Was the lady serious? With the way Lily had cut her samples, that was nearly two pounds of fudge she was giving away for free.

Lily shot him a glare before turning back to her customers. "Not at all." Lily used a pair of tongs to lift each sample onto a disposable plate. "Feel free to sit at the window bar if you need a little time to decide. The fudge is sold in one-pound blocks, but I also sell sampler boxes where you can mix and match."

"This is great. Thank you." Kerry took the plate from Lily and walked toward the counter-height bar that ran in front of the eastern-facing window along Jonathon Boulevard.

Lily dusted off her hands and turned to Declan with a triumphant grin. "Guess I was right."

"About what?"

She came closer and lowered her voice. "Only *some* women find the Top Gun look attractive."

"Hmm."

"What's that supposed to mean?" Her eyes sparked.

"Just that those women took you for a sucker. Look."

Kerry and Blondie were already standing from their stools as they wrapped their fudge in napkins and stuck it into Kerry's purse. When they noticed Declan and Lily's eyes on them, Blondie had the decency to smile sheepishly. "We thought maybe we should have lunch before trying this fabulous fudge, so we're gonna eat at the café across the way. We'll be back to make a purchase though." With a wave, they slipped out the door and headed across the street to Martha's.

"They are definitely not coming back."

"You have such little faith. I'm choosing to believe." Lily stuck her nose in the air and started humming as she re-filled her platter with fresh samples from inside the display case on her side. It was much fuller than Declan's—he'd only had yesterday to make fudge, while she'd had several days to build up a stockpile—but since they'd opened this morning at ten, she'd only made a few sales next to his twenty.

And don't get him started on her record-keeping sys-tem—an old-fashioned receipt stake next to the register compared to his integrated accounting program on his tablet.

He should just let it go. Let her fail. That was what he was here for, to beat her.

But she'd shown him how to make fudge. And without her doing that, there would be no competition.

Declan pinched the bridge of his nose. "Can I give you a tip?"

"I'd rather you not, unless you mean the legal tender sort." She held out her hand for the cash.

"It's not." He stared at her a moment. "It's business advice."

"Now you're going to wave that big MBA around?"

"It isn't like that. You helped me. I'm trying to return the favor." Declan pointed toward her sample platter. "You're giving away too much."

Lily crossed her arms. "I want them to know what they're getting. It's only fair."

"Sure, but you're giving away enough to fill them up, to satisfy them. Give them just a little taste. Enough to make them want more. To tease them."

As if mocking his words, her vanilla scent reached out, hit him. He cleared his throat, moved back to his register. Pretended to dust off his iPad. Stared at it for a moment. Turned back to face her. "The point is, Lily, you've got excellent fudge. You're really talented, and I would hate to see you not reap the rewards simply because your business tactics need a little tweaking."

She winced and turned away. What had he said? But before he could ask, the door opened again and Dani Sullivan stepped inside. A tall man wearing a baseball cap pulled low over his eyes walked in beside her.

"Hey, guys!" Dani said. "How's it going?"

"Great!" Lily's cheer was back as she greeted her friend. "First day officially open and we're already making sales."

"That's fabulous." Like Lily, Dani seemed to have endless amounts of energy, and though just as casual as others on the island in her jeans and T-shirt, she seemed organized. After the mixer two nights ago, she'd already emailed out charts and diagrams of the upcoming Main Street Festival, with a map of the booth, a list of assignments, and an FAQ of all the details the business owners were required to know.

"What can we do for you, Dani?" he asked, eyeing the stranger beside her.

"Oh! Sorry." She glanced over at the man and patted his arm. "This is Asher Quinn, Terry and Angela's nephew, who's looking after their ranch and horses while they're away on their RV trip."

Declan held out a hand over the counter. "Good to meet you, man."

Grunting, the man stepped forward and shook Declan's hand. He wore scars on the right side of his neck that his beard didn't fully cover.

"Yes, hi." Lily came up, smiling.

A lump rose in Declan's chest to see it directed at Asher. Guess Lily wasn't the only one jealous.

"You're staying at the Quinn ranch?" she asked. "My friend Sadie's grandma lives next door. Do you know Henrietta Hudson? She's the absolute sweetest."

Asher glanced at Dani, back to Lily. "Hetty's why I'm here, actually."

Dani leaned on the counter. "I caught him trying to

sneak into Doug's without being noticed, and we got to chatting and he mentioned he was in town to grab a little something for Henrietta's birthday." She eyed him with a smile. "Isn't that sweet?"

The poor guy reddened. "Just being neighborly," he mumbled under his breath.

"Oh, but Henrietta does love sweets," Lily said. "She used to own the bakery here in town, you know."

"That's why I brought him here, to the best place I know to come for sweets." Dani winked at Lily. "Oh, but—sorry, Asher—before you guys fight over him as a customer, I've got two exciting things to tell you, and then I'm off."

"Sounds fun!" Lily said.

Forget fun. Hopefully the news would profit their businesses.

Ahem. *His* business.

"I'll just come back later."

Before Dani could protest, the guy slipped out the door again, hands tucked in his worn jeans.

Dani frowned but turned back to Declan and Lily. "Okay, first, I got you both a job for this weekend."

"What kind of job?" Declan asked.

Lily crossed her arms over her chest. "What Mr. Rude-Pants means to say is, yay! That's so exciting."

Dani laughed. "No, no, that's fair. Feel free to say no, Declan, but it would give Lily a significant lead over you, so I wouldn't if I were you."

"Noted."

"There's a wedding happening on Saturday. So yes, in two days. Caleb Kennedy over at Island House Inn called me asking if I knew of anyone who could do some last-minute dessert catering. Apparently, this couple booked mainland vendors for almost everything, and their dessert caterer had an emergency and can't make it. Their main caterer doesn't have the capacity to add desserts to their order, so"—she waggled her eyebrows—"of course I suggested you guys. The only catch is they want both ice cream and fudge for about fifty people. Is that something you guys can do?"

"I can." Lily smirked at Declan—the same look she'd worn far too often lately when she thought she'd bested him.

Well, two could play at that game. "I can too. The fudge, that is."

"I'll make both fudge *and* ice cream."

Oh, brother.

"Awesome," Dani said. "Okay, one more thing. As you know, the upcoming festival is a small part of my strategy to shine light on Jonathon Island again. To start getting back into people's social feeds, to drum up excitement for next season, when we'll have part of the hotel open for business."

Declan nodded. "Right."

"I reached out to a newspaper in Detroit and told them all about it. They're going to send a reporter out next week—Wednesday, in fact—to interview our shop owners and publish a piece about the re-emergence of our little island. A piece of Michigan, reborn."

"Dani, that's fantastic," Lily said.

"I'm really thrilled. The reporter—Kent Mercer—said

the piece has the kind of appeal that might get picked up for syndication." She paused, as if for dramatic effect. "Especially when I told him about the Fudge Wars."

"Oh no, you didn't," Declan said.

"Really, Dani?" Lily's expression probably betrayed his own.

"Oh, come on. You have to admit there's an interesting story here. A family feud more than fifty years in the making, and the newest generation fighting for the Main Street shop?"

"We'd like to forget that war," Declan said as he finger-quoted the words, glancing at Lily.

Her jaw set tight, her arms folded.

"But it's so small-town," Dani said. "And besides, we all know that it's not a thing anymore."

Hello, did anyone see the *blue line of tape* down the center of the shop?

"I'd much rather people visit us for our fudge," Lily said rigidly.

"Yeah, but the extra press would be good for business, especially if it gets published beyond Detroit," Dani said.

Declan sighed. "I suppose it would get people in here, and that's the goal."

"Exactly."

"When would the article come out?" Lily asked.

"Not sure, but hopefully in the paper's weekend edition so there's a few weeks between it and the actual festival. He's going to promote the festival too. Oh. And the guy wants to sample your fudge so he can give his opinion as part of the piece."

And now, Dani smiled.

Uh-oh. Maybe this wouldn't be good for business after all.

Because in a head-to-head battle of whose fudge would rank better in a food reviewer's opinion?

Lily Hart had it in the bag.

Eight

YOU LOOK PRETTY. YOU HEADING TO the wedding?"

Lily glanced back from the front door into her parents' living room, where Mom sat drinking coffee on the love seat. Her mother had pulled her hair back in a loose ponytail and still wore sweatpants from her early-morning walk around the neighborhood with Dad.

"Thanks. And yes." She smoothed her hands over the yellow sundress she'd selected in her hurry to get out the door.

"You're a little dressed up for catering." Her mother quirked an eyebrow.

"I'm, well, uh—"

"I'm kidding. It's nice to see you out of leggings and a T-shirt. You and Declan are catering together, right?"

Of course she'd heard about that—small town.

"Yes." Lily glanced at the clock over the mantel. "I'm

supposed to meet Declan at ten-thirty to get everything loaded up, so . . ."

"How *is* Declan?" Mom took a sip, eyeing Lily over the lip of the mug.

"Um, fine, I guess." Lily fidgeted in her strappy sandals—the ones that weren't very practical but were definitely cute. "Well, not *fine*, like cute. I mean, fine, as in . . . fine." Yikes. Mom would see right through that one. "I just mean—"

"I think I know what you mean." Her mother sighed. "Lily, your father and I are concerned."

Oh. And this was why she'd tried to sneak in late and leave early—last thing she wanted was an inquisition about the competition.

Which had slowly not felt like competition as they'd worked together this week to fill the order. More like co-workers.

The kind who worked together and most definitely did not think about a near kiss that maybe she'd dreamed up. And refused to wish for.

Because it would never, could never, happen.

Sighing, Lily closed the door. "I know, Mom, but you don't need to be. We're still rivals. And I'm going to win this stupid competition. I told you about that reviewer that's coming in four days."

In fact, between making batches of ice cream for the wedding reception, Lily had spent her off hours experimenting with new fudge flavors for Mr. Mercer's tasting. "I'm not going to let the Kelleys win."

"Oh, honey. You know I don't care a fig about that silly feud."

"Dad cares."

"Does Dad get riled up when he thinks about the past and the pain his father experienced at his best friend's perceived betrayal? Yes, of course. But both of us care far more about you." She cocked her head again. "We just want you to be careful. That boy broke your heart once."

"I know." Lily shook her head, forced a smile. "I'll be okay, Mom. Declan and I, that's ancient history."

Her mother nodded. "Have a great wedding. I can't wait to hear all about how everyone reacts to your wonderful creations."

"Thanks, Mom." Lily darted out the door and hopped on her bike—her knee was nearly fully healed now.

Five minutes later, she pulled up outside the fudge shop. What in the—?

Out front stood two horses hooked up to a short cart with a bench seat.

Dismounting from her bike, she headed inside.

And found Declan—wearing dress slacks and a button-up shirt—pulling one of her ice cream containers from the freezer. He stacked it beside several others already out on the counter.

"Hey. I'm just grabbing everything to load up onto the trailer."

She pointed to the street. "About that—where did the horses come from? I thought they were all off island."

"All but a handful, I guess. Remember Asher Quinn,

who we met on Thursday? How Dani said he's watching his relatives' ranch and horses?"

"Oh. Right. So you asked him if we could borrow a few?"

"Exactly. Thought it might be easier. He said we could use them this morning to transport everything to the inn. He'll pick them up from us, board them next door at the stables for a few hours, and bring the trailer back after the event's over."

Huh. "That's . . . good job. I just figured we'd hook up a trailer to our bikes and make several trips."

"This will be much more efficient." Declan continued to unload the fudge and ice cream containers. "Did you bring coolers and ice?"

"Coolers?" Oh no. "I hadn't even thought of coolers for the ice cream." And she'd told him she had everything handled, that he should just worry about his fudge. Ha. Now, all her treats would melt before the couple's first dance. "What am I going to do?"

"I think we have a few at my parents' place. And I can raid the diner's ice machine."

The man had an answer for everything, didn't he? "Are you sure? I'm sorry I didn't think of that beforehand."

"No sweat. I'll be back in no time." He smiled at her, as if she hadn't totally dropped the ball.

He returned with coolers and ice, and they loaded the food onto the horse-drawn dray. As he got on and took the reins, she glanced at him.

"It's like riding a bike," he said and winked.

And she had nothing as they trotted down Main Street,

a sight that drew a ton of attention and photos from tourists already flocking to the island on this gorgeous Saturday morning. The sun hung high in a cloudless, perfect sky, warming the day.

A glorious day for a wedding.

They headed toward Island House Inn, just south of Blueberry Hill Park between the old livery and Little Stone Bible Church. The charming mid-size inn, with its white Victorian trim, steeply angled roof, and double turrets was host to the ceremony and reception, which were being held outside in the trimmed, green grass of the back courtyard.

An hour later, Lily stood behind the white-draped tablecloths in the shade behind the area set up for the wedding. An arbor had been erected for the happy couple, along with white folding chairs for the guests. Bouquets of peonies, hydrangeas, and roses stood on pillars, and the family had started ushering guests into place. A quartet of musicians started playing a new piece of music.

"Everything turned out really nice." Declan showed up beside her holding a loaded plastic bag and rocking his aviator sunglasses. Paired with his dress clothes, the man was . . . well, okay. He was *fine, fine.*

"I was thinking the same thing." She eyed the bag. "What do you have there?"

Declan pulled two Styrofoam containers from the bag, setting one in front of Lily. "I thought we might not have a chance to eat lunch once the reception's going."

"Oh. Good idea." She supposed it would be poor form to try to snag some of the food arranged on the deluxe charcuterie boards on the table beside theirs, which included fruit and meat cut and folded into roses, plus platters of finger sandwiches that looked gourmet.

"Thanks. What is it—arsenic?" She smiled at him, not sure why.

"Iocane powder. Please. But only because I've worked up a tolerance. Pick one." He held out both containers.

She laughed, took one of the containers, and popped open the lid. The delicious scent of the roast beef sandwich wafted out. "I don't care if it's poisoned. I'm ready to perish."

"I was hoping you'd still like it."

Oh. Right. And suddenly, their past was right there—the date in the park, when he'd snuck her food from the diner. They'd talked and talked till it was far too late.

Their first kiss since the magic of Disney World.

Far more magical because they'd been home.

She cleared her throat. That was then, this was now. "Wow, I haven't had anything of your mom's in forever."

"Really? Even with being back for a few weeks now?" Declan took a bite of his sandwich.

In the background, Pastor Arnie talked about love and commitment. Of finding forever and holding on when you knew it was right, when God had sent you your match.

Lily tossed him a sad smile. "Harts aren't exactly welcome at the diner. Well, I think Cody gets away with it. Maybe Mom. But me? I'm persona non grata over there."

Declan had been about to take another bite, but set his sandwich down instead. Frowned. "That's not okay."

She flicked away a wilted piece of lettuce—the only

flawed thing about the perfectly flaky, juicy creation in front of her. But suddenly, her appetite waned.

Lily closed the lid and pushed the container away. "It's just how it is between our families, Declan. We tried to change their minds once upon a time."

"Maybe we should have tried harder."

Her breath caught as he snagged her hand and guided it back to the container. Before letting go, his thumb swiped the inside of her wrist.

She froze. He let go. "Looks like they're pronouncing them man and wife. Eat up."

Right. She ate half the sandwich, then closed it. But his touch lingered even as the wedding ceremony ended and the reception festivities had begun.

The reception kept both Lily and Declan busy, her scooping ice cream and both of them handing out their fudge. She couldn't help but grin in satisfaction that the guests, nearly all from the mainland, were keen on her unique fudge flavors—several even asking if she'd consider a mail-order option. Lily lost herself in conversation with them all, nearly yelping when Declan sidled up next to her, his face solemn. Cheer up, they were at a *party*.

"What's the frown for?" Lily asked. "You look like you need an ice cream." She twirled the scoop in her hand before setting it down and pulling another box of fudge from under the table.

Declan looked up to the sky. A hard line of clouds hung off the southern tip of the island. "I hope the weather holds." The air had grown humid as the afternoon waned on, tolerable only because of a breeze that cut across the island.

Lily paused while plating more fudge. "Yikes. Me too." She moved the plate to the front of their table and greeted several guests. She pulled another stack of waffle cones from the supply box below the table and handed them to him. "Do you mind?"

He took the stack and slid several into a special plexiglass cone-holder that sat in an arch on the table. "I didn't even know these were a thing."

"Brilliant, right?"

"What's brilliant is the easy way you can pivot."

She stilled, glanced at him. "Um. What do you mean?" And was that genuine admiration in Declan's tone?

"I've been watching you—"

"Well, that doesn't sound creepy at all." She laughed.

He rolled his eyes. "Listen. It's just that you have a really easy way with customers. When you're short on an ice cream flavor someone really wants, you find a way to mix two other flavors to get a new combination they're equally excited about."

"That's the fun of it all. Being creative. Coming up with something new."

"Not sure I'd call it fun, but whatever it is, you excel at it."

Her cheeks burned, and it had nothing to do with the heat. "Thanks, Top Gun. You're pretty good at all this yourself."

And it didn't hurt at all to say it.

Except, his gaze held hers, and she was instantly back in the shop, her back to the table, his eyes on hers—

"Ice cream. Melting." He pointed to the full scoop in her hand.

And right then, the groom's dad came over to the table holding the flower girl's hand. The older gentleman stroked his gray mustache. "Do you have any more of the maple-bacon ice cream? Siena doesn't believe me that it's a real flavor."

"What?" Lily acted shocked.

The girl wrinkled her nose. "Is it really true? Is it good?"

"I think so."

Siena's grandpa pointed at the little chalkboard menu Lily had written in pretty script a few hours earlier. "She also has lemon custard, chocolate-cherry pie, and black licorice."

"Eww, I don't like licorice."

"That's okay. Not every flavor is for every person." Lily lifted an over-stuffed waffle cone to her. "Except for maple-bacon." She winked. "Everyone likes this one."

Siena's eyes widened and she held the cone in her hands for half a second before diving in. "Oh, yummy. This is so good!" She grinned and backhand-wiped ice cream from her lips.

"Great, you're going to be on a sugar high the rest of the afternoon," the man said. He stuffed a twenty in Lily's tip jar. "Thanks a lot."

"Sorry!" Lily called as they walked away.

"No, you're not," Declan said.

"No, I'm not." Lily put her hands on her hips and let out

a little sigh. "This makes me happy." She glanced around. "This whole wedding is like this little snapshot. A glimpse of what island life used to be."

Several children played tag on the lawn. A few others blew bubbles from tiny party favor bottles. A deejay serenaded them with big band music, and couples jitterbugged on the dance floor.

Those halcyon days of childhood. The innocence and naivete—it all tugged at her.

"I remember." Declan's voice seemed full of just as much wistfulness.

A gust lifted the tablecloth and made Lily's dress swirl. She pinned it down against her legs. Looked up at him. And he—he was looking at her too.

She swallowed, throat suddenly dry.

"Okay, you two." The bride's mom slid behind the table, making Lily jump and break her eye contact with Declan. "It's your turn."

"For?"

"Dancing, of course. Come on—you've been working all afternoon. I can't even tell you how good these desserts are. I'm going to stop by and buy some ice cream on our way back to the mainland."

Lily paused. "I don't actually sell the ice cream."

"You should!" Despite her petite frame and her four-inch heels, Mrs. Stevenson gently tugged both Declan and Lily by the arm around the table. "Now go, or I'll reduce your tip. I can handle doling out ice cream and fudge for a little bit. It'll be fun."

"Are you sure—" Lily started, but Declan took her hand.

Oh.

He pulled her to the edge of the dance floor.

"Declan." She stopped and let go of his hand. "Wait. People might talk."

He turned. Met her gaze. "They might." His voice had turned quiet, husky, and it sent a shiver through her. "But none of these people are from here except Arnie and Caleb Kennedy, and neither of them are gossips."

Lily caught sight of the innkeeper, a well-built guy who was friendly and objectively handsome—but *he* didn't make her heart rate skyrocket like the man beside her. "True."

"C'mon, Lil. For old times' sake?" Declan held out his hand.

She shouldn't, but then Etta James's "At Last" came on over the speakers and what was a girl supposed to do?

Lily slid her hand into his. "Just this one."

"Just this one." He squeezed, smiled, and see, his charm *was* hypnotizing. No wonder he sold gobs of fudge.

Then Declan led her onto the dance floor. He slipped his hands around her waist, and she placed her hands on his shoulders. And then he gently rocked to the beat.

Fine. Okay. This might be nice. And she allowed herself to inhale the delicious aroma of Declan. Even let him pull her tighter against his chest.

My lonely days are over . . .

It was all heady, to say the least.

"Lil?" he murmured.

"Hmm?"

"I wish . . . I wish things weren't so contentious between us."

Her too, suddenly. "Let's not talk about that. Not right now."

"It's just, you know why *I'm* doing this. For Grandma. But why are you? Did something happen in Florida?"

Oh. But the last—very last thing she was going to tell him about was failing. Not just in school, but at her job.

Her life.

In fact, since leaving Jonathon Island, and frankly, him, her life had pretty much been in shambles.

After a moment, his chest rose and fell, a sigh. "I wish we could find a way for both of us to get what we want."

She pulled away from him. "But we can't."

"No. I guess not." His eyes searched hers, irises darkening like the sky above them. In the distance, thunder boomed. "What will you do if the fudge shop doesn't work out? Will you . . ." He frowned. "Go back to Florida?"

"No. Florida is a dead end for me. I don't really have a Plan B."

He was still swaying them. "I'm sure there are a ton of places looking to hire a smart, creative genius like you." And oh, the warmth in his smile poured all the way through her, touched her bones.

She just might be a soggy, melted mess if he kept looking at her like that.

Somehow, she found her voice. "Not as many as you might think."

"Oh?"

And maybe, right here, not looking at him, so much of their past in the air, okay. "I got fired from my last job."

He didn't say anything, didn't react, just kept dancing.

So, "But before that, I failed. Out of business school, I mean. My parents don't know and I don't have the heart to tell them. They'd be so disappointed."

Her throat filled. And yet, he still kept moving.

"That's why I need to win, Declan. I'm already an embarrassment to my family. I need to show them I can be successful. I need to make them proud."

Now he stopped. Looked down at her. She raised her gaze to his, and shoot—a tear had dropped onto her cheek. "Aw, Lil." He swiped away her tear and tilted her chin upward. "Don't you know? They're *so* proud of you."

"Only because they believe the lie I told. But if they knew how much I struggled . . ." She blew out a terrible breath. "Who am I kidding? They'll know as soon as you win, and we lose the Hart fudge shop for good."

She put her head back on his chest, not sure why.

Silence. Then, "Don't count yourself out just yet, Lily."

She looked at him again.

"I'm serious. You didn't see yourself today. Your smile, the way you engaged everyone with ease. Looked them in the eyes and laughed. Made each guest feel special." Declan's voice held strength, conviction. "That, plus your incredible creations are a recipe for success."

This man. How did he keep doing this to her? Making her forget the past—the wounds and want . . .

Well, to lift up on her tiptoes and to kiss him.

She swallowed. "You really think so?"

"I really do," he said softly.

And the words of the song swept around her.

For you are mine . . .

"Dec . . ."

His gaze roamed her face, settled on her lips.

Yes. Oh—

Sprinkles, cold splashes on her head, dribbled down her face. The music stopped.

"Rain!" someone from the dance floor yelled, and Declan offered a wry smile and shook his head. Around them people ran for cover, shouting.

But not Declan.

He just stood there, looking at her. Rain dripped from his Roman nose, from the now-loose strands of his hair, and she wanted nothing more than to push her hands through it.

And finally, "Hey you two—get out of the rain!"

The spell was broken. She stepped away from him and he shucked off his jacket.

Held it over her. "We should . . ." His gaze flitted to her lips.

Okay, maybe not broken completely.

"Should what?" Her voice lifted over the pounding of the rain on the dance floor.

"We should probably cover the fudge."

She blinked. "Right. The fudge."

Yes, the *fudge*. The whole reason that kissing him was a terrible, painfully wonderful, disastrous idea.

The stupid fudge.

It had been three days.

Three days of preparing for the reporter's visit tomorrow. Of making fudge and selling to customers and fielding questions from his family.

Three days since the wedding. Since Lily had worn that sunny yellow dress that fitted and flowed off her curves with a gauzy ease. Since she'd pinned her hair up in a loose twist, a few strands sweeping her bare shoulders that had teased Declan all day long.

Three days since he'd almost kissed her.

Again.

And he could probably blame her confession about feeling like a failure—it had gutted him to hear her talk about herself like that.

But if *this* was how she did business, then maybe he could see why the administrative parts of school hadn't been her favorite.

Declan leaned against the door to the small office in the back of the fudge shop, watching as Lily dug through her purse and added two more receipts to a stack in a manilla folder. Beside that sat the receipt spike she used at the register, a few receipts still piled on. "Please don't tell me that's your accounting system."

Lily jumped, her hand knocking the file folder to the ground and sending the entire stack of receipts into the air like a New York City ticker-tape parade. "No!" She dove to scoop up the receipts. Thank goodness she'd gotten her stitches out yesterday or she'd be right back at the clinic. "Why'd you have to sneak up on me like that?"

"Sorry. Didn't mean to scare you. But your system—or lack thereof—scared *me*." He squatted, reaching past her to grab a wayward receipt from under the ancient executive desk and adding it to the fresh pile she'd started. "Lily, you can't keep your books like this."

She rocked back on her heels, putting space between them. "It works for me."

"Does it?"

"Yes." She tilted her chin in defiance.

So stubborn. "Do you want my help?" The words were out before he could think better of them, because what would his parents say? What would Isaac—who'd been by twice in the last few days to spy on him—say? And he didn't want to think about the reaction of the Kelley clan at large.

Harts versus Kelleys all over again, and them caught in the middle.

Then again, why did Declan care so much? His family's feelings on the subject of Lily had nothing to do with whether or not he'd actually win their competition and get to keep Grandma's house. Judging by the number of receipts scattered on the floor, by the way he'd seen customers react to her latest fudge flavors, Lily was already winning.

Which meant he probably needed a backup plan. In the meantime, "Let me help you get organized."

Not that he was giving up. He still had some marketing tricks up his sleeve, parts of his business plan to execute.

But as much as he wanted to win, he also didn't want to see Lily fail. Not anymore. He held out his hand to her.

"Why?" After a moment of intense study, she allowed him to help her stand.

"Consider it repayment for showing me how to make fudge." That wasn't really the reason, but it was the one she'd accept. "Now, we need to get these into order by date." He didn't wait for her to say yes. Just took the stack and began sorting them on the worn brown desktop.

"I can do that."

"So can I." He spied an accounting software box lying next to Lily's open bright pink laptop. His lips quirked.

"What?"

"Nothing."

She swiped a receipt from his hand. "No, tell me. What are you laughing at me for now?"

"I'm not laughing at *you*." The pointed look on her face sent him backpedaling. "Okay, maybe a little, but it's because you're so cute. Most software is sold digitally. You just download it offline. The office programs are for . . ." Would he insult her if he told her that the physical software was mostly intended for old folks and those who were less than tech savvy? Shoot, maybe. "Never mind."

Aw, man, she was frowning. "The ad said installing and using it was so easy, a five-year-old with a lemonade stand could use it." She put the receipt she'd taken from Declan back in the folder. "I've never been at the top of my class, but I graduated high school just fine."

"I know you did. I was there."

She looked at him.

Oops. "Listen, whatever they claim, in my experience, it isn't quite that easy."

"Oh?"

"I can show you a few tricks to get yourself set up right. That'll make a big difference."

"I guess all those years in school have paid off."

He lifted his shoulder. "I learned this working with my dad in high school. They've updated the software in the years since, but the basics are all still the same. It's pretty common business software, and I used it in one of my internships too."

She leaned over her computer, tapped a few keys, and the software pulled up. "I guess that would be okay. I mean, showing you how to make fudge *did* take me a long time."

"I know. Several hours."

"Almost a whole day." She flicked her gaze at him. "You needed a lot of tutoring."

"So much." He smiled.

She smiled back.

Oh boy. "So you'll let me help you?"

Sighing, Lily turned to him. She smelled good—a mix of vanilla and chocolate, and suddenly the office seemed a little too small.

"Fine," she said, but held up her hand. "And then no more helping each other. We duke it out like the rivals we're supposed to be." But despite her words, her tone didn't sound like someone who considered him the enemy.

He'd long ago stopped seeing her that way.

So maybe the Kelley clan was right.

"Lily, make me a promise."

"What's that?"

"Don't ever let your receipts stack up like this again." He tapped the pile of paper. "You're just making it harder on yourself."

"I didn't mean to."

"Set a reminder on your phone until you get in the habit. Every night, make sure you load your transactions into the software, okay?"

"Okay."

He cut her a look. "I'm serious."

"Okay. Fine. I will. And that will be good, because I swear I'm missing some receipts from the last few days."

"What do you mean?"

"It just feels like I've sold more than this."

"And that's the problem. You wouldn't know for sure if you're not entering them daily, yeah?"

"Yeah, yeah," she grumbled, plopping into the chair in front of the laptop. "Let's get this over with."

Over the next two hours, Declan walked her through setting up her business profile, entering her expense accounts, regular vendors, and connecting to her bank accounts. Then loading and reconciling all her receipts.

When it was all said and done, his suspicions were confirmed.

"Wow, you're doing really well," he said as he blinked at the computer screen over her shoulder. "I mean, I'm sorry—but I can't help but see that."

Lily eyed the balance page. "That's better than I thought. Not great, but I won't have to sell a kidney."

"You're doing better than great. In fact, you're leaving

me in the dust." He lowered himself onto the edge of the desk.

She twisted in the chair to face him. "Really? Wow. Fist pump."

"I'll try not to be deeply offended by your enthusiasm."

"I'm sure it won't last now that you're getting the hang of fudge making. Your peanut butter fudge from last night was fairly spectacular."

"You stole some of my fudge?"

"*Stole* is such a strong word." She grinned.

"I'll have to find a way to get repayment." And he couldn't help it—his gaze fell to her lips.

Suddenly, she stopped smiling. Got up.

"Thank you for this." Lily nodded toward the computer. "We were more than even. You really didn't have to."

He took a step back. "I'm glad I could help. No receipt deserves to be treated like that."

"Haha," Lily said, then brushed past him to grab the coffee she'd poured a half hour ago off the bookcase where she'd left it. Then she turned, mug in hand. "So, you asked me the other day what I'd do if I lost. But what about you? What are your plans, win or lose?"

Surely he'd mentioned this to her, right? "The plan has always been for me to go back to Chicago. I've got a job waiting for me there, but only if I leave right after the festival."

"Even if you win?" Did he detect a sort of sadness in her?

"Yes. If I lose, I leave. If I win, I leave."

It suddenly sounded like he'd lose, either way. Huh.

"And how would that work? If you win, I mean? Who would run the shop?"

"I'd help oversee the business from afar and would hire someone here to manage the day-to-day. Maybe my cousin Olive, if she decides not to go to community college on the mainland."

"So, someone your family approves of. No mercy for the Hart you left in the dust, huh?" She said it teasingly, but it fell flat, as did her smile.

"Lily . . ."

"No, I get it. Family always comes first, right? And I wouldn't work here even if you asked me to. I'd bow out gracefully."

"Hey." He waited for her to look him in the eyes. "I meant what I said yesterday. I don't want to fight with you anymore."

"But it's so fun." She sighed. "Just kidding. I don't want to fight either. It's kind of exhausting."

"It is. And you're right—I won't lie that I value family. So do you. But I'm sorry that I let it come between us. That I didn't stand up for you in the moment. Back then, I mean. What happened with Grandpa . . ."

"Hey." She walked over to him, touched his arm. "It was an accident."

"I should have been there."

"Maybe. Yes. But Alzheimer's patients get out all the time. Most of them require round-the-clock care from professionals, and you were an eighteen-year-old kid." She squeezed his arm. "You've got to let go of the guilt sometime, Dec."

He couldn't break free of her gaze, so beautiful, so honest.

Don't . . .

He stepped away, breaking her hold. "Anyway. I just wanted you to know that I'm sorry for the past. For blaming you. For breaking up with you in such a childish way. For putting my desire to be loyal to family above you."

Lily nodded. "I'm sorry too. I shouldn't have left like that and ignored your calls. But when Sadie invited me to spend the rest of the summer in Florida, I didn't think. I just went. And stayed."

"And never came back. Until now."

"Well, except to visit. But yes."

They stared at each other for a long moment, breathing in this change between them. The forgiveness. And Declan's chest . . .

For the first time in he didn't know how long, it felt as if he could breathe again. Finally, "Lily, I think this family feud has gone on long enough."

"I agree, actually."

"Hold the presses." He cupped his hands around his mouth and turned like he was making an announcement. "Let it be known that at 8:52 p.m. on Tuesday, July twenty-second, Lily Hart agreed with Declan Kelley."

"Stop it, you goof." She smacked him on the arm. "So I agree with you. Big whoop. The point is, we had nothing to do with the old Fudge Wars. We don't need to bow to this sense of . . . of *duty* that's decades old, right?" She set down her coffee. "The past doesn't have to rule our lives."

Outside, the sun had begun to set, the colors awash over

the lake, cresting into the room. It picked up the lavender highlights in her hair, settled into her eyes, turning them a deep, rich blue.

"You *are* talking about the business, right?" The question popped out—a more regular occurrence since being around Lily. He'd never been more impulsive in his life. Her influence, once again. "Nothing more?"

"Of course." Her cheeks reddened and she stopped. "Things between us . . . we were just kids. Young. Impulsive. I wasn't suggesting . . ." She held up a hand. "Listen, all these numbers make my brain swim. I'm gonna go whip up some ice cream. Clear my head. We've got a big day tomorrow."

"Yes, we do." Because tomorrow, Kent Mercer was going to taste both of their offerings and give Lily a raving review that would ensure an even bigger lead over him.

But right now, Declan honestly couldn't find it in him to care. Because what if things didn't have to be an either/or situation with Lily? She wasn't his enemy. And, okay, he wasn't sure if she was his friend.

But he was pretty sure that she just might be the one thing that he'd searched the world to find.

Too bad it was on Jonathon Island.

Nine

DECLAN WAS LEAVING.

Win or lose, he was *leaving*.

Why did that devastate her so much?

For the last eighteen hours, Lily had hardly been able to think about much else—like the way Declan had patiently shown her how to wrangle her finances. Or the fact that Kent Mercer was on his way to the island.

No, her brain was all clogged up with the softness in his voice when he'd apologized for the past. Or that almost-kiss at the wedding.

Focus.

"Settle down, girl." Mia laughed and plopped her hand over top of Lily's as she arranged and rearranged the sample box she'd created for Mr. Mercer. "Why don't you make some fudge or something? That always calms you right down." She hooked her thumb over her shoulder, pointing to the marble demonstration table in front of the window. "Haven't seen you use that much. Give the people a show."

"By *people*, do you mean Cody and your children?" From Lily's spot behind the counter, she could see her brother giving two-year-old Maggie a piggyback ride up and down the sidewalk in front of the shop. Five-year-old Finn raced beside him, running a Hot Wheels car over every bench and lamppost along the way. "He sure is cute with them. Can't wait for the day I can call them my niece and nephew."

Mia's mouth fell open, and she let loose an incredulous laugh. "Lily Hart. Don't be saying that so loudly. People will start rumors that we're engaged."

"Oh, please. There's no one here." Lily glanced over at Declan, who was assisting an older couple. *He* certainly didn't seem nervous. Every movement he made was calm and professional, and he spoke in dulcet tones that made her want to—

Her mind really needed to find another topic of thought.

But she knew, deep in her bones, that if she hadn't walked away last night, he would have kissed her.

And she would have let him.

"There's no one here, huh?" Mia's eyebrows rose. She leaned across the counter and lowered her voice. "I see the way you look at him, Lil. Same way you did back in high school. Best be careful or I won't be the only one on the verge of engagement."

"Aha!" Lily lifted her hands in triumph. "I knew it."

Her sweet friend's nose crinkled, emphasizing her freckles. "Not officially. It's just, when you know, you know. It's only a matter of timing now."

The bell jingled as the kids rushed inside with her brother. He came up behind Mia, wrapped her in his arms, and dropped a kiss on her shoulder. "The kids are getting hungry. Want to try the pizza place?"

"It's open?" Lily asked as she slid a small fudge sample toward a waiting Finn and Maggie. Who could resist those big eyes? Besides, she wanted favorite aunt status someday when Mia and Cody inevitably tied the knot.

"This week is the soft opening. Officially open on Saturday. The owner, Antonio, is a boat enthusiast and talked my ear off about it the other day when I was at the marina."

"Exciting. Let me know how the food is. I've missed a good pizza." Till now, Kelley's Bar & Grill was the only place to get one and, yeah. Clearly that hadn't been an option.

The bell sounded again and another few customers walked in, headed straight for Declan's counter.

"Sorry. We're crowding you out." Mia ushered the kids toward the door, glancing over her shoulder. "Let's get together soon, okay? I want to hear all the details." Then she shot her gaze toward Declan.

Oh. *Details*. Right. "Sure."

As she and the kids vacated, Cody tapped his knuckles on the countertop, his eyes trained on Declan, who had finished up with the older couple and now was busy with the new customers. "Is he treating you well, or do I need to remind him that nobody messes with my big sister except me?"

Lily rolled her eyes. "I admire your sense of justice, but let's just lay off the fisticuffs, okay? I'm going to beat him in my own way."

"Oh yeah? How's that?"

"The newspaper reporter is coming today."

"Oh, right! Well, good luck. Knock 'em dead. Break a leg."

She laughed. "Pretty sure that last one is just for show business."

On the other side of the store, Declan's customers chuckled at something he'd said, then headed for the door.

"I wanted to be sure all my bases were covered." Cody stuck his hands in his pockets. "For real, Sis. You've got this, and I love ya."

"Aw, thanks, He-Man," she said, pulling out a childhood nickname he'd earned when he was four and refused to wear anything around the house except for He-Man underwear and a cape.

"On second thought, you are dead to me." Cody winked at her and turned toward the door, pulling it open for another man before slipping outside to join Mia and the kids.

The man, who held a large cup from Jill Kelley's coffee shop, glanced around the lobby. He reminded Lily of an eagle. Tall, with a shock of silver hair that lifted off his scalp despite his apparent best efforts to slick it down. It gave the otherwise imposing man a little humanity.

Declan may have gotten the others, but this customer was all hers.

"Hi there," Lily sent him a smile. "Welcome to Hart Family Fudge."

"And by that she means welcome to Kelley's Classic Fudge." Declan appeared out of nowhere, slipping in front of the counter and into the lobby, hand outstretched. "Mr. Mercer, welcome to Jonathon Island. I'm Declan Kelley."

This was Kent Mercer? She'd pictured someone much more affable, with laugh lines and a large belly. Kind of like Santa, but without the red suit. But this man didn't look like he enjoyed sweets at all. He was lean, and the upward curl of his lip reminded her of her gym teacher in elementary school who had scolded Lily one too many times on her lack of performance on the basketball court. And soccer field. Basically anything that had to do with sports.

She followed Declan around the counter. "So nice to meet you. I'm Lily Hart."

"I gathered as much." After setting his coffee on the counter and pulling a small notebook and pen from the pocket of his blazer, he perused their cases, reading through the labels on the various offerings.

"How was your trip to the island?" Declan asked, returning to his side of the counter.

"Windy." The man didn't even look up.

Frowning, Lily side-glanced at Declan. *Just breathe*, he mouthed.

Right. Yes. Breathe.

"All right." Mr. Mercer stood in front of them, his hand poised over his notebook, which he held in the air. He studied them with that hawkish gaze. "I want to sit down with you both and ask lots of questions, but first, the fudge. It's why we're all here, yes?"

"Absolutely!" Lily's falsely bright voice grated on her own ears.

"We've created two fudge flights for you." Declan lifted his box of boring, albeit delicious, fudge samples. "I recommend you start with our dark chocolate and move toward our sweetest fudge, the double-milk chocolate rocky road."

"Okay."

Lily lifted her box from the counter. "And, for a real treat, I've selected my favorite offerings." She wanted to make note of the order he should eat them in, but really, it didn't matter. Hers were all too different to organize in any order. But she'd slaved over them, agonized over which flavor profiles to feature. In the end, she'd chosen four: blueberry lavender, caramel salted peanut, dill pickle, and—her signature—bergamot.

"Thank you." He took the gift box from her hands.

"You're welcome to eat them at the window bar, but with a day this nice, we recommend the sidewalk seating." Declan pointed out the window to the small café table with two chairs he'd set out earlier this week for this express purpose.

The man should get a taste not just of our fudge, but of Jonathon Island as a whole. And what better place to do that than on iconic Main Street?

The guy really was a business genius.

"That sounds perfect." Grabbing up his coffee, Mr. Mercer excused himself. With Declan holding the door for him, he navigated through a few incoming customers, weaving his way back to the sidewalk and settling down at the table with his two boxes of fudge and trusty notepad.

"The flowers are a nice touch," Declan said. The fresh lilacs cascaded over the lip of the broad vase Lily had placed them in, adding fresh summer ambiance to the table. "But, I'd say if you get any closer to the window, you're going to leave a nose print."

"Hush." She waved him off but vacated her spot nearest the window.

Lily returned to the counter and helped a couple customers, catching glimpses as Mr. Mercer drew Declan's first slice of fudge to his nose. Inhaled. Then studied the texture, turning it over in his hand, before taking a bite.

Considering it against his palate.

Lily licked her lips. She could almost taste it too. She might tease Declan about bland and boring, but, in truth, his fudge was anything but. Sure, they were classic flavors, but he was a classic kind of guy. They were still melt-in-your-mouth deliciousness that could put someone into a sugar coma in blissful delight.

The door closed behind the last customer and then both she and Declan were back at the window in seconds.

"I can't tell if he likes them or not." Declan was so close to her, Lily could feel his breath against her ear.

"Guess I'm not the only one who wanted to spy," she teased. "And of course he likes them. He's going to give us both rave reviews."

"And then I guess we'll have to let the customers decide who wins."

She squeezed his elbow. "Can we not? For just a minute,

can we revel in the joint victory here? This article is going to be great for Jonathon Island. And for whoever wins."

And if that was Declan, so be it. After last night . . .

He nodded, bumped her shoulder with his. "Yeah. You're right."

"Ooo, is it my turn to make a fake announcement to the empty room?" She swung a smile his way. "Declan Kelley agrees with me, everyone!"

They both laughed before settling into silence, watching Mr. Mercer make notes on his paper pad as he ate each one of Declan's samples. For many long minutes, the man hovered over Declan's box of fudge, as if he were consuming a five-course meal. Taking polite bites, slowly chewing, making notes on his pad of paper. Pondering—clearly even relishing—the fudge flavors.

"He takes his job very seriously," Lily said, her toe tapping against the tile floor. "What, does he fancy himself a food critic or something?"

"Maybe. Or could be he's just enjoying the benefits of his job. Free travel, free stay on a beautiful island, free fudge. And who doesn't love fudge?"

Finally, Mr. Mercer took a drink of coffee and opened the second box.

"I hope he starts with the bergamot. That's my personal favorite." She'd put her whole heart and soul into this batch. It was special. And Mr. Mercer was about to find out.

The man withdrew a sample and lifted it to his nose, as he had every other sample. His brow lifted and he turned it, likewise, studying the texture, as he'd done with Declan's.

From here, it appeared to be the green fudge. "Oh no."

"What?"

She touched the glass. "That's the dill pickle fudge. It's a really yummy blend, but it does take a certain adventurous spirit to enjoy it. Oh, maybe I should have told him to start with the caramel one. But I wanted to stand out."

"That'll stand out, all right."

She elbowed him, and he grunted out a laugh. "Come on, Lil. If he doesn't like that one, he'll love the rest, and he can chalk it up to individual taste. We'll make sure of that."

We.

Like they were on the same team instead of . . .

Oh, her heart. So many *what if*s. Things she couldn't think about right now.

After considering the fudge for longer than Lily liked, Mr. Mercer finally took a bite. Made a face. Took a long draw of coffee. Made a note on his notepad, shaking his head, and then reached for what looked like the bergamot. To anyone else, it looked like plain fudge, but Lily knew Mr. Mercer's world was about to change.

She grabbed onto Declan's sleeve and hopped on her toes. "Here goes . . ."

His chuckle went straight to her heart, but instead of looking up—and inevitably getting lost in his crystal blue eyes—she kept her gaze trained on Mr. Mercer, who bit into the fudge.

And stilled.

"Why is he not chewing?" Lily whispered.

"I'm sure he's just letting it melt in his mouth."

Mr. Mercer lifted a napkin to his lips, covering his mouth. Lily watched in horror as the man politely and ever-so-discreetly spat the fudge into the napkin and deftly wrapped it into a wad before grabbing his coffee.

"Good grief, does he have to chug it?" Lily's hand dropped, making a fist at her side.

"What?"

"His coffee." Lily pressed a hand to her forehead. "This is awful."

"What?"

Lily covered her face, leaving room between her fingers to watch the horror unfolding before them. "He just spit it out."

"He did not."

Except, even Declan couldn't deny what was so very clearly visible to Lily. Mr. Mercer stood, then looked around before dropping the wadded-up napkin along with Declan's empty box into the nearby trash can. Replacing the lid on Lily's box, he straightened the collar of his shirt and walked toward the front door, but not before taking another long drink of coffee.

Lily scurried away from the window and toward the counter. Declan smoothly did the same, much less panic in his movement. His hand found hers, wrapping her with the kind of comfort she wanted to wholly cling to, despite every good sense that she shouldn't.

The door opened behind them, and they turned to face Mr. Mercer as he walked in. "Thank you for letting me taste that very . . . interesting combination of flavors, both of you."

Lily pasted a smile on. "Of course. So happy you enjoyed them."

Mr. Mercer set Lily's box on the counter. "Would you mind if I used your restroom before we proceed with the interview?"

"Of course not." Declan flashed Lily a look of sympathy. "It's just down the hall. I'll show you the way."

When they were gone, Lily turned and opened the box. There sat the half-eaten slices as well as the two undisturbed pieces of fudge—he hadn't even bothered to try the caramel or lavender, probably because he'd hated the first two so much. She understood he might not be a fan of the pickle, but the bergamot? Come *on*!

Maybe, well, it was possible something had gone wrong with the batch. She rarely tried her creations once she got the recipe down. She never needed to. But perhaps her ego had been her downfall.

Snagging a fork from the dispenser on the counter, she sank the tines into the opposite end of the bergamot fudge and shoved it into her mouth.

A terribly bitter, overly salted taste filled her mouth, and she raced to the trash can to spit out what had once been her pride and joy. Her signature creation.

Lily turned and stared at the open box. How . . . ?

But there was only one answer that made sense. Only one explanation.

Once again, she'd allowed herself to get so distracted—

this time by Declan Kelley—that she'd somehow ruined this batch of fudge.

And, in the process, probably her reputation too.

If anything could make this day better, it was Mom's famous chili fries.

Declan flipped the fudge shop sign to Closed, gave one fleeting look at Lily—who had been polite but distant for the last three days, ever since Kent Mercer's visit—and locked up behind him.

It couldn't have been that bad. But even he'd wanted to cringe when Kent Mercer left with another box of his fudge, and a tight smile and handshake for Lily.

Something had gone terribly wrong, and Lily knew it. Hence why she'd barricaded herself in the kitchen, whipping up another batch of signature fudge.

She might want to spend all of her Saturday evening obsessing over ways to win this competition, but Declan needed air.

Needed to figure out what to do next. As in, what to do if he won. Because, if Mercer's article was any indication . . .

He should start looking for a manager.

He waited on the porch while a few evening cyclists toured downtown, then stepped into the road and crossed to Martha's on Main, which was hopping if the line out the door and wrapped all the way down past the public library was any indication. A breeze kicked up off Lake

Huron, and clouds gathered in the distance. Perhaps another storm on its way.

But Declan could only handle so many, and the one inside him raged on.

He nodded at the people waiting, many of them perusing menus, and pushed his way inside, where the smells made his stomach grumble.

He'd eaten nothing but a couple fudge samples today, thanks to a stream of customers. More than a few held the article and wanted to take home the double-milk chocolate rocky road that Mercer had raved about.

Thankfully he'd called ahead and had Mom prep a to-go container. Nothing sounded better than plopping down in front of his parents' TV and catching tonight's Tigers game.

Martha's was always a bastion of busyness, especially on Saturday evenings, and tonight was no exception. The booths along the right wall and all the tables scattered throughout the cozy diner were filled to capacity. The upbeat rhythm of rock oldies, Mom's favorite, mingled with laughter and the low hum of conversation.

A table of older gentlemen pointed at him.

"Declan!" Seventy-something Lyle Graves waved a copy of the Detroit paper in the air. "Wanna sign my copy? Great job, boy." Beside him, Dad flashed Declan a thumbs-up.

Whoa. He hadn't seen his parents since the article had released this morning, but apparently it had earned him some respect among his family.

"Maybe later, Lyle," Declan called back across the room.

Next Declan passed Mia and Cody and her two kids, and another few tables of locals, each one with one of those stupid newspapers sitting beside their plates of meatloaf and bowls of potato soup.

He wasn't surprised. Dani had pre-ordered five hundred copies so she could hand them out all over town and at the Tourism Bureau. Of course, upon reading Mr. Mercer's assessment of Lily's fudge, she'd been just as dismayed as Declan—and Lily, who'd rushed to the bathroom with "something in her eye" and had returned with red, puffy eyes—but since the paper also had great things to say about the rest of the revitalization efforts, Dani had felt bound to distribute them.

He squeezed past his old Sunday school teacher, Vera Graves—Lyle's wife—who was carrying a large platter of food toward the back corner booth. "Hi, there, honey. Good to have you home. You make us proud."

And he couldn't deny the words found a crack in his heart, filling it up with warmth. "Thanks, Mrs. Graves."

The kitchen door beside the booth swung open, and Isaac walked out with his busboy bucket. His little brother wore his work uniform of dark jeans and white button-down shirt. He started to bus an abandoned table.

Declan just wanted to get in, get out, and get home so he could relax and think. About ways to capitalize on the good business about to flood his way. Ways to make his processes more efficient so he didn't spend so many hours at the fudge shop—the long hours and days were starting to wear on him, and would on any employee he left in charge.

And then there was Lily. He needed to think about her. About their situation. Did they even have a situation?

There was no better way to think than greasy food and baseball.

He finally approached the wooden bar, where a blonde woman sat on a stool chatting with a brunette waitress cleaning glasses behind the bar. Jordi Chamberlain, the pastor's middle child, flashed him her winning beauty-pageant smile that was more friendly than flirtatious. "Well, Declan Kelley. Hi, there. Look, Holland, it's our local celebrity."

The blonde—Jordi's best friend, Holland White—turned in her chair and grinned. "It is indeed." A copy of the infamous paper was spread in front of her.

The front photo, of him and Lily in the fudge shop lobby, facing off, arms crossed and frowning like rivals, caused a hitch in his chest. Dani had taken those photos when she'd first learned about the reporter. She'd had to do many takes because Declan and Lily couldn't stop laughing. It had been a good day.

Now he didn't know if he'd hear Lily laugh again. The article had said some pretty terrible things about her fudge.

Declan groaned at the women's attention. "Not you guys too."

Holland rolled up the paper and smacked his arm with it. "Nah, we know better. We remember what you looked like in junior high with those braces. And you had zits just like the rest of us. Now you're a big *star*."

"Oh, yeah." Jordi grabbed a bagged-up Styrofoam container and slid it across the bar to Declan. "And remember that time his brother snuck in and cut part of his hair in his sleep?"

Holland snorted. "Declan was sooooo upset about his precious hairdo."

"Understandable. He had to shave his whole head and his ears stuck out like Dumbo."

"Thanks for keeping me humble, ladies."

"Always." Jordi's smile faltered. "I do wish they hadn't done Lily dirty like that, though. I mean, just look what he said about her fudge!" She grabbed the paper from Holland, her eyes scanning the article. "Ah, here. *The fudge was a symphony with out-of-tune instruments, honking and blaring, as if not even attempting to play the same sheet of music.* I mean, come on. Who says that?"

"Well, the man has a point." Isaac plopped his bucket next to Declan, and water sloshed over the sides. "Have you guys had her fudge? Way too salty in my opinion."

"Didn't she, like, go to school for candy making? I'm guessing her creations are exquisite." Jordi wiped down her counter with a rag. "Go away if you can't say anything nice, Isaac. In fact, I see a dirty table over—"

"School or not, she's got an overinflated sense of her abilities. I'm thankful that *someone* finally brought her down a notch." Isaac turned to face Declan, practically lounging against the bar. His eyebrows lifted in challenge. "What about you, big brother? You seem upset, but you should be reveling in your victory over her."

He started at him. Since when was Isaac on his cheer squad? "I don't wish her to fail, Isaac."

Except, wasn't that was this competition was about? Someone had to win, and someone had to lose. A.k.a. fail.

"Whatever, dude." Isaac walked off whistling toward the kitchen.

Holland frowned. "Tell Lily that those who know her know that she's talented. In fact, I'll be by soon to grab some of her fudge. Oh." She seemed to realize who she was talking to. "I mean, I'll buy some of yours too. For the competition. I just want Lily to know we support her."

"No, it's okay. Go give her a boost. It'll make her feel good." He lifted the bag to Jordi. "Thanks for this."

Maybe the chili fries hadn't been worth all this. Probably he should have gone in through the kitchen. Declan hauled it across Main Street and up Jonathon Boulevard toward his parents' house, where he'd finally, at last, be blessedly alone.

Except maybe not.

Because when he got to the front steps, he heard someone calling his name. Brandon came out of Grandma's house and jogged over.

"Hey, man. It's been a few days." Brandon smacked Declan on the back. "Seems things are going well if that article has anything to say about it."

"Don't start."

"Whoa, what's eating you?" Brandon sniffed. "And are those chili fries I smell?"

"Yeah. Mom's." Declan turned to the door. But much as he loved his cousin, if he let him in, he wouldn't leave for hours. Instead, he sat down on the front stoop, setting the container of fries next to him. "Wanna join me for a sec? How's Grandma?" He had been so busy with the competition, Declan hadn't been able to stop by and visit much since coming home. Hopefully she'd be at church tomorrow.

"Doing okay. She just fed me a can of soup and some grilled cheese before heading to bed."

"In other words, you're still starving?"

Laughing, his cousin flexed. "You think soup's gonna sustain these bad boys? Of course I'm still starving." He plopped down beside Declan, the fries between them. "Don't mind if I do. But you've gotta tell me what's going on."

"Uh, pass." Declan opened the container, the top of which was slightly damp with steam. The golden fries were hardly visible under the layers of chili, cheese, and onions. He pulled out one of two plastic forks—Jordi must have thought he was sharing with someone—and handed it to Brandon.

"Come on, dude." Brandon stabbed a fry and, leaning over the container, managed to get it and a mountain of chili into his mouth without spilling a drop. After he chewed, he pointed the fork at Declan. "You haven't given me an update for over a week, when you said, and I quote, 'Working in the same place as my high school flame might have been a mistake.'"

"I still stand by that statement."

"So." Brandon shifted on the step, leaning back against the staircase post. "Have you kissed her yet?"

"What? No."

"But you want to."

Declan leaned forward and buried the bottom part of his face in his hands, groaning. "I don't *want* to want to."

"And why not?"

"Because it's complicated."

His cousin took another stab into the chili fries. "From what I can tell, you guys complement each other really well. And you clearly care about her."

"Of course I do. We're friends, I think. Like today when everyone was waving around that newspaper, I could see her sinking in on herself and I just, I don't know. I want to help her."

Brandon swallowed. "Friends? Does she know that?"

He sighed. "Not sure. Maybe. The other night, we put some of the past to rest. Apologized. Agreed that the family feud was stupid. But yes, I don't know. There are these moments when I think, maybe . . ."

"You could fix things. Go back to the past."

"I don't want the past. I want . . ."

"Her."

He sighed.

"I knew it!" Brandon hit him on the shoulder. "You're crazy about her."

"Crazy's a little over the top."

"Cra-*zy*, cuz. You always were."

Yeah, he had been. In fact, that's why he lost his head a little around her. Why he'd gotten into trouble. So maybe he should pay attention.

"Maybe. But it changes nothing. I'm still leaving for my job in Chicago in a few weeks."

"You wouldn't consider staying?"

"What would I do here?"

"You're a smart guy, Declan. You'd figure something out." Brandon looked down at the container, which was almost empty. "Sorry, man. I ate all your food. You want the last bite?"

"You go ahead. I'm not hungry anymore."

Shrugging, Brandon polished it off, then tossed the plastic fork into the container and closed it, sitting back against the railing again, studying Declan.

"What?"

"You said what would happen if Lily won, but what about if you do? After that article, it's a strong possibility if it wasn't already."

"It is. But if I win, I'm still going back to Chicago. I'll hire someone to run the place here."

"What about Lily? Why not hire her?"

It was the same idea he'd had—and thrown away—earlier this week. "She definitely wouldn't want to work with Mom and Dad with me gone."

"You're not thinking, man." Brandon reached over and smacked Declan's head.

"Hey!" He rubbed the spot. It hadn't exactly hurt, but still. "What was that for? What am I not thinking about?"

"The fact that nobody is *making* you go back to Chicago. Your parents would love it if you stayed. And if you stayed, you and Lily could work together. Really put the family feud behind you."

"I'm not sure she'd work in a Kelley shop. That might be too much for her."

"You'll never know if you don't ask." Brandon reached

over to smack him again, but Declan strong-armed him back. Brandon laughed. "And you'll never know if she is feeling the same way if you don't just man up and kiss her."

Ten

NORMALLY, CHURCH UPLIFTED LILY. Reminded her that God was bigger than her problems. But not today.

It wasn't Pastor Arnie's fault. He'd given a riveting sermon on the parable of the talents—the parts she'd heard, anyway. Her brain had crowded out the other parts, unable to settle, to quiet.

Even now, after service had ended, as she stood with her parents, who were talking with Cody and Mia at one end of their wooden pew, Lily should be finding pleasure in her day off. She and Declan had mutually agreed they would close the shop on Sundays, at least until one of them won and could afford to hire someone to work limited Sunday hours. Because nobody could work seven days a week without burning out.

Of course, it didn't seem to matter how many days a week Declan Kelley worked. He always came out on top, as judged even in church by the crowd of people surrounding him. He stood like some anointed prophet on the other side of the small sanctuary, near the stained-glass window of Jesus with the lost lamb. Someone slapped Declan on the back, and he grinned that thousand-watt smile of his. Laughed.

Lily huffed, and Mom turned toward her. "You okay?" She looked pretty today in a flowing skirt and blue sleeveless blouse, her hair down around her shoulders.

"Yeah, I'm fine. Just thinking about going into the shop later and experimenting some more. Gotta find the perfect recipe."

"Everyone knows you make amazing fudge. That reviewer didn't know what he was talking about."

Except, he *had* known. Lily had yet to tell Mom the real reason he'd spit out his fudge. She'd let everyone assume it was because his tastebuds just weren't quite refined enough.

Only she knew the wretched truth.

But how had her fudge turned out so terribly? She knew fudge. It practically flowed in her veins.

Apparently, her over-salted veins.

"Thanks, Mom," she said. "But there's a bit more to it than that."

Cody and Mia left, likely to grab her kids from the children's classrooms in the building next door. Dad turned from them, faced Lily. A gruff man with skin a bit brown and leathery from all his years in the sun, today his sharp gaze was softened by the powder-blue polo he wore. "Listen to your mother, Lily."

Lily's eyes widened at her father, who didn't speak unless he had something to really say. "Yes, sir."

"I mean it." He took a step closer, kissed her on the temple—a rare display of affection. "You can't let that boy get you down."

That boy. That's all Declan had ever been to Dad. He'd never known him like Lily had. Had never needed to know anything more than that Declan was a Kelley. But he hadn't seen how Declan had helped Lily. How he'd lent her his professional expertise, even though it wouldn't benefit him—might even hurt his chances at winning.

I think this family feud has gone on long enough.

"It's not Declan. Dad—"

But her father held up his hand. "You're a Hart and that means you're going to succeed." Turning, he found Frank and Martha Kelley, who now stood by their son. As if expecting it, Frank met Dad's stare—and both of them glared.

"Oh, for goodness' sake." Mom grabbed Dad's arm. "We're at church, Randall."

"What? I didn't say anything."

"You didn't have to." Rolling her eyes, Mom looked at Lily. "Mia and Cody are joining us for lunch. How about you?"

Lily shifted her purse from one shoulder to the other. "Thanks, but I think I'm going to head to the shop."

Mom frowned, but nodded, patting Lily's cheek. "Just don't stay too long, all right? Everyone needs a day of rest. Sometimes the best ideas come when you're resting." She winked. "Surely you learned that in business school."

The words landed like a punch.

Maybe Declan deserved the fudge shop after all.

As her parents left through the front, Lily headed for the back door. She walked outside, the sunlight warming her skin. A large Dutch elm tree spread its branches over the manicured lawn with its surrounding walking path. Lily started to turn right, toward the concrete path that led to Jonathon Boulevard, but stopped when she heard her name being called from inside the church.

Well, she'd *almost* escaped.

Turning, she found Tara Chamberlain approaching. Just like her daughter Jordi, the pastor's wife was always the height of fashion, and today was no exception in her wide-leg trousers, silk blouse, beige kitten heels, and pearl hoop earrings. "Hey, girl." Arms outstretched for a hug, Tara offered her a smile. "I was trying to get over and say hi before service started but you know how it is."

"I don't, actually," Lily teased, accepting Tara's hug. The woman smelled like lavender. "We can't all be as popular as you."

"Popular is one word." Tara stepped down onto the sidewalk. "It's mostly people wanting to complain about something either church-related or town-related."

She smiled at that. "I saw Jeb's in town?"

"Yes. Just for the weekend. He's going hiking today with some of his buddies, and Arnie has a counseling session before he'll head home. So." Tara tilted her head with a sly smile. "Will you indulge me with a short walk around the green? It's such a nice day."

She didn't fool Lily. "Did Mom ask you to check on me?"

"She might have mentioned you were having a rough time since that article released yesterday."

Lily groaned. "It's so embarrassing. And the worst part is, it's true. My fudge *was* terrible."

And somehow, without meaning to—because Tara was just *that* good—Lily spilled the whole story about Mr. Mercer's visit. The aftermath too. "It really, truly tasted awful. I still don't know what happened."

In the distance, historic Fort Jonathon overlooked the lake, its limestone walls standing thick and strong. Tara's heels clicked on the sidewalk that meandered along the edges of the church's property. She stopped and looked at Lily, her eyebrows pinched together. "Lily, you're sure . . . well, I don't want to suggest . . . Hmm."

"What is it, Tara?"

"It's only, you don't think Declan sabotaged your fudge, right? I wouldn't think him capable, but then again, your families have been fairly contentious over the years. Perhaps the pressure of the competition got to him?"

"No." The answer came quick and sharp. "He wouldn't do that."

"You're positive?"

"Yes." Not a question in her mind. "This was *my* fault. *I* messed up. When Declan told me I was in the lead last week, I couldn't believe it. Maybe I got distracted." She sighed. "I'm not sure I'm really cut out to be a business owner."

"Now hold on right there." Tara pulled out her mom

voice, though it was still soft and pliable, caring. "Just because you made a mistake doesn't mean you throw everything away. You're every bit as capable as Declan."

"No, I'm not."

Tara raised an eyebrow.

Aw, she'd already told her so much . . . "I failed out of business school because I was too focused on the creation process. I didn't want to worry about the numbers, because the numbers were hard and I'm not naturally inclined toward them. But the numbers matter when you're running a business."

"They do. But they're not everything. I'm guessing Declan is beginning to see that."

"What do you mean?"

"It means you have something he doesn't—a love for creation. A business isn't ever going to succeed without true spirit and heart behind it."

"Declan has heart. He cares about his grandma. Cares about his family's legacy just like I care about mine."

"And you also care about him." A smile edged Tara's lips. "Don't try to deny it. It's written all over your face."

Once again, Lily groaned. "I don't want to care."

"And yet, you do. It's why I asked you if you thought he was trying to sabotage you. Oh my, the defense."

Lily laughed, incredulous. "You didn't really think he was. You just wanted to see if *I* thought he was. To see if I . . ."

"Love him? Yes, dear."

"Love?" Lily sputtered the word. "Ha! No. I tolerate him, sure. He's easy on the eyes, I'll admit. And he's got a surprising amount of kindness in him. And he apologized for the past."

"So far I'm not hearing a *but*."

"But"—Lily said, with emphasis—"he's leaving, Tara. And I don't think, well, he's never said he would want to be with me or anything like that. Plus, we're *competitors*." She stopped and placed her hands on her hips as she faced Tara. "That's a lot of *but*s standing in our way."

"True. There were a lot of buts standing in mine and Arnie's way too. You know the story."

Lily swallowed. "I do." She knew how a girl named Tara Montgomery from a rich Bostonian family had visited Jonathon Island the summer after her high school graduation and met a poor seminary student named Arnie Chamberlain. How they'd fallen for each other and, despite the disapproval of her family, she'd chosen him and a young marriage over the fancy college education her parents had planned for her.

"Then you know that when it comes to love, nothing is ever one-hundred-percent easy. It takes work and commitment." Tara squeezed Lily's arm. "But when two people decide it's worth it, oh, honey, it's worth it."

What if . . . Oh, the thought weirdly filled her chest. No. No—that wasn't . . .

Well, she'd been down that road of dreaming of a future with Declan Kelley, and look where that had gotten her. And this time she *knew* he'd abandon her, so . . .

"I appreciate that, Tara, but right now I have bigger problems. I don't know how to come back from that article." Her eyes started to burn. "I don't know if I should even try."

"You should *definitely* try. God has given you a talent, Lily Hart, and it's your job to do your best with it—like Arnie said today, don't bury it. And sure, things may not turn out the way you envision. They may not even turn out the way you want. But His ways are infinitely better, and when we give our talents back to Him, then it's so fun to watch and see what He will do."

Tara smiled at her, and it sank into Lily, along with her words. Tara held out her arms and Lily stepped into the embrace. "Thank you."

"And one more thing. Regarding that article." Tara pulled away and looked into Lily's eyes. "There's no bad press that can't be overcome with a little brilliant marketing. And if I recall, you have a best friend who just happens to know a lot about marketing."

Sadie.

"Oh my goodness." Smiling, Lily smacked her own forehead. Yes, Sadie would know what to do.

This game wasn't lost yet.

You'll never know if she is feeling the same way if you don't just man up and kiss her.

For five days, Brandon's words had played on repeat in Declan's head.

Especially seeing the rekindled fire in Lily. On Monday, he'd come into the fudge shop to find a new woman there.

One with a new spark, a new confidence, a new determination in her eyes.

In truth, it made her even more beautiful.

Man up. Kiss her.

"Earth to Declan." Mom's voice broke through the haze and snapped him right back to his parents' table, where his family was gathered on this Thursday evening. It was Mom's night off from the diner, so instead she'd spent the evening whipping up an eggplant lasagna that was to die for.

He'd probably gained a few pounds during his stay on Jonathon Island.

"Sorry, what?" Declan stabbed a crouton on his salad with a bit too much force, sending it streaking across the white tabletop.

"Your mother was asking how business was going." A bit of sauce dripped down Dad's chin, and Mom reached over to swipe it off with a napkin.

"Yeah, Decky." Isaac leaned back in his chair, lifting the front two legs off the ground. "How *is* business going since that Hart girl somehow managed to spin the article in her favor?"

"Is that true?" Mom's gray eyebrows disappeared under her wispy bangs. "How'd she do that? And has it affected your numbers?"

"My numbers have held steady." It was the truth, if not all of it. Because yes, Lily had found a way to spin Mr. Mercer's advertising, embracing his criticism and invoking a scarcity mindset around her most unique flavors. *Get this flavor before it's gone* had become her favorite saying.

Not that she'd said it to Declan himself. She hadn't been rude, but ever since the article came out, their easy camaraderie had slipped back into a cordial professionalism. Mostly, she just left the room if they found themselves alone together.

And he hadn't a clue how to get it back. Or if he should.

But Brandon's words . . . they still wouldn't let go of him.

Or maybe *Declan* didn't want to let go of *them*.

Mom set her fork down and leaned forward as if inspecting him. "You should be furious, or at least working furiously to beat her. The festival is in less than a week and a half! Do you know who is beating who?"

He dabbed his mouth with a cloth napkin. "No, I haven't seen the latest numbers." But his sense told him Lily was ahead.

"It's clear he's losing, Mom." Isaac tossed his napkin right into the mess of leftover sauce on his mostly empty plate. His brother's lips twisted into a smirk.

"Shut up, Isaac."

"And this is why you shouldn't have trusted him with saving Grandma's house."

What was the matter with this kid? "Oh, like she should have trusted *you*—the guy who busses dishes down at Mom's diner? Hello, how old are you? Twenty-two? I'd graduated *summa cum laude* by then—"

"Declan!" Mom said.

And maybe he should have held back, but someone had to say it. And nobody else would. "No, come on, Mom. Look at him. He's done nothing with his life. A twelve-year-old in a twenty-two-year-old's body, playing video games every off hour."

"You're just jealous," Isaac said, lifting a shoulder.

"Of what, exactly? That you get to freeload off Mom and Dad? That *you* aren't the disappointment in the family even though you've worked for years to do everything right after the one thing you did wrong?" Declan pushed back from his chair, the legs scraping against the wood floor. "Sure, Isaac. I'm jealous. Or maybe it's *you* that's jealous of *me* because nobody even thought to ask you for a solution to saving Grandma's house. They had to call me in all the way from Chicago."

His chest heaved with the exertion of finally speaking his mind.

"Now, Declan," Mom tsked. "That's not fair. Your brother lived part of high school through the pandemic. It's just taking him a little longer to get up to speed. And we called you because you're the one with the expertise we needed."

His brother slow clapped. "Nice speech, bro. But you forgot what I said about expectations. And also what I said about Lily Hart—"

"What about Lily Hart?" Mom's fully loaded fork lowered to her plate as she looked between them.

"Nothing." Declan gathered up his plate and moved to wash it in the sink.

"Decky still has a thing for her."

"Is that true?" Mom repeated.

The plate clattered from Declan's hands into the sink. Thankfully it didn't shatter. He picked it up again and scrubbed it with the brush, the bristles scraping against the ceramic surface.

"Declan, *do* you have a thing again for Lily Hart?"

A *thing*. Like that could adequately describe what he felt for the most vivacious, amazing woman he'd ever met. He turned back to face his family. "So what if I do?"

"So what if you . . . Declan!" Mom glanced at Dad, then back at Declan. "That girl nearly ruined this family."

"Yeah," Isaac said. "And she's not even that hot."

"Seriously, Isaac?" Declan started toward his brother, ready to grab him by the collar, rough him up. "I said shut up—"

Dad slammed a fist on the table. "That's enough, you two."

Declan halted, and his hands lowered into fists at his side. Isaac's eyes laughed at him. Why had Declan even bothered trying to talk sense into anyone in this family?

"Now, let's sit down and talk through this like adults," Dad said, pointing to Declan's chair. "And you can tell us how you were just joking with your mother because you would never be so stupid as to fall for a Hart a second time."

He *was* an adult. Twenty-eight years old. And yet, right now in this moment, he felt eighteen again.

Declan's phone shattered the silence, buzzing against the granite countertop. Reaching for it, he noticed Lily's name on the screen. She never called—only texted. His heart thudded in his chest. "Hello?" A whooshing noise filled the background, and a woman yelped. "Lily?" A pause. "Lily? You okay?"

"Sorry." She came onto the line. "Declan, I wouldn't have called you but Cody's with Mia having dinner on the mainland, and I couldn't get ahold of my dad and I didn't know what else to do."

Her panicked voice shot immediate worry through him too. But that wouldn't help her.

His family stared at him with wide eyes, but Declan ignored them, striding toward the front door and grabbing his keys on his way out. "What's going on?"

"Just come to the shop. I was here working late and cleaning up and there's a minor leak situation going on."

Uh-oh. "Where?" Declan headed for his old bicycle leaning against the side of his parents' house.

"Kitchen. Right underneath the sink." Another yelp.

"I'm coming." He hopped on the bike and started pedaling, one hand gripping the phone, one on the handlebars. "Can you shut off the water valve?"

"I tried, but it's stuck. Please, hurry." Then the line went dead.

Declan flew down the road. Lily had needed someone, and she'd called him. Sure, she'd tried her family first, but that was normal, right? Her calling him had to mean something.

Maybe just that finally, she trusted him.

He left his bike lying sideways behind the store and burst through the alley door. Lily was on her hands and knees in a huge puddle of water, her head stuck inside the bottom kitchen sink cabinet. Water had inched across the kitchen floor and was heading toward the pantry.

"Lil?" He headed for her, steadying himself as he nearly slipped. Whoa.

She sat back on her heels holding a thick roll of duct tape. Her hair was plastered to her forehead and neck, her soaked blue shirt clinging to her. "Oh, thank goodness."

He squatted down. Lily's pink toolbox sat on the other side of her. "What happened exactly?" The pipe under the sink appeared to be wrapped with several towels and the tape, but water continued to drip. Lily's temporary fix wouldn't last long.

"Um, well." She pushed her hair back. How was it possible for her to look so incredibly attractive even sopping wet?

"Hold that thought." Clearing his throat, he rummaged in her toolbox for a flathead screwdriver. Then he examined the valves. Seemed easy enough. "Okay, go ahead."

He inserted the screwdriver into the hot water isolation valve and turned it clockwise one quarter—it turned easily.

"I was working late and noticed a small drip under the sink and thought, hey, I'm a grown woman. I can fix that."

He held back a smile. "Did you now?"

She slapped his arm, and he fumbled the screwdriver.

Declan chuckled as he moved the screwdriver to the cold water valve, which didn't turn so easily. "Guessing it didn't go well?"

"Understatement. And when I called Cody, he said he wasn't surprised a pipe busted since he's pretty sure this place hasn't been re-piped in a while. Apparently it's been on his list of things to do for Seb. But you know. Cody's been a little busy."

"I'll say." His eyes met hers as he fumbled with the pipe valve. "He and Mia seem to be heading for happily ever after."

He met her eyes.

She met his.

His entire body started to tingle.

He let out a grunt and the valve moved, the dripping of water through the towels tapering until it died. "There. It's off."

Lily stood. "I should have known you'd come riding in like a hero, Top Gun."

"I'm always happy to come when you call, Lil." Then he stood too, and his hand brushed hers in the process.

She blinked at him for a long moment before moving away quickly. But as she stepped backward, her sandal hydroplaned across the floor, sending her upper body backward. She twisted, trying to catch herself.

Declan stepped forward to steady her, his arm catching around her waist. Too bad he also hit the slick spot.

She crashed down on top of him with a *hmmph*.

"Are you okay?" The cold water soaked through his jeans, through his T-shirt. But all he cared about was his arm around her, her body in his arms.

She blinked down at him.

His gaze went to her lips. *Just kiss her.*

"Sorry." She clambered upright. Her wet clothes clung to her every curve.

Shutting his eyes, Declan lay there in the puddle, trying to set his hammering heart right.

Lily nudged him with her foot. "Come on."

He opened his eyes and found her standing over him, hand held out. Declan took it. Stood, but then Lily's feet slipped again. This time, he held her steady. "I've got you."

"Thanks."

And aw, man, he couldn't help himself. His fingers looped through her hair, loosened a lock that clung to her check, and tucked it behind her ear. "Are you okay?"

"You already asked me that."

"But you didn't answer me."

She looked back at him with those crazy blue eyes. Those eyes he'd fallen for at eighteen. And that same forbidden longing crested inside him. Turned his legs weak. Stole any common sense he might have left.

Just kiss her.

"Lil?" His voice rasped. "*Are* you? Okay, I mean?"

She nodded. Swallowed, her gaze locked on to his.

A heartbeat and then, his head dipped toward hers, his arms enfolding her. The kiss felt a little wild, unfettered, and as he deepened it, a moan escaped her, a soft little sigh of surrender.

And it set him on fire. He moved her back against the counter so they'd be in no danger of slipping again, and then his fingers plunged through her hair, the skin of her cheeks soft when he drew his thumbs across.

It was even better—even sweeter—than he remembered.

Lil . . .

Suddenly, Lily stilled. Pulled her head back. She blinked, her eyes alight with the kind of delight that could captivate a man. Mesmerize him. "We shouldn't—we can't . . ."

"Why not?" The words were out there before he could stop them. And maybe he should regret it, but he just couldn't. Not when it meant Lily was here again, in his arms.

Just where she was always meant to be.

"Because." Lily started to draw away, slip from his grip. He should let her go. Shake off the water. The kiss. Clean up. Instead, he gave her hand a little squeeze and she froze. Looked up at him.

"That's not a reason, Lil."

Her lips were still parted, a delightful shade of pink on her cheeks and her hair mussed in the most bewitching way that he had to stop himself from running his fingers through it one more time.

But then she leaned toward him again. Let her hands fall on his chest before they slowly—agonizingly—made the trip upward to wrap around his neck.

And then he hoisted her up onto the counter, wrapped his arms around her, tilted her slightly back, and found himself kissing her again. Being kissed by her. The fascination of it—of Lily—thrilled his senses. It didn't matter that their wet clothes clung to them, the chill burning against the heat of his skin. Didn't matter that they didn't have all the answers about how anything beyond this moment was going to work.

Kissing Lily Hart was coming home. Belonging. Where he was loved not for his successes but for himself.

He could drown in that.

The front door rattled open. "Lily? Are you here? I came as quickly as I could."

Lily gasped and pushed at Declan's chest. "Cody's here." Then she slipped from the counter, still standing in Declan's embrace. "Back here," she called to her brother.

Then Lily started to step away from Declan.

But before she could escape, he pressed his lips to her ear. "We are definitely going to talk about this later."

Because the rules of the game had suddenly changed.

Eleven

ALL DAY, THE ONLY THING DECLAN could think about was that kiss.

And his promise: *We are definitely going to talk about this later.*

Later hadn't come last night, since Cody had stayed to help clean things up. He'd given Declan more than a once-over, his gaze wary. As if he knew what had happened. As if he knew how Declan felt about Lily.

Well, Declan was tired of holding it back.

And if Lily responded to the note he'd slipped her during their evening rush—if she came here, now—he was finally going to tell her.

I'm falling in love with you.

Of course he'd known it—maybe even weeks ago, but . . .

Yeah, that kiss had confirmed it. He could still feel her in his arms. Maybe had never forgotten really. But he couldn't escape the feeling that she *belonged* there. And him, with her.

He glanced at his watch again. 9:06. She was late. But not *too* late. And Lily was known to lose track of time. That could be all her lateness meant.

Then again, maybe *late* in this case meant *not coming*.

Huffing out a breath, he shifted the picnic basket from one hand to the other, scanning Blueberry Boulevard and the eastern end of Main Street from his spot in front of the Blueberry Hill Park sign. A couple stepped out of Doug's Market across the road, and some tourists meandered down Main, but there was no sign of the lavender-haired beauty that had stolen his heart for the second time.

The sound of children's giggles reached his ears from the playground, but there were fewer families inside the park now that the sun had almost made its descent for the day.

With his free hand, Declan pulled his phone from his back pocket, stared at his notifications—all emails, all trying to sell him something that would make his life better. But he didn't need a coupon to Chicago's finest restaurant, or the latest time-saving app, or a membership to the coolest gym.

He just needed Lily. Here, with him. Preferably in his arms again.

And then, like a vision, she appeared at the end of his line of sight. She was riding that pink bike down the cobblestone street, bouncing as she flew, the edges of her purple skirt fluttering with the movement.

She was wild and fierce and beautiful, his Lily.

Declan swallowed against the dryness in his throat, just

watching her as she slid her bike to a stop in front of him, breathing hard. "I'm so sorry I'm late!" She dismounted and secured the bike into the rack. "I had a very chatty customer right there at the end."

"I thought maybe you'd decided not to come."

She made a face. "I'll be honest. I considered it. But after . . ." Even with the dimming light, he could see her cheeks flush a gorgeous pink. Was she thinking about their kiss? "Well, I thought maybe it would be best if we talked."

"Good." He cleared his throat at the hoarseness there, straightened, lifted the basket. "But first, let's eat. You hungry?"

"Oh my goodness, starving!" She eyed the basket. "More of your mom's food?"

"Not this time." After his confrontation with his parents at dinner last night before his kiss with Lily, he'd avoided his whole family all the rest of the evening and today. "Thought we could try the new fish and chips place."

"Yum! Lead the way."

They walked toward a grouping of picnic tables under the shade of some elms. A few cyclists or pedestrians passed, out for a moonlit ride or stroll along the main park pathway, but for the most part, it was just the two of them.

Declan set the basket on the ground and pulled a red-and-white-checkered blanket from inside. He spread it on the old wooden table, covering a few stains and sticky spots. Then he grabbed a small plastic vase with a bouquet he'd purchased from the new florist near the fudge shop. He placed that in the middle of the table.

"Look at you, getting all fancy," Lily teased, but there was a delighted sparkle in her eye.

"Nothing but the best for you, Lil." Declan winked, and his chest lightened to see that blush steal over Lily's cheeks again.

He liked this version of Lily. The version that didn't hate him. The version that felt very much like the one he'd fallen for, only older, with a deeper sense of self.

The kind of woman that could make a guy stick around? Maybe.

He finished setting up for dinner with two disposable clear plates, two sets of silverware rolled up into napkins, and containers with their food—battered slices of fish, coleslaw, and crisp fries, with enormous brownies for dessert.

"It looks amazing. Thank you for going to all this effort." She slid onto the bench across from him.

He reached over the table for her hand. When she placed it inside his, he squeezed. "You're worth it." Then before she could respond, he bowed his head, prayed, and asked the Lord to bless their food.

He added a silent prayer for strength and a clear head to say what he needed to say. Maybe some courage too.

Then they dug in, falling into easy conversation about everything but their kiss and the growing awareness between them. She told him about Florida and how, despite loving being home, she missed Sadie and the warm weather. He talked about Chicago, how she'd love some of the art galleries there. Before Declan knew it, an hour had flown by. Their food had been eaten, including those brownies—the chocolate of which he could still taste on his tongue—and other than a chorus of cicadas that had joined their conversation, they might as well be the only two people in the world.

It was time.

At a pause in the conversation, Declan pushed away from the table. Stood. "Want to take a walk?"

"Sure. I could use it after all that rich food."

Together they cleaned up their table, tucked the picnic basket behind a tree to grab on their way out, and turned onto the trail that looped the park.

For a while, they were both silent. Because how did he begin to talk about something so huge? And maybe it wasn't so huge to her, but it had taken up all the space in his head.

Their future.

Please, let them have a future.

Before Declan could figure out how to start, Lily said, "So. One week left until the festival." In the light of the full moon, the blue cast lit the meadow of fresh-cut lawn. "How do you think things are going?"

Declan stuck his hands in his pockets. Not exactly the beginning he'd had in mind, but he'd go with it. "Your latest marketing tactics seemed to have really brought in the crowds. I think you might be ahead again."

"And how would you feel about that if I was?"

"I'd be proud of you." He glanced over at her, uncertain what she might read on his face. "I *am* proud of you."

Her eyes shone. "That means a lot. I'll admit, doing this well has surprised me, especially after what happened with business school." As they rounded the bend, her face suddenly grew serious again. "I couldn't have done it without you, though. And I don't want you to resent me for that. If, *you know*, I do win."

"I'd never resent you, Lily." How could he?

Because Brandon was right.

He *was* crazy about her. Lily was his sunshine and laughter, and she grounded him. She was the bergamot to his milk chocolate. The lavender to his rocky road.

"Maybe you wouldn't, but your family sure would." Her beautiful eyes were full of emotion.

"Just like your family would resent me if I won." He stopped walking, turned toward her. "But are we going to keep letting them determine what we do with our lives?"

Because, yeah. His family would never, ever accept how he felt about her. So what was he going to do about it?

She frowned. "Maybe it's futile." She kicked off her sandals and walked across the grass, only a step in front of him. In the moonlight her pale blonde hair glowed like a halo.

"It doesn't have to be." He reached for her, captured her hand, and turned her around to face him. "Lily, I can't stop thinking about that kiss. About you." He swallowed hard. "About us."

It took her a beat, a moment that lasted far longer than it should have, but finally, she said, "I can't either." Before he could breathe out a sigh of relief, she added, "But it doesn't change the fact that our families hate each other. Or that you're leaving."

"I don't have to." The simple truth of Brandon's words

flooded in. "I could stay, or you could leave with me. Come to Chicago. We could go anywhere, really. Back to Florida, if you wanted. We could find a way, Lily, if we really wanted it."

I know I do.

"I just don't see how it would work." She dropped his hand and resumed walking barefoot in the grass. "We tried it once, and it ended so badly. I don't want that to happen again. Now that we're friends again, I couldn't stand to live in a world where you hated me."

"I could never hate you, Lily. I never did." At her serious side eye, he shook his head. "Besides, like we've both said, we're not kids anymore."

"You're right. We aren't, but we are still who we are. A Kelley and a Hart. One of us is still going to lose our fudge shop." She made her way toward the now-deserted playground, stepping up onto a balance beam on the ground. "Our two families still can't let go of decades-long hurt and hate."

He followed alongside her. "*We* could be different."

"And do what? Leave our families?" She hopped off the balance beam and headed right for a pair of swings. "I don't know about you, but being back here, I guess it's reminded me how much I missed home. And I don't want to leave again, not if I have a choice." Tossing her sandals to the side, she lowered herself onto a swing.

He joined her, turning on his swing to face her. "Then don't. We can stay. We can fight. Whatever the results of the competition, we figure it out from there. As long as we're on the same page."

She stared at her pink-painted toenails, buried them in the sand before starting to sway. "Who are you kidding, Declan? You'd never go against your own family." Lily said it softly. Not in admonishment. Just stated it right there, like a fact.

And it *was* a fact. Or at least, it had been. But something had broken in him last night, when he'd dared to finally speak up against his family. When he'd chosen Lily by walking out on family dinner.

"You're right. Family's important to me. But so are you."

"And you're important to me too. But with your family, it just seems, I don't know." She kicked her foot, sending a spray of sand flying forward.

"It just seems what?"

She sighed. "Almost unhealthy. Like you're doing it out of guilt or fear, not love."

Her words shook something loose inside him. "No, Lily. But maybe there is a part of me that wants to break free of everything they expect of me."

"Why? What happened to make you feel like you couldn't be your own person, that you had to do everything your family asked of you? Is there more to it than what happened with your grandpa?"

How did she do that—cut to the heart of everything he'd struggled with his whole life and make it sound so cut-and-dried? So simple?

Declan planted his feet on the ground and leaned forward. "When I was a kid, my mom's brother married someone the family didn't approve of. They met when she was visiting Jonathon Island, and she got the flu. My uncle was on call at the clinic that night. I don't know if you remember him, but he was a physician and planning to take over my grandpa's pediatric practice. He split his time between that and the clinic."

Uncle Craig. He'd been so generous and kind to Declan, had encouraged him to follow his dreams, wherever they might lead.

Lily reached over, slipped her hand in his. Squeezed. "And?"

"And, Gert was from Germany. They fell in love really quickly and decided to get married. The only problem was that she didn't want to leave her own parents who lived in Frankfurt, so he told his parents he'd be moving."

"I'm guessing they didn't take that too well."

"Not well at all. They basically said if he moved, Uncle Craig was dead to them."

"Not cool."

He smiled at how succinctly she'd put it. "Not cool at all."

Another squeeze at his fingertips. "So what happened?"

"Uncle Craig chose love. He moved. And I never saw him again."

"Wait, *seriously*?"

"Unfortunately, yes. When I asked my mom what had happened to him, she told me, 'Family always comes first. He was selfish to prioritize his own happiness and leave the rest of us in the lurch.' All because he wasn't here anymore to take over the practice."

"Wow. I'm sorry, Dec. But you know she wasn't right in that, yeah? That was her own fear talking."

He shrugged. His thumb swiped across the back of Lily's hand, so soft in his. "Looking back, yes, I'm sure she was speaking largely out of hurt. They were really close, and she missed him."

"It's not like he was dead, though. She could have still had a relationship with him."

"In case you haven't figured it out, my mother is an all-or-nothing kind of person."

She'd come to face him, resting her head against the swing's chain. Offered him a small smile. "I did kind of guess that. But she was wrong, you know. It isn't selfish to want to be happy."

"I know that now. Or at least, I'm trying to." He inhaled a deep breath. Here it went . . . "And do you know what's made me happier than I've been in years?"

Lily pressed her lips together, eyes wide as she shook her head.

Declan looked her straight in the eyes, without blinking, and uttered the one word that might finally change everything between them. An admission with the power to blow up their worlds—for better or worse. Hopefully, mostly better.

"You."

And there it was.

The thing they'd been building toward since Declan had kissed her senseless in the kitchen last night—though to be honest, for her, it had started long before that.

Had there ever been a moment, ever since that Disney

World trip when they were eighteen, when at least some part of her hadn't loved Declan Kelley?

Maybe not.

And Lily was oh-so-tired of pretending, of holding back this living, breathing, and yes, growing desire inside of her.

Which was why she bounced to her feet, rounded on Declan, and grabbed on to the swing ropes on either side of him. She leaned in, her breath mingled with his as her hair fell forward over her shoulders.

Declan reached up and gingerly pushed it behind her ears, his large hands cupping her face, his eyes liquid in the moonlight. "What do *you* want, Lily Ann Hart?"

"I want . . ." She inhaled and decided to be brutally honest. "For just once, I want someone to choose *me*. Not just when it's convenient. Not just when it feels right. But always."

He flinched. "I know I already said this, but I'm so sorry for what happened in high school. I shouldn't have—"

"I know." She leaned closer. "It wasn't just you."

"What do you mean?" His gaze darkened. "Who else hurt you?"

"Nobody of consequence now." Straightening, she backed away from Declan. A sudden breeze had her wrapping her arms around herself—but it was the memories too that chilled her.

Declan stood, drawing her to himself, tucking her in. "Please tell me."

"Okay." She relaxed into his embrace. "Back in Florida, I dated this guy, Tony."

"I hate him already."

Lily laughed and pinched Declan's side. His low chuckle filled her ear, filling her up. "So Tony and I dated for quite a while in school. We were partners for this creative project. Even won a free trip to Paris."

"What? That's amazing, Lil. I'm guessing it was your creation that led to it too, huh?"

"It was the bergamot. Gets the judges every time."

"Of course it was." His hand lightly stroked her back, and she couldn't help but lean into his touch. "So what happened with Baloney Tony?"

She snorted. "Baloney Tony ended up being a phony."

"I see what you did there. How was he phony?"

"Um." This part, ugh. "A few days before our trip to Paris, he broke up with me. Said he'd rather take Jessica, another chef in our class, instead."

"What an absolute . . ." He cleared his throat. "I hope you said no way and went to Paris and amazed all the chefs there."

"Not quite." Her words were soft, filled with the aching of those days. "I should have. But I spent the week holed up in my room claiming a cold, and my teacher let Jessica go in my stead."

Declan held her tighter. "I'm so sorry, Lily. That shouldn't have happened. Sounds like you dodged a bullet, but I imagine that hurt. Especially after what I did."

She nodded into his chest. "I'll admit, for a long while, I wondered what was wrong with me."

He pushed her away slightly so he could look down at her. "Absolutely nothing. You are perfect."

"I'm hardly that."

"Maybe you're just perfect for me, then."

Oh, her heart. Her fingers tugged on his belt loops. "All right, I spilled. Now what about you? Any exes to report?"

Something shifted in his gaze. "You don't want to hear about her."

"Ah, so there is someone." And why did the thought of it make Lily want to find this woman and feed her *on purpose* the same batch of fudge she'd accidentally fed to Kent Mercer?

"*Was* someone." He lifted her chin. "But she was never you, Lil."

Oh, Declan. "Still. I want to know. If you'll tell me?"

Sighing, he kissed her temple and pulled her back to himself, settling his chin on top of her head. "Kim and I dated for a few years in Chicago. We were serious. At least, I thought so. I was working hard at my current job and applying for grad school. It took me a few rounds of application to get into the program I really wanted. But Kim didn't stick around long enough to see me succeed."

"What do you mean? You're not saying she dumped you because you didn't get into grad school on the first try?"

"That's exactly what I'm saying."

Now it was Lily's turn to hold her tongue when she really wanted to call this Kim character some colorful names. "But why?"

"She was from a rich family and said she could never be with someone who couldn't provide her with a certain standard of living. Guess when we started dating, I had all these ambitions, and she thought I was her meal ticket to the fancy life. She never wanted me for, well, me."

Looking up, Lily brushed her fingertips across his jawline. "It's her loss, then."

"You think so?"

"I do."

His heated gaze consumed her, especially when it flitted from her eyes to her lips.

"Lil . . ."

"Yeah?"

"You told me what you want—but you didn't tell me how you feel about me. Because in case it isn't clear, I kind of really like you."

She couldn't help but giggle. "Okay. Well, then, I kind of really like you too."

Understatement of the century.

Something flashed in his eyes and he pulled her close, angling his mouth close to hers.

But before their lips met, she whispered, "I still don't know what we're doing here. Or where this is going."

"I don't either. But at some point, we just have to make a leap of faith and believe that it will all work out."

"Faith, I can do. I'm willing to weather the storm with you. But Declan, please don't kiss me if you can't choose me this time." The plea fell from her lips straight from her heart before she could stop it. "Don't start something that you're not willing to finish. Please."

"Aw, Lil." Once again, he cradled her face in his hands. "Do you trust me?"

"I want to." Oh, how badly she wanted to.

"Then trust in this."

And he kissed her.

Oh, he kissed her.

The kiss was gentle at first, a tender exploration filled with unspoken promises. Lily's fingers curled into the fabric of his shirt as she melted against him.

Declan's hand slid to the small of her back, drawing her even closer. His other hand stroked the nape of her neck, fingers tangling in her hair. The kiss deepened as they poured years of longing and uncertainty into this one perfect moment.

Lily's lips parted with a soft sigh against his mouth. The taste of him, the scent of his cologne, the warmth of his body against hers, it all overwhelmed her senses. He was hers, and she was his, and nothing else mattered in this moment.

Oh, she loved him. Loved every part of him. The tenderness, the steadfastness, the protectiveness. How could any woman have turned away from all that he was simply because he didn't make enough money?

Kim's loss had definitely been Lily's gain.

And Lily kissed him again and again to prove that she loved him for *him*—for all that he was. Just poured out her heart there in the moment, on that grassy knoll, with the stars shining overhead and the emphatic hoots of a barred owl.

Finally, Declan rested his forehead against Lily's, his eyes closed as if savoring the moment. "I choose you, Lily," he whispered, his voice husky with emotion. "I choose us. No more doubts. I don't know how things will go with the fudge shop or our families, but this, right here, with you, is where I want to be."

Lily's thumb traced his lower lip. "Promise?" she asked, her voice barely audible even to herself.

"I do." Declan captured her lips in another fiery kiss—a seal to his promise.

And as they stood there in the moonlit park, wrapped in each other's arms, Lily knew that this time, it was real. This time, they were choosing each other.

No matter who won this stupid competition.

Twelve

ONE WEEK LATER, AND TWO THINGS were clear.

Lily had a real shot at winning the fudge competition.

And she was terrified at the prospect.

Because winning meant the real work of running a fudge shop began. There would be no margin for error. No backup plan. No Declan there to talk her through it.

Unless he agreed to come work with her. But he'd said nothing about the future since their kiss, their words in the park. There they were, a whole decade later, their love still held under the secrecy of the moonlight.

But maybe she was overthinking it. He'd been working with her all week, glancing in her direction, occasionally trapping her in a kiss.

So, maybe that conversation would come *after* the festival, when they knew the final winner of the fudge shop competition. When they'd both agreed to finally tell their families about what they meant to each other.

Lily closed her eyes and blew out a breath. Right now, she needed to focus on getting everything prepped for the Main Street Festival. She and Declan would have separate booths from the time the festival began at ten until it ended at eight, and she'd been making fudge all week in preparation.

Lily hefted a stack of decorative boxes from the storeroom and carried them to the work counter in the kitchen where Mom was dutifully slicing and boxing the last of the decadent confections. She hadn't wanted to ask her mother for help, but Mom had insisted.

"These are the last of them." Lily set the boxes on the counter. "Are you sure that doesn't hurt your hands too much?" She glanced at the clock. "I can always finish up alone. Declan doesn't need the kitchen for another hour or so."

"Nonsense. I'm doing fine. Besides, I miss being here." Mom continued her methodical slicing and separating. She'd pinned her hair back with a clip, like she had so often when she'd worked the fudge shop.

The memory swirled in Lily's heart, stirring up all the nostalgia and history. "There's something about this kitchen, the way sugar and chocolate pervades the air. It's like every breath is a treat." Lily folded another box into shape and lined it with parchment paper.

"I never thought of it like that, but you're right. And it smells even better now with you here. So many new scents mingled with the old. Your creativity at work. It's beautiful to witness." Mom held up a slice of the specialty fudge in front of her. The pale cream base held dried rose petals and pistachios pressed into the top surface. "What did you call this fudge?"

"Saffron black cardamom." They'd already spent a few hours boxing up the bergamot, lavender, toffee-chunk, and many other pounds of Lily's unique offerings.

"It looks, smells—and yes, I'll admit it—tastes amazing."

"Mom!"

"What? You can't expect me to slice all of this fudge and not take a tiny sampling. Or two. Or five." Mom winked and got back to work. "Everyone else is going to love it too."

"I sure hope so." Lily had gone to a lot of extra expense. And, while it wasn't a traditional fudge, its unique flavor profile would either make her a winner—or solidify her as the loser.

"The flowers really make it look special." Mom placed the delicate fudge squares into one of the boxes Lily had prepared.

"I had those organic rose petals shipped from Pennsylvania." She handed her mom a slice. "Declan usually helps me source ingredients, but these are top secret. They're originally from Egypt."

"Wow." Mom examined the piece Lily had given her. "They're gorgeous. Simply gorgeous." Her mother blinked, still staring at the fudge for a moment longer before setting it into the box.

"You really *do* miss it, huh?" Lily reached out and placed a hand over Mom's.

Mom's eyes watered. "Quitting the shop was like losing a piece of my identity. But then, having you come back. Being able to be a fudge family again. Even though I can't do the work, I'm seeing our legacy—seeing you—carry on that tradition. I can't wait to see what you do with all of it."

The weight of the shop—everything it meant. All the past and the future rolled over Lily, the weight of it nearly toppling her. "Maybe I should have made more of the regular fudge recipes."

"What are you talking about? These are beautiful."

"Yes, they're beautiful—but do people *want* to eat flowers? What was I thinking?"

Mom stared at the box of fudge in front of her. "I thought you told me that customers had been flocking to your unique fudge ever since Sadie helped you tweak your marketing."

"Well, yes, but they love the traditional flavors too—Declan's still sold a lot. And that's what worries me."

"What's that?"

"What if the people who come to the festival tomorrow are largely into traditional fudge? Then it won't matter how well I've done before this. The festival could tip everything over the edge in Declan's favor."

Mom gave her a soft smile. "That's business, sweetheart. You just don't know what they'll love, what they'll go for. There's risk. But you're a risk taker, Lily Ann. You always have been."

"But maybe I shouldn't be." Look where her "risk taking"—or flightiness, or whatever it was called—had led her before this. Failing out of business school. Losing her job. "Maybe this was a mistake. I could have just stuck with peanut butter fudge, cookies and cream—the stuff that's guaranteed to sell."

"But then you wouldn't be true to who you are, and can I just say it? You are amazing." Mom rounded the counter and gave her a hug. "Win or lose, I'm proud to call you mine."

A tear streaked down Lily's cheek. "Aw, Mom. Thank you."

"I mean it. But I still think you'll win, and I'm not going to lie. Seeing the look on Martha Kelley's face when you do will *not* make me overly sad."

Lily pulled away, giving Mom a knowing look. "I thought you said the feud was silly."

"Did I?" Mom winked, moved back to her fudge slicer, and resumed her duties. "I'm just kidding. I do think it's silly—especially since my daughter has fallen for a Kelley."

Lily froze. "Wha—"

"There's no need to deny it," Mom said, slicing as if she hadn't just rocked Lily's world with that statement. "I knew from day one that it was a possibility."

Lily slumped onto a barstool near the counter, the un-assembled boxes to her left. "I didn't mean to. I assure you, I tried very hard not to."

Mom's laughter warmed the space. "How does someone try *not* to fall in love?"

"I reminded myself of all the ways it could never work.

I mean, we don't even know what will happen with the fudge shop."

"You can always hire him when you win." Mom lidded the full box. "Hand me another empty."

When you win. Mom really did think she could do it.

She passed Mom a box. "I thought of that, actually. Seeing if he'd work here with me. But I don't know if he would, not with a great job waiting for him in Chicago."

"Didn't you tell me he wasn't sure they'd hold it for him?"

"As of last week, his boss still wants him back. And I can't help but wonder if that's what's meant for him. Will a fudge shop really keep him happy when he's always been ambitious for more?"

Would *she* keep him happy?

"He's a grown man, Lily. He can make his own decisions."

"Maybe." She blew out a breath. "He says he wouldn't resent me if he doesn't win, but how could he not? The only reason he really did all this in the first place was to save his grandma's house. How would he not be upset if I won and took that from him?"

"So rent it back to her. Better yet, just give it to her." Mom looked up at her. "Even if you weren't head over heels for a Kelley, you're too kind-hearted to kick an old woman out of her home anyway."

The words smacked Lily in the chest. "Of course I always felt terrible at the idea, and kind of assumed I wouldn't win. But I can't afford to live anywhere else, and I don't want to stay with you and Dad forever—no offense."

"Sure, sure." Mom winked. Then she waved the slicer in the air. "Why not have Cody help you fix up the storage room overhead? There's plumbing up there already, and it would take some work, but surely you could find a way to convert it to a decent living space."

Lily blinked. It was the perfect solution—if she did actually win. "Mom, you're a genius!"

"I have my moments." Mom pretended to bow. "So are you going to tell Declan? Maybe it would relieve some of his tension."

Lily placed another sheet of parchment paper into her box and started a second row of fudge. "Maybe I will. Or maybe I'll surprise him with it if I win. Soften the blow of defeat." She grinned.

"That's a nice idea too."

Hmm. A nice idea indeed.

They worked in silence for another half hour. Finally, Mom added another lid. "I think that's all of them. Those are winners, right there." Mom held up her hand for a high five and Lily gave it a pat. Interlocked their fingers.

"Thanks again, Mom." Lily gave Mom's hands the gentlest of squeezes, aware of the tenderness.

Mom released her hand and gave her another hug. "What's next?"

"You can head home. I'm just going to get all these placed into those large boxes and stage them for easy transport in the morning."

"I can help you finish up. Dad's grilling tonight, so I don't need to be home just yet."

"If you're sure."

They stacked the boxes and then set them against the back wall of the kitchen, ready for the hand-cart in the morning.

"That's the last box." Lily straightened, stretching her back. "Dinnertime."

Mom looked around the shop. "Where are Declan's boxes?"

"Remember? He's coming in soon to finish making his batches and package everything up."

"Right. You sure you don't want to stay and help?"

Lily shook her head. "No, his parents insisted on helping him."

"Those pesky parents." Mom tsked, a smile on her face. "Always in the way."

"Stop." Looping an arm through Mom's, she tugged her toward the alley door. "I couldn't have done it without you today."

"You're much more capable than you give yourself credit for."

"Thanks, Mom. Guess we'll see tomorrow."

But as she glanced at the boxes stacked high, holding her creations—expressions of her very soul—for the first time in a while, Lily didn't feel like a failure. She felt like someone with the doors flung wide open, possibility and hope and success—and yes, even love—right at her fingertips.

Finally.

Ah, yes. Lily Hart was *finally* on her way.

Declan's nerves buzzed wildly when he stopped in at Martha's on Main. The entire last month had come down to this.

The Friday night crowd was dwindling at this late hour, but neighbors still waved to him, welcoming him as if he'd never left the island. Could this really be home again? And did he really want that?

He wanted Lily, and he wanted to win Grandma's house back for her—that was all he knew. And for now, that was enough.

Declan caught sight of his dad near the bar, chatting with an off-duty Police Chief York, and headed to look for Mom. He found her in the kitchen, black apron still thrown on and her graying hair pulled back. "Hey, Mom. Are you ready?"

Steam billowed around Mom as she stirred something on the cooktop. "I'm sorry, we got a rush right before closing and Jordi's home sick, so your dad hopped in to help serve." She nodded her head when Isaac swung through the doorway in his hoodie, chewing his gum, AirPods in. "Your brother offered to help you at the fudge shop while we take care of closing up here."

Declan folded his arms over his chest. "He offered, or was volun-told?" The last thing he needed tonight was Isaac in his business. Ragging on him again.

Isaac pulled out an earbud. "I offered, of course. I care about this family too."

Biting back a sarcastic remark, Declan shook his head. "It's not necessary. I can handle it myself." His parents had been insisting for two days that they help. Otherwise, he would have just worked with Lily to get all of their boxes ready together. Of course, she might cause a tiny bit of distraction, but Declan never minded her kind of distraction.

In fact, maybe he could call her now.

Except Isaac was already turning to him. "Let's get going."

"Seriously, you don't have to help."

"Too bad."

"Have fun, guys," Mom called as they headed for the door. "And Declan, be nice to your brother."

Wow. Okay. "Sure."

They headed into the night and crossed the street to the darkened fudge shop. When they entered the kitchen, it was still warm, and even though Lily wasn't here, Declan sensed she had been. There was the telling scent of vanilla, the sink overflowing with dishes and a Post-it Note saying she'd clean them later with a smiley face and a heart that made Declan grin. Besides all that, Lily had a few hundred boxes stacked, ready to go—a daunting reminder of all that Declan and Isaac still had to get through to reach the end of this horrible competition.

"Tell me what to do," Isaac said, washing his hands.

"There's something I don't hear every day." Declan stepped up to the sink and scrubbed.

"Haha, funny man." Isaac dried his hands and passed the towel off to Declan. "Seriously, though. I know I was a jerk last week, but I'm here to do everything I can to help out. To give you that edge."

It wasn't exactly an apology, but it was probably as close to peacemaking as they were going to get. And it would all go much more quickly with a partner. If it couldn't be Lily, then maybe Isaac would do. "All right. I need to make a few more batches of fudge and box up what I've already made."

Declan flicked on an old radio in the corner and, while classic rock filled the kitchen, together, they set to work. Pulling the ingredients, heating the copper pot, and creating fudge—the Kelley recipes, but made the Hart way, exactly as Lily had taught him. Isaac didn't need to know that, of course.

They'd made some good progress when Declan snatched a few water bottles from the fridge and tossed one to his brother. "Thanks for your help. This is actually coming along well."

"You sound surprised." Amusement clear on his face, Isaac popped open the water and took a swig.

"I mean, you're not always the most diligent worker." Declan tried to add teasing to his voice, but maybe there was too much truth to it for it to really be considered a joke.

Thankfully, Isaac laughed. "That's fair. I just gotta have the right motivation, I guess."

"And bussing tables at Mom's restaurant isn't enough motivation?"

"Nah, that place will sink or swim with or without me." Isaac downed the rest of his water, smashing the plastic down onto the countertop before tossing the compressed bottle into the trash. "But you . . . this place . . . you need me."

"Do I, though?"

Isaac gestured toward the fudge they'd piled up in the middle of the three tables—sixty pounds of new candy, nearly ready to be cut and boxed. "Think you could have done all this so quickly by yourself?"

"All right, sure. You've been helpful."

Isaac nodded and pulled another piece of gum from his pocket. "Look, I know we haven't always seen eye-to-eye, but I care about the family as much as you do." His fingers worked to unwrap the yellow gum. "I want to see the family succeed. And your success here, it matters. Not just for Grandma, but for the family legacy."

"I know. It's a lot of pressure, though." Declan's eyes flicked toward Isaac. What would his brother think of his confession? "So your help really does mean something."

"Not that Mom and Dad will ever see it. But that's okay. As long as Grandma gets her house." Shrugging, Isaac moved for the slicer, but Declan held up a hand to stop him.

"Now, wait. Seriously. I'll be sure to tell Mom and Dad how great you're doing here." Because maybe his brother really did want to change. Maybe he just needed someone to believe in him, the way Lily had believed in Declan. "You've got a lot of talent—way too much to waste. Maybe if we win, you can come work here."

Isaac raised an eyebrow. "You'd want me to head up the fudge shop when you go back to Chicago?"

Declan cleared his throat. "Well—"

"Ah, I see. You might not be going back to Chicago, now, huh?" Looking away, his much-too-perceptive brother started slicing fudge.

"I'm not sure what I'm planning to do." Declan grabbed a handful of boxes Lily had left unassembled on the counter and started popping them open. "But yeah, I don't know. Maybe, if I win this competition, you could split your time between Martha's on Main and the fudge shop. If you wanted to." It was a huge olive branch, and one Declan wasn't sure he should offer. But this was his brother. He was family. "You've got what it takes. And yeah, maybe you'll fall like I did, but maybe you'll learn from my mistakes too."

"Oh, I have." Isaac rolled his eyes, the twitch of a smile on his face. But it wasn't a sneer—it was almost like camaraderie. When was the last time his brother had actually felt like a friend? Probably not since grade school. The six-year gap between them had started to feel so wide then. But now? If Declan stayed, maybe this was yet another relationship he could work on mending. "And there have been a lot."

"I know, right? But I'm serious, man. Think about it."

"Aw, now you're just going soft on me. What happened to the big brother who was ready to pummel me at dinner last week?"

"He's still here in case you step out of line again, because you deserved that."

"Yeah, guess I did. I should know better than to insult your girl."

Maybe his brother said it to rile Declan, but the truth was, Lily *was* his girl—and tomorrow, he'd be declaring it to his family. What did telling Isaac one day early matter? "Yes, you should."

Instead of some smart remark, Isaac just kept slicing fudge, chomping away at his gum. They settled into a rhythm, working to box up the fudge while Bon Jovi sang about livin' on a prayer.

Finally, Isaac looked up at him. "You said *if* we win. Do you think we will?" He set the slicer down, leaned back against the counter, arms crossed. "Do you think Grandma is going to lose her house? And are we really going to lose this shop to the Harts? No disrespect to your girl, but that would be really embarrassing for the family legacy."

Declan ran a hand through his hair. "Honestly? I don't know. I think Lily might have an edge. But at this point, I've done all I can do."

"Hmm." Frowning, Isaac circled back to the fudge, slipping slices into boxes that Declan had prepared. "And you really think that Mom and Dad will be okay with you dating the woman who took Grandma's house from her? Who took our legacy away?"

"Look, I know it's hard to understand, but none of this is Lily's fault. It's not mine, either. We've just been victims of our circumstances, but we don't want to be anymore. We're going to forge a different path for our families. End this feud."

Isaac whistled. "Pretty tall order."

"Tell me about it."

"And what happens if Mom and Dad never accept Lily? What if her parents never accept you? You gonna go all Romeo and Juliet on us?"

Declan elbowed Isaac as he handed him another box. "Don't you wish."

"Solo heir to the Kelley throne does have a nice ring to it." Isaac waggled his eyebrows. "But seriously, man. Have you really thought about the consequences of this? I know, I'm the last one to talk, but I'm just looking out for you. For all of us."

"It's nothing I haven't already considered, believe me. But I'm just hoping that time will buffer the hostility."

"I hope so too, for all our sakes. Especially Grandma."

Maybe his brother didn't mean it, but his words were an ice pick, twisting in Declan's heart.

By the time they poured the final batch of fudge onto the marble table, Isaac had taken over paddling it into shape. He'd insisted on cutting it and boxing it.

Declan's phone buzzed, and Isaac looked up from the table. "Go ahead and take that. I can finish up."

Lily's name popped up on the screen. "It's okay. I can call her back."

"Just go, man." Isaac waved him off. "There isn't much more to do here, and I'll finish up—cut these, wash the dishes. Leave me the key and I'll lock up."

He glanced down at his phone again. Maybe there was time for a quick meetup with Lily, just to say a proper goodnight. "You sure?"

"Absolutely. Like you said—you've done all you can do, and you've got a big day tomorrow. Let me take care of the rest."

Huh. Well, if this wasn't the biggest seismic shift in the

world. "All right. Thanks, man." Declan tossed his keys to Isaac.

"No problem. And tell Lily I say hey."

Declan blinked at his brother for a moment, looking for signs of sarcasm, but they weren't there. Isaac just kept on working.

If Isaac could accept Lily, if he could make such a one-eighty, then maybe the rest of Declan's family could too.

Thirteen

I T WAS MAKE OR BREAK TIME. GO TIME. The beginning of the end.

Whatever cliché Lily wanted to use, today's festival earnings would determine the winner of the fudge shop.

But that was almost secondary to the buzzing giddiness inside her at the thought that she and Declan would finally publicize their feelings for each other. He'd been so sweet to stop by last night, but she was tired of sneaking out to meet him in the darkness.

Even though she appreciated a moonlit goodnight kiss.

Hopping off her bike, she shivered at the early-morning chill in the air. The festival didn't start for another few hours, but she'd woken before the sun and figured she might as well get over here to start setting up. At the very least, she could spend some time exploring the upstairs storage room. Ever since Mom's suggestion that she clear it out and make it a habitable living environment, Lily had been excited to get up there, to check it out and start dreaming.

Might have done it last night, but then Declan had stopped by and all thought of anything but taking a stroll with him flew from her brain. And then she'd woken today—a day all about second chances. New beginnings. Possibly a win under her belt too.

Humming to herself, Lily stuck the key in the back alley lock, opened the fudge shop, and watched her big win float right out the door along with five-hundred-million gallons of water.

And, even if that was an exaggeration, the destruction inside the fudge shop kitchen wasn't.

"No—no—no!" She ran inside, the cold water flicking up her bare legs and her sandals sliding on the wet tiles. The bottom few inches of everything—walls, workbenches, tables—had all been wicking water.

"What *happened*?" Declan's voice came from behind her.

"I don't know. I just got here."

Oh no. It looked like a leaky pipe in the ceiling—positioned almost directly over her boxes of fudge—was the culprit this time. She just stared at the place where pieces of the soggy ceiling plaster had collapsed all over her boxes of fudge.

"My fudge . . ." She held out her hand, braced it on a marble top.

"Hey. It's going to be okay. Let me turn the water off." Declan disappeared in the direction of the shop's main shutoff valve.

Lily couldn't move, the cold water chilling her feet, her heart.

Her fudge, destroyed.

She didn't want to look, but she had to know. Inhaling a sharp breath, she moved toward her neatly stacked boxes. Not only had the top boxes been crushed by the falling ceiling, but the ones that hadn't wicked water up from the floor had been sprayed from the side.

Declan was wrong. It wouldn't be okay.

He returned carrying a mop and bucket, his forehead furrowed. "We should have had Cody look at all the pipes when the last one busted. He said that most might need replacing due to the age of the building." He stopped and looked at her. "Oh no. All of your fudge." Leaning the mop against the counter, he strode over to her. "Is any of it salvageable?"

"Maybe a few boxes in the middle." She cleared some of the rubble off the top boxes and finally got to a box that wasn't crushed but was still soaking wet. Opened it. A mushy mess of chocolate and flowers greeted her. She couldn't breathe. "It's all ruined."

"Oh, no, Lil." Declan wrapped his arms around her from behind. "I'm so sorry."

Wait. She straightened. Looked around. "Where's your fudge?"

Declan dropped his arm from her waist, took a step back. Scratched behind his ear. "In the back storeroom."

"Oh." *Convenient.* She bit back the word and swiped a tear.

Frowning, he cupped her elbow. "Since we were using

the same boxes, I wanted to be sure we didn't get our offerings confused, so that's where I told Isaac to put it."

"Isaac?"

"Yeah, he came and helped me out last night. He even closed up so I could come see you." He sighed. "What can I do?"

"There's nothing *to* do." She pulled the large trash can over from the corner and opened the fudge boxes one by one. "Almost all of my fudge is ruined, and the festival begins in a few hours."

It was over. She'd lost.

Declan looked at the clock. "Make more. You still have time, and I'll help."

"There's no way." Lily lifted her hands. "Besides—look at this place. We can't make fudge in here."

"We can use the tables out front. Maybe the water won't have reached that far." Declan dried his hands on a nearby towel. "Come on, Lil. You're the one who's always able to pivot. To roll with things."

"I just don't know how this time."

"We can mop the floors, sanitize. There's no reason you can't make batches of fudge this morning—the shop won't be open to the public anyway." He reached for her hand.

She sighed, let him take it. He squeezed, and the look in his eyes stole her breath. This seemed bad—like end-of-her-little-world bad. But Declan was here, and he wasn't leaving or gloating. He was pitching in, trying to help her find a solution. Choosing to stay.

Lily flung herself into his arms, burying her face in his chest. "Thank you."

He kissed the top of her head before pulling back, then cupped her face with his hands. "You've worked too hard to give up now. In fact, your ability to never surrender is one thing I love about you."

She placed her hands on top of his. "Love?" And now was so not the time to be having this conversation—because hi, they still stood in several inches of water and her fudge was ruined and the kitchen was a wreck—but the one-word question just slipped out.

And she let it hang there.

Declan smiled, his thumbs stroking her cheekbones. "Yeah, Lily. Lo—"

"What's going on here?" a man's deep voice rumbled.

Squeaking, Lily twirled to find a red-faced Frank and Martha Kelley standing in the kitchen doorway. A key dangled from Martha's hand.

"What are you guys doing here?" Declan asked.

"We thought we'd check and see if you needed anything since we couldn't help last night and we won't be setting up my booth for a few hours. Isaac gave us the key." Martha's glare stayed trained on Lily for a few long moments before her gaze swerved, taking in the damaged kitchen. "Oh my. What happened in here?"

"A pipe burst in the ceiling." Declan stepped between Lily and his parents, almost as if sheltering her from his parents' wrath.

But no. They were in this together, right? Lily moved to stand beside Declan once again. She hooked their pinkies together.

Martha's eyebrows shot up at the action, but she didn't

say a word. Declan's dad either didn't notice or ignored it as he carefully stepped sideways so as not to slip on the wet floor. "Is that your fudge, Declan?"

"It's Lily's. Mine's in the storeroom."

Martha's shoulders visibly dropped with relief, and Lily looked away from the smug gleam in Frank's eyes.

"This place *does* need a total renovation," Martha added. "We'll definitely be speaking with Seb about that when he gets home this week."

Lily winced.

The jab landed a direct hit. Martha was so sure Declan would win.

And now, with so much fudge ruined, he probably would.

"Don't count Lily out just yet. She's going to make more fudge before the festival." Declan grabbed his inventory checklist off the magnetic fridge. "I've still got half a gallon of vanilla extract, plenty of butter, and there's more than two hundred pounds of sugar in the dry storage. I know it isn't that fancy recipe you made, but—"

"Wait a minute, son." Frank hitched up his pants as he strode forward, tapping the clipboard with his index finger. "You just said those are Kelley fudge supplies." He shook his head. "You're not going to hand those items, paid for with our money, over to her."

"She has to make more fudge, and I'm sure she'll pay us back." Declan looked over at Lily.

She nodded, smiling. Because he was really doing this. Standing with her, no matter what. Her heart soared—

Then she caught the looks on his parents' faces.

Utter disdain. Contempt. Withering glares.

Oh. Her throat thickened. "I—"

But Frank wasn't done. "Declan, I feel like all that money spent on your MBA was a complete waste if that's the kind of business sense they taught you. This is a *competition*."

"Oh, come on, Dad, you can't be serious."

"I'm completely serious. You *do* understand your grandma's place is on the line here, right? Do you want to watch her heart be broken because you were too weak to do what needed to be done? Because you sold out your family?"

Now, wait just a minute. "Declan's just being a decent human being. And as for his grandma's house—"

"Frank." Martha looked from Lily to Declan. "I think this is something we should talk about in private."

Private.

Because this was a family matter.

And Lily would never be family—at least as far as Martha was concerned. To her, she was only a Hart. The enemy.

Declan's jaw tightened, his gaze flicking between Lily and his parents. "Fine. Let's talk."

Everything in Lily screamed for Declan not to go. Not to listen to his parents—but he followed Frank and Martha right through the swinging kitchen door. Lily couldn't hear Frank's words, but she *could* hear his hammering tone. And, when Lily peeked out into the lobby, she could see Declan's face fall. Saw the way he scrubbed a hand through his hair.

His pinched reply. "Yes, sir."

Lily's eyes filled with tears as she fumbled her way back

toward her ruined fudge and began tossing more boxes into the trash can.

Finally, Declan pushed through the kitchen door, holding it and calling over his shoulder, "I'll be out in a minute" before turning to Lily.

"So? Can any of it be saved?" he asked.

Lily shrugged, still feeling the sting of his desertion. But he was here now. He was going to help her. That was what counted. "Maybe like forty pounds?"

"All right. Look, I've got to go set up the booth—"

"Wait, what? You're leaving me with this mess?"

"Hey—" He reached out and took her hand. "We will clean this up together, but for right now, I've got another plan for your booth. Trust me."

Right.

But he left her there as he disappeared into the kitchen. He returned moments later holding an ice cream container. "You have plenty of ice cream left over from the Stevenson wedding a few weeks ago, plus what you've made in between batches of fudge to, as you say, *fuel your creativity*. Sell that today, with whatever fudge you can salvage."

"Ice cream?" Lily took her own mental inventory. She had been making a lot of fudge—and yes, ice cream too, as a way to ease the stress over the last few weeks of the competition. "I don't know."

"You can do this. You've got all those creations sitting in there." Declan waved toward the walk-in freezer. "Besides, even if I were able to help you make the fudge, I don't have all your specialty ingredients and—"

"And your dad would never speak to you again if you loaned me supplies."

"Probably." He glanced toward the door, where his parents were likely still waiting. "But I'm working on him, Lily. I am."

"He doesn't seem like he'll ever come around. Your mom, either." Her chin trembled, but no, this wasn't the time for tears. It was the time for bravery and fortitude. The time to focus.

Declan's gaze softened and he pushed a strand of her hair behind her ear. "I'm still in this if you are."

Lily's mouth opened to respond, but the kitchen door swung open with a bang. "Are you coming?" Frank stood there, glaring at them once again.

Sighing, Declan dropped his hand from her face, took a step away, and looked at her. "You've got this, Lil." Then he joined his parents.

"I sure hope so," Lily whispered to herself.

Two hours later, Lily stood under her tent along Main Street, her vendor display nearly complete. Dad had rounded up every fan on the island to dry out the fudge shop, though they'd tripped the breaker and had to dial back her production.

The last thing she needed was to burn down Jonathon Island.

Mia dropped a box of supplies onto the extra table at the back of the booth. "I bought every cone I could find and cleared out the disposable bowl and spoon section in the market," she said. "Cody will be here in a minute with the rest."

"You're a rock star."

Mia gave her a hug. "I'm happy to help. And look at you—your display is so bright and cheerful." She pointed to Lily's yellow sign—the one Declan had helped her order. It was indeed cheerful, and the purple lettering stated "Hart Family Fudge" in gorgeous cursive.

"Thanks. I considered adding 'and Ice Cream' to the end of the font in permanent marker, but didn't think my chicken scratch would look very appealing."

"Even then, it would still catch more eyes than the Kelley's Classic Fudge sign." Chuckling, Mia thumbed over her shoulder across the street, where Declan's booth sat between Martha's and Patrick's—a unifying of the Kelley family.

She couldn't help but notice the dividing line of Main Street between them.

Or the handsome man behind the booth—the one she'd completely lost her heart to, despite the very unimaginative black-and-white sign with touches of red. Classic indeed, just like her Declan, though his aviators disguised him as a rebel.

But maybe, if he really *was* willing to defy his family's expectations and be with Lily, he was more of a rebel than she'd thought.

I'm still in this if you are.

She dearly hoped so.

Lily shoved all negative thoughts away and laughed with Mia. "Guess we'll see tonight."

"I believe in you, Lil. Dani does too. She's racing around

here somewhere, but wanted me to tell you how proud she is of you. You've got this."

Right. "Thank you." At least she had plenty of pistachio, coffee toffee, and even maple-bacon ice cream, along with her forty-five pounds of fudge.

All was not lost.

Sunshine warmed her face and filled her with the kind of nostalgic hope of a Norman Rockwell painting.

Colorful flags fluttered from the lampposts along the cobblestone street—which was closed off to all but foot traffic on either side of the long stretch—and the bustling atmosphere developed a buzz as all the vendors completed their displays and early arrivals began venturing through.

Cody dropped a stack of cardboard boxes behind the stand and surveyed her display.

"Oh, wow. You really *don't* have a lot of fudge."

She dumped another bag of ice into the bath her ice cream buckets sat in. "It's okay. We're due for a hot day, and everyone will be screamin' for ice cream, right?"

Please, God, let it be true.

Either way, Lily had done her best. And maybe, just maybe, success was still at her fingertips.

If anyone looked up *cad* in the dictionary, Declan was certain his picture would be found.

Even though he'd left Lily with a plan, he still felt like he'd also left her hanging. Again.

But he'd also seen how close Dad had been to exploding. Hadn't wanted to expose Lily to that. And his parents' surprise appearance hadn't given him time to figure out how best to express to them his true feelings for Lily. He wanted them to accept the relationship, but with the competition still going on, now wasn't the time.

Still, walking away from Lily for the second time was one of the hardest things he'd ever had to do.

And he hoped with everything in him that she understood.

Declan hefted another box onto his decorated table and placed the wrapped fudge onto his display. The Beach Boys sang "Don't Worry, Baby" over a stereo system, the perfect song for the summer day vibe—and an ironic one too, given Declan's currently spiraling thoughts. Lily's booth was straight across from his, so bright that the sunlight caught the glittery surface of her banner and dutifully blinded everyone walking by.

Thankfully, his suggestion about the ice cream had paid off, because for hours now, she'd been bombarded with tourists, filling order after order and laughing.

It distracted him more than he should admit.

Isaac—who had shown up to help run the Martha's on Main booth—had even had to call Declan out a few times, reminding him to tend to his own customers instead of staring across the way.

Of course, that had earned more than a few frowns from Mom, though she had yet to actually say anything about finding him and Lily so close this morning in the fudge shop kitchen. Surely, it was coming, but she too was focused on the Main Street Festival today, running back and forth between her kitchen and the booth to serve up mini meatloaves, turkey sandwiches, sweet potato fries, chili, and a variety of other items off a limited menu.

Declan had already seen so many townspeople and tourists come through, their arms loaded down with purchases from the antiques shop booth, from Mia's small booth featuring her own paintings, from the maritime-themed booth run by Grace Marconi. Aunt Whitney had even helped Grandma walk through earlier, when it was much cooler out and not so crowded. She'd taken a sample of fudge, closed her eyes, smiled, and said, with tears in her eyes, *Just the way my Barry and I used to make it.*

Then she'd patted Declan's cheek, told him how proud she was, and shuffled to Mom's booth.

Hopefully, he wouldn't let her down. He'd sold a lot of fudge, but Lily'd had a steady line throughout the day. The crowd had filtered through, winding among the vendor booths, making their way back after hitting the carnival-type games set up in Blueberry Hill Park, eating lunch beneath the trees in the park or at the picnic tables spaced throughout Main Street.

Despite the competition, it was thrilling to see people back on the island. It wasn't as extravagant as past events, and there weren't fireworks or a concert or any other things that had made past festivals great. But it was a start—a literal small spark. As construction continued on the Grand Hotel, with targeted recruiting, Jonathon Island really might return to that former glory.

A part of him didn't want to miss that.

"How's it going?" Interrupting his thoughts, Brandon

walked up to the table and perused the offerings. He carried a generous green scoop in a waffle cone.

"It's going great, no thanks to you, traitor."

Brandon licked a drip off his cone. "Oh, yeah—sorry. But, she's got pistachio, and it's really good."

"Whatever, dude." Declan waved him off. It's not like he was actually upset, but it was fun to tease his cousin. He'd miss him when Brandon left town—

Wait—what? Apparently, his heart had already made up its mind.

"I'll buy from you too. It'll cancel my purchases out." Brandon bit into the ice cream. "Seriously, though. This stuff is amazing."

"I know." And Declan was okay with that—because, deep down, he really did want Lily to win, despite the fact that he had no idea what kind of aftershocks it might cause Dad if they lost the fudge shop. If Grandma lost her house.

But they'd figure it out, together.

Because he'd finally found someone to share his life with. Someone who saw him as more than a problem solver, more than a title, more than a suit.

Lily saw Declan for who he was—flaws and all—and she accepted him. More than that, she wanted him.

Declan looked over and caught a little smile from Lily. It was the reassurance he'd been needing all day. He grinned back at her.

"Dude, you've got it bad." Brandon leaned in closer. "So I've gotta ask—did you take my advice?"

"What advice is that?"

Brandon gave him a look.

Declan busied himself with plating a few fudge samples. "I don't kiss and tell."

"My man!" Lifting a hand for a high five, Brandon laughed. "So you did kiss her."

He pushed Brandon's hand down. "Shh." Declan glanced at Mom's booth, but thankfully she was busy with a customer. "I haven't told my family yet. That's a conversation for after the contest, when we know who won."

"Why does that matter?" Brandon took another bite of his ice cream.

"I just don't want it between us anymore. Maybe my family will be able to deal with the news of our relationship better if we win."

"And if you don't win? Won't that just make them even less inclined to accept the two of you?"

Declan blew out a breath. "Maybe."

"Seems to me that maybe there is no perfect time."

"Oh, just go eat your ice cream and leave me in peace."

Laughing, Brandon saluted and walked off without buying any fudge.

Before Declan could call after him, several customers approached his booth and there was a constant stream of traffic the rest of the afternoon. A few hours before sunset, Uncle Patrick came by, leaving Olive and her fourteen-year-old brother, Scott, manning the booth for the Bar & Grill.

"You'll be closing your tills at eight," he said. Tills—Declan's and Lily's. And then it would all be over. "Jim Michaelson from the bank has volunteered to tally everything up so there's no room for error. He'll hand those numbers over to Dani, who's already got your accounting totals from the prior sales to date."

"Sounds good."

The next hour saw a handful of new customers, but for the most part, things were winding down. Even so, there was a certain satisfaction in it all, despite the soreness in Declan's feet and the ache in his neck from bending over the table, taking people's money. It was so different from being stuck behind a desk, in boardrooms, in meeting after pointless meeting.

There was legacy and good work and family here. And, for at least a little while, he'd been a part of it. He'd been accepted back into the fold. Forgiven.

And he could rest in the fact that he'd done everything he could to make the Kelley fudge shop a success. To save Grandma's house.

Hopefully his family would see that, if Lily won.

A bullhorn crackled. "Hello, everyone!" Dani Sullivan stood at the far end of the row of vendor booths. "Thank you so much for coming out today, but it's time to say our goodbyes. Please make your final purchases, and then join us down at the park for the exciting announcement of our Fudge Wars winner!"

A murmur went up from the crowd. A few stragglers rushed Lily's booth, cleaning out the few pounds of fudge remaining on her table and a few ice cream cones too.

Declan started packing away fudge samples and taking down the sign he'd designed weeks ago for this day. Gray-haired Mr. Michaelson stopped by, opened his register, and pressed his thin lips together as he counted Declan's money. Then he asked to see Declan's credit card sales. While he did that, Declan finished clearing off his booth and slipped over to help Lily with hers.

Cody and Mr. and Mrs. Hart were already there. As Declan approached, Lily chatted with her family, her hands flying as she spoke. "And then this man came up and gave me his card and said he'd love to talk with me about franchise opportunities—for the ice cream, of all things—and I said—" She stopped talking as she caught sight of Declan, blinking. "Oh. Hi."

He stuck his hands in his pockets. "Hey."

Her family stared at him—Cody, who was breaking down her awning, seemed to be enjoying the awkwardness, if the grin on his face was any indication.

Declan risked a glance back at his own parents. Yep. They too were looking this way, at Lily and Declan.

He should just haul her into his arms and kiss her—show everyone what she meant to him.

He took a step forward, but then Mr. Hart put a hand out, stopping him. "Looks like your mother could use some help over there." His voice was steely. Protective.

And Declan couldn't blame the guy. He'd broken Lily's heart so many years ago. But this time was different.

"Dad—"

"Declan!"

And man, if Mom didn't have the most rotten timing.

He glanced her way, and she waved him over. "I need your help with this!" she called, pointing to her own awning. "It'll hurt your father's back."

Never mind Isaac, sitting right there, legs propped up on a cooler while he scrolled on his phone.

Clearly, this was a ploy to keep him away from the Harts.

The Harts—at least one of which didn't seem to want him here either.

Declan had known it would be tough, getting their families on board, but perhaps he needed to think through the best way to explain things to them all. Logically. Sometime other than this emotionally charged one, when the fate of the fudge shop hung between them.

Huffing out a breath, he flashed what he hoped was an apologetic smile at Lily. "I need to go. But I'll see you at the announcement?"

She tugged on a lavender curl, nodded—some sort of uncertainty in her eyes. "See you there."

He headed for his mom's booth. Started helping to break it down, to put things back the way they'd been. Then the lampposts flickered on, and Dani gave a five-minute warning for the announcement, so Declan and his whole family left the partially disassembled booths and headed down to the park.

A small crowd had gathered there near the playground and kids' bounce houses—mostly friends and neighbors who cared about the fate of the fudge shop.

Setting her bullhorn on a picnic table, Dani stood on the bench. "Would Declan Kelley and Lily Hart please join me up front and center?"

Yeah, this was it.

Declan shuffled up front and stood on the ground

to Dani's left. Lily emerged from the crowd and stood on Dani's right, her face a jumble of emotions. Her eyes flicked first to Declan, then to the ground. Then she rubbed at a spot of chocolate on her leather leggings.

Declan held back a smile.

Yeah. Whatever happened, he wanted this woman in his life.

"Thanks again for coming out today," Dani said. "This was an excellent way to kick off the first of many Jonathon Island events, and to show our community that we're still here!"

Cheers lifted from the crowd. Liam, who stood nearby, whistled loudly.

Declan blew out a breath.

"Okay, I know that this past month has been an exciting time for our chocolatiers. Is that what I call you? Fudge-tiers?" Dani asked. She looked from Lily to Declan before continuing. "Whatever you're called, we've all enjoyed the fruits of your labors. I can't imagine a tastier competition. But now, we face the final verdict. Which one of these two has won the right to own and operate the Jonathon Island fudge shop? The final tallies and winner have been provided to us by our local banker, Mr. Jim Michaelson." She pulled an envelope from her back pocket and waved it in the air. "I'm so nervous for you both. Okay. I know, you're nervous too, right?"

Lily looked unnaturally pale. Declan wanted to reach across, comfort her.

But there in the front row stood his parents. Grandma, her hand clutching the edge of her sweater.

Declan's stomach twisted.

"Drumroll, please," Dani continued.

The crowd whistled and hollered and began patting hands against legs to create an appropriate sound effect. Dani struggled to get the envelope open.

Declan looked over at Lily, who tried to give him a smile, but it fell flat.

Dani slid the card from the envelope. "Here we have it. The winner of the Fudge Wars competition and recipient of the fudge shop on Main and the house on Poppy Place . . . Oh, my goodness—Lily Hart! Congratulations!"

Lily's hands flew to her mouth.

Whistles. Applause. Declan clapped. Lily's gaze met his, so many questions in them. He hoped in his own she found the answers.

He was proud of her. He loved her. She'd worked hard, and she deserved every bit of praise to go with it.

Cody, Nancy, and Randy, along with several other friends, swarmed her, and she disappeared behind a swath of hugs.

Dad stepped into view in front of Declan, a steely glare carved deep into the lines of his face.

Seeing the joy on Lily's face, seeing her rightly secure her family's fudge shop . . . he just wished it hadn't come at the price of letting down his family. Losing Grandma's house.

"This can't be," Dad said, stepping closer. His jaw flexed and his fists balled until he lifted one, with his finger pointed. "She must have cheated somehow. Did you give her an edge? Don't think I didn't notice the way you held her hand this morning. How'd she trick you again?"

Declan's mouth fell open. "Seriously, Dad? Lily earned this all on her own. Our relationship has nothing to do with it."

"Oh, it's a *relationship* now, is it?"

"You two are making a scene," Mom hissed from behind Dad. There was a deep crease in her brow. "But really, Declan, how could you have fallen for a Hart *again*? We warned you about this. And we all know what happened last time. I didn't think you'd be so foolish."

"This has nothing to do with that." His eyes flicked toward Grandma's retreating back. Apparently this was all too much for her, because Brandon was leading her away, his arm wrapped around her, supporting her.

Aw, Grandma.

Declan's hand gripped the back of his neck.

"I can't believe, with all your fancy degrees, that you lost," Dad ground out. "Clearly, you weren't on your game."

Isaac took the spot next to Dad, red splotches across his face visible in the light cast from the park's lamplight. "How did she win? She wasn't even selling fudge."

"She couldn't—it was destroyed."

"Wait—those receipts weren't for fudge?" Dad said.

"The rules were specific," Mom said. "It was whoever sells the most *fudge*."

"You're right. They were." Dad lifted his head, swiveling to look around. "Where's Patrick?"

"Don't do that." Declan tried to step in front of Dad, but Dad shouldered his way around him.

Then he stopped, turned, and poked Declan in the chest. "Don't do what? Save the family legacy? Do what you weren't able to do?"

Ouch. While the words were technically true, hearing them like this . . .

Words stuck in Declan's throat.

"I do think someone needs to mention the rules," Mom said. "It's unfortunate what happened with her fudge—I get that. But rules are rules. I think the numbers need to be examined in light of that."

It didn't take a single one of Declan's business skills to calculate out the winner. Without today's ice cream sales, he'd have Lily beat.

And he was right back at the beginning, wasn't he? Family versus Lily.

Rules versus rebel.

"What's it going to be, son?"

Fourteen

HOPEFULLY DECLAN WOULD GET LILY'S text to meet up here at the fudge shop, because they needed to talk—and she didn't want to wait until tomorrow to assure him that his grandma's house would remain hers.

She'd tried snagging him at the park, but he and his family had been embroiled in what looked like a serious conversation—Frank especially looked none too happy—so Lily and her family had returned to breaking down her booth and then back to the fudge shop to make sure there wasn't anything else that needed doing.

Correction: *her* fudge shop.

She'd really done it.

She'd *won*.

A thrill traveled up her spine as she tucked an ice cream container into the kitchen freezer. Thankfully, other than the hole in the ceiling and some damaged cabinets under the countertops, the kitchen looked repairable. Dad and Cody had gotten the fans here quickly enough and the heat of the day had helped to dry out the water on the floor.

The door swung open, and her brother and parents came in, each carrying more pieces from the booth. They'd been in the middle of breaking it all down when Dani had called them to the park.

"You can just prop the canopy up in the storeroom." Lily closed the freezer.

Cody nodded. "We'll put it with the table." He and Dad went through the side kitchen door toward the hallway.

Mom set a stack of empty ice cream vats on the counter next to the sink. "Do you want me to wash these now?"

Lily looked at the clock. "It's getting late, and it's been a long day. I can do them tomorrow."

"You don't want this mess to sit until morning."

"It'll be okay. I still can't believe it's finally over."

"You deserve this—you're the exact right person to carry on the Hart tradition," Mom said.

"Lily? Tradition?" Cody laughed as he and Dad came back in.

"You know what your mother means," Dad grunted. But for once, even he was smiling.

Mom laughed. "Yes, not the literal tradition—though, of course, you can always crack out those recipes too." Winking, Mom lifted the lever on the faucet.

Nothing happened.

"The plumbing—I forgot, Declan turned the water off because of the leak."

Cody examined the hole in the ceiling from below. "We'll need to get in and fix up the pipes, make sure there's no residual moisture that will mold. Dad, you want to help with that next week?"

"Sure. I can round up a few of the guys to help. Mac is dying for something to do with his free time. Retirement has him bored stiff."

"I'd love to have the work done quickly so I can open up ASAP and enjoy the rest of the season," Lily said.

Though the thought of opening the shop without Declan at the other end of the counter caused a pinch in her throat.

"You could use the front tables to make fudge. It'll be a little noisy while the guys work, but I don't think you need to miss out on sales in the meantime." Mom leaned against the sink. "Though maybe you should plan a bit of a remodel. Then a grand reopening."

"I don't want to make a big fuss about it."

"It *is* a big fuss—you're carrying on the family business. You get to marry the old with the new. Make it exactly what you want it to be."

Cody lifted a shoulder. "Besides, if you have to do repairs anyway, you may as well put in a few design elements to bring the shop into the new century."

Mom held up her hands. "Wait a minute—we're not talking industrial modern, are we?"

"You said whatever Lily wants it to be." Cody grinned.

"And Lily does not want that." Lily cut Cody a look. "Whatever I do needs to be in alignment with all the charm of Jonathon Island." She crossed the room and poked her brother in the arm. "Ignore your son, Mom. He only knows fishing-chic."

Cody pushed her away. "Hilarious."

"Okay, good." Mom placed a hand over her heart. "Just making sure."

She and her family laughed—even Dad—and there was only one thing that would make this moment better.

Declan.

Hopefully, he'd arrive soon. If he hadn't gotten her text, she might need to go in search of him. His face had seemed to say he was okay with not winning—at least, she'd hoped that was it. But then, she'd also seen Frank step in and she couldn't imagine that was going to be a pleasant conversation.

She just hoped it wasn't so bad Declan would be driven off the island. Back to Chicago. But he'd assured her that after the contest was over, they could make decisions about their future—together.

It would finally be them against the world.

Lily hoisted the last bucket of ice cream and stowed it in the freezer. "I'm just going to do a few more things here, and then I'll head home."

Mom grabbed her sweater and purse, and Dad ushered her out the door.

Cody turned to her. "You're meeting Declan, right?"

"And if I am?" She lifted her chin.

"Hey, I know I tease you—which is my right as your pesky little brother—but I just want you to be happy, Sis." He wrapped his arm around her shoulder and squeezed.

"If he makes you happy and he treats you well, then it's all right with me."

"He does, on both counts. Let's just hope his family is as okay with it as you are."

"If they aren't, that's their own fault." He ruffled her hair before stepping away. "And if he hurts you, you know where to find me." He winked.

Lily laughed. "Yeah. Mia's house."

He grinned. "Speaking of, Mia should have the kids down, and we're going to watch a movie. Would you mind if I took some leftover ice cream?"

"Knock yourself out."

"Thanks, sis." Grabbing a container of chocolate mint ice cream, Cody slipped out the door, and Lily headed for the storeroom to put away a handful of items she'd used today.

A few minutes later, she heard voices in the lobby. She froze. Had Declan brought his family here, now? Before they'd had a chance to speak privately? Surely not.

She slipped into the hallway and down toward the lobby, where she found Dani, Tara, and Patrick Kelley.

Tara wore a stricken expression, and Dani took a breath, swallowed. Patrick just stood there, arms crossed over his broad chest, a sort of glimmer in his eyes.

Lily stilled, a sick roil curling in her stomach. "Um, what's going on?"

"I don't know how to say this," Dani said.

Nothing good ever started out that way. No one ever said *I don't know how to say this, but you've won the lottery. I don't know how to say this, but you're the lost heir to a throne.*

I don't know how to say this, but you've been promoted to master chocolatier.

"Lily, I'm so very sorry," Dani said.

"What is it? What's wrong?" Lily asked.

Patrick cleared his throat, but Dani held up her hand to him. "No. Let me." She wrung her hands together. "It was brought to the council's attention that the original rules agreed to for the fudge shop competition stated that the winner would be the person who sold the most *fudge*."

"Fudge," Patrick said. "Not ice cream."

Oh, thanks for that. Like she hadn't understood the words herself.

Lily didn't need to open her books back up to know that Declan would have her beat. He'd had a good stream of buyers for the entire festival, and without her ice cream sales . . .

"I didn't win?" The full weight of the truth caused Lily to sag back against the display case.

She'd lost her family's shop.

Gone.

The door opened and Declan and his parents walked in. His jaw was drawn tight, and his lips were pressed into a thin line.

Lily moved her attention back to Dani. "That's ridiculous. This is my family's fudge shop. There never should have been a competition in the first place."

"But there was," Tara said, sympathy in her expression and voice. "Everyone agreed to it."

Lily's eyes met Declan's, and her feet stupidly took her closer. So close, she could smell his aftershave and see the flecks in his blue eyes. And that made it hurt so much more. "Aren't you going to tell them how unfair this is?" The question came out a whisper, a raw scrape.

"I..." His lips flat-lined, and he glanced over his shoulder at Patrick, who watched them both with a shrewdness that made Lily want to disappear. "The rules..." He closed his mouth, swallowed, his Adam's apple bobbing up then down.

She got the eeriest case of déjà vu—sure, maybe she wasn't standing on his parents' front porch in the rain surrounded by wet trees, but it was still him once again standing by while his parents dismantled her world.

Unbelievable.

"I can't do this right now." Lily turned on her heel, rounded the counter, and smacked the kitchen door open with her palm. Hopefully it would swing back and hit Declan in the nose, because oh yes, he was following her.

"Come on, Lily. Let's talk about this."

"Why bother?" She reached for her bag on the counter. She needed space, room to breathe, to think.

"Because we're in a relationship."

Lily headed for the alley door. "Are we?"

"So you're just going to run away again?"

Halting, she spun and strode across the kitchen, her finger lifted in the air. "Don't you dare say that to me. You're the one who wouldn't speak up for me out there."

"I'm in a weird spot." He pushed both hands through his hair. "And the rules were clear."

"Yeah, and very convenient for you—the guy who told me to sell ice cream today in the first place. What I think is, you're weak. Underneath all that polished exterior is a man who can't think for himself."

"Hey—!"

"No, you hey. You've let them push you around all your life, afraid to go against the family." She finger-quoted her words. "And I get it. I do. But I'm not going to play the game anymore. I'm done being your dirty little secret. Your mistake."

He reached for her elbow. She twisted away, not caring now that tears burned her eyes.

A sodden piece of ceiling plopped at her feet from above. She glanced up, where the leaky pipe was now partially exposed. "You know it's awfully suspicious that your fudge was miraculously saved and mine was ruined—and your brother was the last one in here last night."

His eyes widened. "What's that supposed to mean?"

"I think it's pretty obvious."

"I know Isaac has his problems, but he wouldn't sabotage you like that. That's crazy."

She held up her hands. "Of course I'm the crazy one."

"I didn't say *you* were crazy—just the idea. Isaac may be a jerk sometimes, but he's family."

And there it was again. "Yep. Family." She stepped away from him. "I gotta go figure out what to do with my life now that my shop has been stolen from me for the second time." Lily turned again toward the door.

"Lil, stop. You don't have to go. Stay here. I'll hire you—I don't care what my family says. You can run the shop."

And he could have punched her with less pain to her chest. "What? Are you kidding me?"

"Then marry me. You'd be a Kelley and then—"

"That's your solution? To propose? You think that will solve all of our problems?"

Before she could move away, Declan was in front of her again. "It would unite us. Our families wouldn't have a choice but to accept us then. It just makes sense. And you're not a mistake. I love you, Lily."

The words she'd longed to hear from him her whole life. But not like this. "Really? It doesn't feel like it. It feels like you're compromising to save face in front of your family. Trying to make everyone happy. Taking the easy way out."

"That's not what's happening here. I'd already intended to tell you I loved you. I was fully ready to support you running the shop, regardless of what it meant for my family—or Grandma."

She lifted her chin. "First of all, I wasn't going to kick your grandma out. I fully intended to let her keep the house. Was going to have Cody help me remodel the upstairs into a livable space. It was going to be a surprise."

His eyes widened.

"Yeah. See, one of us had a plan. Surprise, surprise. But it doesn't matter now. Now that your family is deemed the winner—under questionable circumstances, I might add—your answer is to sweep those circumstances under the rug. I'm sorry, but how can you really think that I'd marry you like this?" A sob worked its way up Lily's throat. "I don't always want to play second fiddle. That's been me my whole life. I'm sick of it. And I want someone to choose me for once."

"Lily, come on . . ."

"No, Declan. The ironic thing is that I thought *you* were that someone. That you were a man of integrity, a man I could respect to do the right thing, no matter what. But it turns out the man I fell for was just another fantasy. The real thing was just a disappointment in disguise." She tipped her nose to him. "I thought you were more, but turns out that all you are is a Kelley, through and through." And now tears dripped off her chin. "And Harts do not marry Kelleys."

Then she pushed out of the door and into the night.

He may have won the fudge shop for his family, but he'd lost Lily.

For good this time.

And Harts do not marry Kelleys.

Declan winced at the memory of Lily's words, still banging around in his head. He'd spent the last hour mopping the fudge shop kitchen floor—which was probably pointless, since he'd need to find someone to fix up the pipes and there would only end up being drywall dust and other debris here soon.

Or maybe he didn't need to do anything at all. He was due back in Chicago. He still had his job. And sure, when things had changed between him and Lily, he'd been planning to give his notice, but that was before she'd ripped his heart open with her accusations.

What I think is, you're weak. Underneath all that polished exterior is a man who can't think for himself.

Hello, he could think for himself. He wasn't weak.

Except, a review of the past few hours—and really, the last few weeks—said differently.

Maybe, if he had stood up to his parents so many years ago . . .

Well, life would have been different. And maybe he'd needed the past ten years to become the man who returned to Jonathon Island.

To become the man who could stay. And this time with the woman he loved.

Except, maybe she didn't want him. Not with the baggage of his family. She actually thought Isaac caused the disaster. That was a reach—and he might be upset with his parents for ruining Lily's victory in the first place, but he couldn't really blame them. They'd wanted the fudge shop and Grandma's house secure. Besides, the pipes were old. It was unfortunate, sure, but Isaac wouldn't—

Let me take care of the rest.

Wait. Those had been Isaac's exact words to him last night when his brother had volunteered to finish up here.

Declan dropped the mop, and it clattered to the floor. What did that mean? Was Lily right? Surely not.

But this time, he wasn't going to blindly believe. He had to know.

Declan headed out the back alley door and stalked up Jonathon Boulevard. The last of the tourists would have caught the ferry by now, and the night was inky black with a bright canopy of stars and a crescent moon—enough to light his way to his parents' home.

When he got there, he twisted the handle with so much force he was afraid it'd break off in his hand.

The TV blared from the living room, and Declan walked with purpose through the foyer and kitchen to find Isaac sitting on the couch, a beer bottle in his hand and an old ball game on the screen.

Declan grabbed the remote off the coffee table and hit the Power button, then turned to his brother, whose eyes were slightly red.

"Hey!" his brother protested. "I was watching that."

"Did you do it?" Declan ground out through clenched teeth.

"Do what?"

"Did you damage that pipe somehow?"

"What are you talking about?" Isaac rubbed his hand across his mouth.

"The pipe at the fudge shop—the one directly over Lily's fudge. The one that suddenly burst open and destroyed her fudge. Which basically guaranteed I'd win the competition."

"You said so yourself. The pipes in that building were old. That's why you had trouble last week." His brother took a swig, but there was something shifty in his gaze as he looked away from Declan.

A nauseating roll swept through Declan's gut. He stared at his brother for a moment, tried to collect himself. Still, his words came out tight and his fists balled. "And you took full advantage of that, didn't you?"

Isaac said nothing.

"I trusted you, man. Let you work beside me." Declan paced the room. "How could you do this?"

"Do what? Save Grandma's house? You're welcome."

Declan stilled. "You think I wanted this? Do you know what you cost me tonight?"

"Oh, boo-hoo. Poor Declan, oh favored one. Don't worry. At least you'll get all the praise for saving the day. Again."

"What are you talking about? Up until now, I've been the family pariah for what happened to Grandpa."

Isaac's face tightened. "At least they even thought to ask you to stay with Grandpa. They didn't trust me to go anywhere near him."

"You were twelve."

"And you were only eighteen, but Declan Kelley could do no wrong in Mom and Dad's eyes." Isaac drained the rest of his beer, set the bottle on the side table, stood. "And then you left, and Mom couldn't talk about anything but how much she missed you, how much she wished you'd come back. I saved you. Now you can go back to your fancy job, the conquering hero. You saved Grandma's house *and* the fudge shop. You're welcome."

"You cheated so we'd win."

"And it finally worked," Isaac mumbled as he headed for the kitchen, stumbling a bit.

"Wait, what's that mean? You did other stuff to sabotage her?" Then, as if the lightbulbs clicked on, the chain of events of the past weeks clicked into place. "Did you steal Lily's recipe cards? Her receipts?"

Isaac shrugged. "The Mercer thing was tricky. Not so easy to replace Lily's fudge with something awful, but she never knew the difference since I knew her stupid 'secret' ingredient." He brushed past him, on the way to the kitchen.

Declan just stood there. Oh, he'd been an idiot. He marched into the kitchen.

Isaac held his hands up. "Back up."

Nope. Declan grabbed the front of his brother's shirt and pressed him against the wall. "How dare you." The words came out thin and narrow.

Isaac tried to pull away. "Let go of me."

"You're a punk, you know that?" Fury burned in Declan's veins. This? This is what pride and hate had driven his family to.

"Why? Because I'm actually willing to do something to save Grandma's house and our family business?"

"Grandma's house was already saved!"

"What are you talking about?"

"Lily was going to give it to Grandma if she won. Because she's mature enough to see past this ridiculous family feud. But you—"

"Declan!" his mother's voice.

He glanced at the door as his mom stood in the frame, wearing a stricken expression. His dad walked in, took one look—

"What's going on in here?" Dad roared.

"Let go of your brother," Mom gasped, dropping her purse on the counter.

Declan held tight. "Tell them what you did."

Isaac shook his head and Declan wanted to wipe the smug look off his face.

"Tell them!"

"Let him go," Frank's voice bellowed. He stepped forward and took a grip of Declan's jacket.

Declan released his brother, holding his hands up.

Isaac stepped away and smoothed out his shirt. "He's out of control. Completely lost it because of Lily Hart."

"Is someone going to tell us what's going on?" Mom asked.

"Isaac caused the water damage at the fudge shop."

His dad turned on Declan. "What are you talking about? That's ridiculous—everyone knows that shop's had plumbing issues. You told us about one just last week."

"And that gave him the idea to ruin her fudge with a leak. He all but admitted it to me."

Dad turned to Isaac. "Is Declan right? Did you do it?"

Isaac lifted a shoulder, opened the fridge. "It isn't a big deal. It's the Harts."

Declan turned to his parents. "Is this what you want? Does that make you happy that you've fostered so much hate for people you don't even really know—all because, what? Because Grandpa had a falling out with his best friend? Is that okay with you?"

"It isn't okay." Dad lifted the paper. "We'll deal with this."

"Deal with it how?" Declan asked. "By ignoring it? Lily should be declared the winner."

Mom held up her hands. "Hold on. Let's just think this

through. There's no proof that if the pipe hadn't broken, Lily would have won."

"Do you even hear yourself?" Declan pointed to Isaac. "He *cheated*. Cheated—sabotaged the competition. And the ironic thing was, Lily was going to give Grandma her house, so it's all for nothing."

"Well," his mother said, "that *is* the right thing to do, of course."

"And it's also really generous, Mom. It's totally within her rights to keep it."

"Not anymore," Dad said. "Because the shop belongs to the Kelleys."

"It shouldn't, though."

"Declan, be reasonable." Mom placed a hand on his shoulder. "This is our family legacy we're talking about."

"I thought it was all about *Grandma's house*."

Mom shrugged. "It was. But the legacy, that's important too. Remember, family comes first."

"Yeah, that's what you've been saying my whole life." Huffing, Declan shoved past Dad and pivoted in the doorway. "But I'm starting to wonder if that's really the motto I want to live by if my family is nothing but a bunch of cheats."

Because by association, it made him one too. And whatever Lily thought about him, Declan wanted to be more than a Kelley.

Starting right now.

He headed out the door.

Fifteen

THE MOONLIGHT GAVE HIM NO AN-swers.

Declan's feet crunched along the rocky marina shore. The water caught the reflection of the moonlight, a line from here to the mainland.

He'd gone by Lily's house. Knocked on her door.

She'd refused to see him, of course. And maybe he didn't need to be a jerk and barge past her father.

So, hands in pockets, he'd walked the shoreline between the yacht club and Fort Jonathon. The wind had kicked up off the lake—maybe he should have grabbed his leather jacket. But that's what impulse did—put you in a place you didn't expect.

Like falling back in love with the one woman he'd never forgotten.

Leaning over, Declan picked up a large stone and

skipped it across the waves. It disappeared after a few plinks.

"Now I *know* you can do better than that."

Declan turned at the familiar voice to find Pastor Arnie. He wore a flannel jacket, walked with his hands in his pockets.

"What are you doing here?"

"Thinking about tomorrow's sermon. I like to get alone, hear it in my head. Great show today. Tara told me about the dilemma. Said you got the shop and your grandma's house." He clamped him on the shoulder. "Congratulations."

"Yeah, well, it doesn't feel like a win."

"This wouldn't happen to have anything to do with your second chance with one Lily Hart, now would it?"

Declan coughed. Small-town living had its downfalls sometimes. "More like feeling under my family's thumb."

"How so?"

"Let's just say they have a certain vision for my life, and it involves forsaking everything to support the family legacy."

"You mean the fudge shop?"

Declan's shoulder lifted. "And the feud with the Harts."

The paster scooped up a rock and sent it sailing. It skipped into the night. "Ah, so they're not in support of you and Lily?"

"They never were. Surely you remember what happened in high school?"

Arnie palmed another rock, smoothing his thumb along the surface before handing it to Declan. "I know there was a tragic accident. I know that young love wasn't allowed to bloom. That two young people Tara and I loved went their separate ways, made lives for themselves elsewhere, and despite all odds, were thrust back together in what I don't believe was a coincidence."

"You don't really believe it was a divine moment, do you?" Declan squeezed the rock in his hand. It was calming, cool and solid just like this man of God beside him. "Especially with the way things turned out."

Arnie studied the lake, and the breeze rustled his hair. "What I believe is that people and their opinions—our own too—can often distract us from hearing what God wants for our lives."

"And what's that?"

"Peace. Joy." Arnie looked at him sideways, smile lines appearing at the corner of his eye. "Love."

The word twisted Declan's insides. "I thought maybe this time would be different, you know? That Lily and I would find a way. But then my stupid brother sabotaged Lily's fudge."

Arnie turned to face Declan a bit more, eyebrows lifted. "Oh?"

It felt good to admit it out loud to someone. Too bad Arnie couldn't be the one to go to the town council with the information, but he'd never break a confidence. Declan nodded. "I found out tonight, after the results of the competition were reversed. He's been sabotaging Lily all along. I had no idea," he rushed to say. "But when I told my parents, they . . ."

"Didn't want to tell the truth?"

"More like didn't want to admit that she might have won. They convinced themselves that maybe even without Isaac's sabotage, I would have won."

"And is that true?"

"I saw the numbers. She was ahead. But it's true that I still might have sold more fudge than her. There's just no way to know."

"And does it really matter?"

Right. "I want Lily to have her fudge shop, but I also know it's important to my parents. And ultimately, I want to do what's right. But does that mean outing my family to the whole town, exposing us as cheaters? That might have unintended consequences. People might boycott their businesses, their livelihoods. What if I'm the reason my family sinks or swims?"

"Son, you aren't God. You don't have the power of life or of death—real or metaphorical."

Declan blinked. "Of course not. I didn't mean that. It's just, I want to do the smart thing. And I want to keep the peace." He sighed. "Lily called me weak. And maybe I am."

"It takes real strength to do what is right, even if it costs you. But it also takes strength to keep the peace. You have to stand up, make sacrifices. This is exactly what Jesus did—he made peace between us and God by doing what was right and making the ultimate sacrifice." He chuckled, maybe to himself. "Sometimes what the world thinks is the smart thing isn't the same as the right thing. God could be leading you in a completely different direction than what others—including your family—would say is the right way."

He looked over at Declan. "You can ask Tara about that one. She had to go against her family's wishes when she and I fell in love, but this little island was where God was leading her."

"And her family didn't disown her?" His thoughts skipped to Uncle Craig.

"Oh, they weren't happy with her for a while. And there were many painful conversations. Some silent periods. But when her family saw she was respectfully standing her ground, they decided they'd rather have her in their lives than not." Arnie flashed a wry grin. "Plus, they decided I wasn't so bad."

Declan laughed, though there was a hollow echo in it. "I'm glad it worked out for you. Not sure my family would be so forgiving, though."

Pastor nodded. "We have to do what's right regardless of what may or may not happen, or how other people might react. The Bible says, 'There is a way that seems right to a man, but its end is the way to death.'"

Declan's fist gripped the stone until his hand muscles ached. "If that's true, then how are we supposed to know what way is right?"

"God will show you, but you've got to pray about it. Maybe fast. Ask advice from someone you respect."

He couldn't think of anyone he respected more than Arnie. "So what should I do then, Pastor? Tell the town council about Isaac and possibly ruin my family's reputation? Or stay quiet and ruin the dreams of the woman I love?" Declan stared at the ground. "It seems like an impossible choice."

Arnie clapped him on the shoulder. "The Bible is full of men and women making impossible choices. But each one had to listen to God as the ultimate authority in their lives. Because as much of a blessing as family is, they are not the ones we will answer to in the end."

Declan stood there, nodding. Had he been making his family and what they wanted for him his god? Had he been seeking their love and acceptance—their forgiveness—over God's?

His grip on the stone loosened, and it slid from his palm to his fingertips, waiting. What would it be like to let it all go? To fling away the burden of his family's expectations? The fear that he'd lose them all? The worry that he'd never be known for who he really was?

With a twist and a step, Declan tossed the stone Arnie had handed him across the surface of the lake.

The rock neatly skipped and skipped and skipped until Declan couldn't see it anymore.

He took a deep inhale of the fresh air, closed his eyes, and started—finally, for real—talking to God.

And now she didn't have a clue what to do with her life.

Light streamed through her childhood bedroom window, and Lily flipped over in her bed, facing the wall she'd once upon a time painted a bubble gum pink. The true-life application to the dreams in her head. Happy. Fun.

Too bad real life hadn't matched her expectations.

She snuggled deeper into her thick white comforter. Maybe she'd stay in bed for the next three days. A week.

Whatever. It wouldn't matter. Nothing changed the fact that she'd ruined everything.

How could she have accused Declan and his family of sabotage? The fresh air and some ranting to her parents had helped her see the truth.

Cody had warned her about the pipes. If she'd been a smart and savvy business owner, she'd have gotten them fixed ASAP.

Instead, she'd spent her time dreaming and kissing and falling in love. Same old head-in-the-clouds Lily, doomed to repeat her mistakes.

Lily sighed and closed her eyes again, but a knock at her door had her sitting up.

Mom poked her head inside. "Hey, sweetie. Can I come in?"

"Sure."

Nudging open the door, Mom came in. She lowered herself onto the bed beside Lily and stroked Lily's hair. "You should know, Declan stopped by last night."

Yes, she'd heard him. And her father's words after he turned him away.

She'd nearly gotten up, nearly gone down to apologize, but what would it matter?

She'd already lost everything.

"It's almost two in the afternoon."

"What?" She sat up.

"Yes. Dani and Mia stopped by after church, but you were still sleeping." Mom studied her a moment, sighing. "I know things are hard right now, but they *will* get better, love."

"I'm sorry, Mom." The whisper eked from her lips.

"Sorry for what?"

"For being an airhead. For not focusing on the right thing. For losing the shop." She leaned back against her headboard, pressing her lips together. "I'm such a failure."

"Don't talk about my daughter that way. You are *not* a failure."

"What would you call it, then? I'm certainly not a raving success."

"Success is overrated, and so subjective." Mom held up her hands. "You think I don't have days I feel like a failure because my body doesn't work the way it used to?"

"That's different. That wasn't your choice."

"And neither was this. It was the result of some bad luck, that's all."

"No, Mom, that's not all. It's a pattern for me. No matter how much I want to be different, I get distracted and then I fail to live up to the person I want to be."

Mom shook her head. "Lily, where is all of this coming from? God made you exactly as you are, and you're amazing. You don't have to be anyone but you."

"And yet, Grandpa chose Cody. Oscar chose Carlos. Tony chose Jessica."

And Declan . . . he'd chosen his family over her.

"Okay, the Tony and Jessica reference I get, but you're going to have to back up and explain the others to me."

She ran her hands through her hair. Oh, she needed a shower. Inside and out. She sighed and met her mother's eyes. "The reason I came home from Florida . . . it wasn't just because I wanted to run the shop. It's because I got fired and was literally out of options."

"Oh, Lily. I'm sorry."

"It was my own fault. I thought . . . well, I got carried away, just like always." She looked away, not wanting to see Mom's face—the inevitable disappointment—when she told her the rest. "It's why I also failed out of business school. Why I didn't graduate."

Mom was quiet for several long moments before finally speaking. "Why didn't you tell me?"

"I was ashamed." A tear rolled down her cheek. "I wanted so badly to make you proud. To prove that I had what it took to someday take over the fudge business, just like Cody was going to do with the fishing company."

"Why in the world would you think that graduating or not graduating would prove anything?"

She glanced at Mom. But there wasn't disappointment, just confusion etched into her features. "In case you've forgotten, neither your father nor I graduated from college. Your father never even attended."

"I know. But you had common sense. A business mind. I didn't. I don't. You remember the things Grandpa would say."

Mom's lips screwed into a frown. "Yes, I remember. He wasn't the nicest man. He'd say them to me too, you know."

"Wait, what? I didn't know that."

"It's true. But even if it wasn't, I'm sorry you ever felt like we weren't proud of you. We were." Mom reached for her hand, squeezed. "We *are*."

Lily swatted away yet another tear. "Thanks, Mom. I just wish I'd been able to keep the shop."

"I do too, but for *your* sake. Because you love it."

"I love the creating part, that's true. Maybe not the business stuff, though."

"That's why there's such a thing as a *business partner*. You find someone who complements your strengths with their own. You don't have to do everything alone." Mom tilted her head, smiled. "It's that way with a life partner too."

"Yeah, well, I think things are even *more* dismal in that department."

"I'm sorry things didn't work out with Declan. He was starting to grow on me."

"Even though he's a Kelley?"

"You know as well as I do that it's not the name that makes the man." Mom pressed a hand against her heart. "It's what's in here."

Lily grimaced—because what she'd said to Declan . . . not only was it mean-spirited, but it also wasn't true. He was so much more than his family name. Just like Lily was so much more than her success or failure.

Maybe success really *was* overrated. And maybe it had more to do with the state of her heart than a list of her accomplishments.

The thought was a balm—but maybe a thorn as well.

Lily sighed. "I think I really hurt him, Mom. But he hurt me too."

"Your dad and I hurt each other all the time. Not intentionally, and not in an abusive way, but it's called a relationship between two imperfect people. The important thing is what you do afterward."

"I don't know *what* to do now—with my life, or with Declan. He's probably on the first ferry off the island, anyway." The thought made her want to roll under the covers and never emerge.

"I don't think I'd count him out just yet."

Lily sat up straighter, pushing back the comforter. "Why do you say that?"

"Because I saw him at the door, looking very sad. And how he looked at you when he thought you'd won."

Goosebumps covered her arms. "How did he look at me?"

"Proud. Maybe even adoring. I think Declan recognizes how very special you are. He looked like there's nowhere he'd rather be than by your side."

Oh, Declan. "I don't know if that's true anymore."

Mom leaned in, kissing the top of Lily's head. "Even if it's not, just know that my love for you will never subside. And neither will God's. No matter what you do, no matter how you fail or succeed, you are precious because you were created in His image. You are exactly who you are supposed to be. Because He said so."

Lily sniffled.

"Who knows. Maybe Declan Kelley will surprise you."

"Him? Surprise? He's as straitlaced and predictable as they come." Reliable and solid too. At least, he had been.

"Ready to get up and take a shower? I have soup on the stove." Her mother stood. "And soup solves every problem."

Lily climbed out of the warm covers. "Yeah, but not as well as ice cream."

Her mother laughed. "That right there is the Lily I love. Always thinking outside the box." She kissed her cheek and headed out the door.

And right then, Lily knew exactly what she was going to do.

Sixteen

FTER A HANDFUL OF DAYS SPENT praying hard, a right course had finally settled in Declan's heart.

But the response hadn't been what he'd expected.

"What do you mean, not enough evidence?" Declan paced inside the Tourism Bureau, where Dani had asked him to meet her Thursday afternoon. "I told the council everything Isaac admitted to me."

He'd met with them this morning, in a closed meeting—Uncle Patrick and Mom had been informed about it, but had not been invited. They didn't know the particulars, only that their presence would be a conflict of interest. Mom had probably guessed at the meaning behind it, because she'd been blowing up Declan's phone all day saying she needed to talk with him.

Or maybe it was about the fact that Seb Jonathon had arrived back in town on yesterday's ferry. Probably Lily and her mother had been the first one in his office this morning, trying to wheedle back the shop.

He didn't blame them. Maybe it really did belong to them, despite the terms of the contest.

Seb and the council had heard his argument, quietly, no comment, and now, while the council deliberated, Declan had hidden out in the fudge shop, overseeing the repairs to the kitchen until Dani had summoned him.

"I know." Dani leaned back against the large wooden desk at the entry. "But the council said they didn't think they could change everything based on hearsay, even though they all admitted they believed you. There just wasn't precedent for it . . . though to be honest, there's not really precedent for any of this—the contracts, the competition. None of it."

Declan stopped, looked up at Dani. "You're right. There's not." His mind raced, putting all the details together. "What did Seb say about the lease?"

"He said that in his absence, he'd abide by the council's ruling."

"Good."

"I feel like I've missed something . . . Good?" Dani cocked her head.

"Yes, good. I think. I need to go home and check something out." If he was right . . . why hadn't he thought of it before? "Thanks, Dani!" Declan headed for the front door.

"I don't feel like I did anything, but you're welcome!"

Declan strode down Main Street, turning up Jonathon Boulevard, waving at neighbors as he sped toward his parents' house. He heard voices in the living room but raced up the stairs to his room, digging in his desk for the fudge shop contract the town had given him.

Sitting in the chair, he skimmed the contract language until he confirmed what he'd been looking for.

He smiled to himself and smacked the edge of the stapled document against the palm of his hand. "Thanks, God."

Then he put the contract back in his desk and made his way down the stairs quietly, managing to avoid the squeaky third and tenth steps.

But somehow, Mom heard him.

"Declan?" She popped out from the kitchen, her glare finding him on the stairs. "Family meeting. Now."

He groaned. This wasn't when or how he'd wanted to tell them his plans, but Declan was learning that he wasn't in control of everything. Never had been.

Sending up a prayer for fortitude, he rounded the corner into the living room, where Mom and Dad sat on the couch, Isaac on the love seat—and Grandma Kelley in the recliner.

Oh, man.

Flicking on a smile, he went to her, leaned down and kissed her paper-thin cheek. "Good to see you, Grandma."

"You too, young man. I haven't even seen you since the festival." Her eyes shimmered. "Haven't been able to thank you for everything you did to save my home."

"I did my best." He swallowed, glanced at Mom and Dad, who watched him with accusatory expressions. Isaac sat, arms folded, mouth pinched.

"Sit, Declan," Dad said.

"I'll stand. What's going on?"

Dad opened his mouth to speak, but Mom placed her hand over his. "Declan, I was very surprised to hear that there was a meeting of the town council today. One I wasn't invited to. Do you happen to know what that was about?"

He didn't want to fight. But he had to do what he knew was right regardless of his desire to keep the peace. "I asked the council for a private meeting that would remain confidential." He cleared his throat. "I told them about the sabotage."

Isaac shot forward and turned in his seat. "You did what?"

"What were you thinking?" Dad yelled.

He looked up. "I was thinking that I couldn't live with myself if I went back to Chicago knowing the truth."

"And what is that?"

"We don't deserve that fudge shop."

His words shut down the room.

Grandma looked at him, something he couldn't place in her gaze.

"You're going back to Chicago?" Mom asked.

"That was always the plan. You know that."

"I know, but . . ." Her nose wrinkled. "You're still here. I figured you'd decided to stay."

He shook his head. "I asked Ned for an extra week. He was gracious enough to give it, but I *have* to be back by Monday at the latest or my job is definitely gone."

"But you don't need that job. You can run the shop."

For the first time, Mom's voice shook with emotion—one that wasn't anger.

Maybe Isaac had been telling the truth. Maybe Mom really *had* missed him.

But that wasn't enough. "I can't, because it isn't ours to run."

"So that's it, then?" Dad lifted a hand to Mom's back, rubbing circles into it. "The council gave the shop back to Ms. Hart?"

"No. They said there wasn't enough evidence."

Mom blew out a breath. "Thank goodness."

"No." Declan shook his head. "Not good. Lily deserves that shop and I—"

"Your grandma deserves her house, and even if *you* do, *I* don't trust that Hart girl to give it to her if she owns the shop," Dad said. "Case closed."

"No, Dad. It's not. I won't let you take this away from the woman I love."

Dad's eyes widened. "Do you know how much we've done for you? How much we've sacrificed? You have a responsibility to do what's best for all of us."

"Actually, I have a responsibility to do what God's leading me to do. And in this, you're wrong. I won't stand by and let you—"

"*Let* me?" Dad stood abruptly, advancing toward Declan.

"Frank, sit down."

The words, spoken so loud and clear and strong, halted everyone, who turned to Grandma where she sat in her chair. Her eyes flashed.

Dad stared at her. "Mom?"

"I said, 'Sit. Down.'"

Huh. Declan couldn't remember the last time—if ever—he'd heard Grandma raise her voice.

His dad sat down.

Her eyes seemed to glisten. "I never wanted this."

"Wanted what?" Declan asked softly.

"This division. For all of you to feel the burden to help me out of my mess. For you to stoop to *cheating* to do so. I'm the one who didn't pay the back taxes, who allowed the sadness to weigh me down so deep that I stopped caring about anything but how much I missed your grandpa."

Declan's eyes burned. "But I'm the one who let Grandpa get out. I should have been there—"

"Oh, Declan." Grandma lifted a shaking hand and wiped away her tears. "Surely you know? That wasn't the first time he'd escaped. It wasn't on you. He was a tricky old sneak, even at the end." She smiled, however.

"What do you mean, Edna?" Mom sat up straighter. "Why didn't you say anything?"

Grandma sighed. "I'd been in denial for a while. Thought I could care for him here, but he should have been in a home. I just didn't want to let go."

Declan allowed her words to sink in.

"It wasn't my fault," he breathed out.

"No, Dec. It wasn't. You were a boy—of course it wasn't. It was a terrible, tragic accident. No one is to blame."

Of course, that didn't stop the sting of his family's blame for the last decade. Leaning forward, he reached for Grandma's hand. "Which means it wasn't yours either."

"I know that now, child. With much counseling and prayer. Doesn't mean I don't miss him terribly, but I'm at peace." She patted his hand. "The thing that's threatening this peace, though, is you all fighting. Your grandpa never wanted a fudge war. He was a peacemaker and didn't even want to open up that competitor's shop, but *his* father convinced him that it would be better for the family. Sound familiar?"

Dad had the decency to look chagrined.

Grandma's cool fingers wrapped around Declan's wrist, not quite reaching all the way. "And no, your grandfather didn't steal William Hart's recipes, but the damage was done. That rift between friends, it festered with unforgiveness. And that spilled over into our current situation—with generations of hating and fighting that doesn't do anyone any good. Not only between the Harts and Kelleys, but among all of you."

She turned to Dad and held out her other hand.

Frowning, he took it.

Grandma spoke again. "Here's what I've learned in my long life, though. God keeps no accounting of our wrongs. If God keeps no accounting, then who are we to keep one?" She turned her face toward Declan. "You may not agree with your father, but I don't want to see you running off to Chicago before you've talked through your issues."

"Yes, ma'am," he said. "But what if he won't listen? He's kind of stubborn."

Dad coughed. Didn't say anything.

And Grandma laughed. "Yes. You're a lot like him in that way." Then she turned to Dad. "And you. You may be fifty-seven years old, but I'm still your mother, and you still have to listen to me." Her mouth twitched with the announcement. "Your son is not a fool to be in love. If I recall, you were once young and in love. Try to remember what that was like."

"But—"

"But nothing." Grandma tutted. "Get past the fact that he's fallen for a Hart, and ask yourself if your unnecessary hatred of another family outweighs the love you have for your son."

Dad slumped. Mom did too.

Maybe with a little forgiveness and understanding, they really *could* get past this . . . even if—no, *when*—Declan enacted his plan.

Isaac stood. "Well, this has been fun—"

"And then there's you, young man."

Declan nearly laughed at the way Isaac zipped his lips and plopped back down on the edge of the couch while he listened to Grandma stick it to him straight.

And it wasn't lost on Declan that perhaps Arnie was right—that his being here hadn't been a coincidence after all. That there was a bigger purpose to it all.

He might have lost his chance to be with Lily, but he'd still be leaving a changed man.

One who did what was right in God's eyes, even if everyone else called him a fool.

Her parents' kitchen wasn't as spacious as the fudge shop, but it would have to do.

With hands on her hips, Lily surveyed her working space. Mom's ice cream maker—which had appeared two nights ago on her doorstep, with a note from Declan that Lily had yet to open—took up nearly one-third of the small kitchen island, and her ingredients, bowls, and kitchen tools crowded out the other two.

She flicked open the curtains on the kitchen window to find a bright Saturday morning shining its hope straight into her soul. A breeze rustled the treetops of the tall oaks in Mom and Dad's backyard, and Lily smiled as she pulled her hair into a ponytail.

Yep. Her heart might still be sore, and there would be hard days ahead, but she had everything she needed right here.

"Morning." Mom stepped through the front door dressed in her jogging pants and sweatshirt, a baseball cap pulled low over her head. Her cheeks were wind-chapped and red.

"Hi. Did you have a nice walk with Elise?"

"We did." Mom tugged off her cap and smoothed down a few flyaways. "She told me all about her cruise, and then she talked non-stop about Finn and Maggie, and I told her how much I wish Cody and Mia would hurry up and get married so I'd have grandkids." Mom froze and blinked at Lily. "Goodness, I'm sorry, honey. That was really insensitive of me."

"It's okay, Mom." Lily grabbed her mixing bowl and started to measure milk into it. "If I can't have my happy ending, then I'm glad someone else gets theirs. And I also can't wait to be an auntie. Those kids are awesome."

"They are that." Mom approached and kissed Lily's head, then she turned and tapped the yellow envelope held on the fridge with a years-old Hart Fishing Company magnet. "Have you read it yet?"

"No."

"Why not?"

Shrugging, Lily measured out the sugar. "I don't know."

"Okay." Mom grabbed a water bottle from the fridge, cracking it open and taking a drink. "But you know, maybe it's an apology."

"And maybe it's a goodbye. Maybe it's a lot of things." Lily set the measuring cup down, sighing. "It's dumb, I know, but opening that letter feels like an ending."

"Or maybe it's a new beginning." Mom looked at Lily's setup. "Speaking of, I'm so glad you've decided to try your hand at an ice cream company. You've gotten so many compliments on your flavors, I'm sure you'll have lots of business in no time."

She'd gotten the idea when the ice cream maker had appeared. If she couldn't do fudge, then this just made sense. At least, for now. "I'm not sure it'll be a success."

"But remember . . ."

"I know. Success is subjective."

"Exactly. And you are more than welcome to live here with me and Dad for as long as you need to while you get things going."

"I'm going to pay rent."

Mom waved her off. "Once you're making an income, sure. But for now, just enjoy the process and don't worry about the business part. Start small. Oh! Speaking of that,

I told Elise what you were doing and she wants to hire you to cater an ice cream social at ladies' Bible study next week."

"Really?"

"Yes! You can text her for the details, but I thought it would be a perfect first gig for you." Mom winked. "Although, really it's more like a third gig after that wedding and the festival."

"True."

"I'm proud of you, you know. Pivoting like this. I know it isn't fudge . . ."

"It's actually okay. Fudge is in my blood, and it always will be. But I really like the ice cream too. It's like a mini therapy session every time I make a new batch." Lily grinned. "And I have a feeling I'll need lots of therapy over the next little while."

Mom opened her mouth to reply, but Lily's phone started blaring.

Lily glanced at the screen and froze. Why was Declan calling her?

"Aren't you going to answer that?"

"Um. I'm not sure." Lily blinked at the phone, hands itching at her sides. By the time she finally stirred the courage to reach for the phone, the light blinked off. The music ended. Silence.

She took a breath, watched for a voicemail to pop up, but it didn't. Instead a text message came through.

Declan

Are you coming?

"Coming where?" she murmured. She lifted the phone and replied with three question marks.

Declan

Did you read the note I left?

Lily swallowed.

Mom watched her. "Well?"

"He wants me to read the note."

"Ah." Mom took her water and gave Lily a hip bump. "I'll support whatever you do. But maybe it would be good to hear him out. Don't run this time. Face it head-on."

"That's kind of frightening."

"All the hard things are. But often, they have the highest rewards too." Then Mom left the room.

Lily stared at the envelope on the fridge door, her name written in Declan's clean, crisp block letters. Then she strode forward, snatched it off, and opened it.

LILY,

I KNOW I HURT YOU. PLEASE GIVE ME A CHANCE TO MAKE IT RIGHT.

I'M HOPING YOU'LL MEET ME ON SATURDAY AT NINE IN THE MORNING, AT THE FUDGE SHOP.

YOURS,
DECLAN

She clutched the letter to her chest. Somehow, despite the professional tone of the letter, this man still made her *feel*. Lily didn't even think more about it. She had to go.

If she didn't, she might just regret it forever.

She ran to her room, tugged on her favorite pair of leather leggings and a flowing tank top she tied at the bottom corner. Tossing on some lip gloss, she headed out the door and toward her bike.

A chill hung in the air, fog over the harbor as she rolled past the Grand Hotel and the Center for the Arts. Ahead of her, Martha's on Main already had a line waiting on the sidewalk, and Main Street itself had lots of foot traffic even though many of the shops wouldn't open for another hour. Lily might not have a shop anymore, but it was still thrilling to see her hometown coming back to life.

She approached the old Hart fudge shop—which she'd successfully avoided all week. She expected to see the Kelley name already plastered across the door and sign.

Instead, there hung a simple hand-painted white and yellow wooden sign with purple lettering. Squinting, Lily parked her bike on the porch and read it.

The Fudge Shop on the Corner.

She blinked at it. That was the name she'd created for *her* fudge shop. The one in her very simple, pitiful business proposal.

What was that all about? It seemed a bit cruel, but maybe Declan was trying to pay her some sort of homage?

A flash of white filled the window—and there he was, on the other side, staring at her.

An ache hit her chest. He looked as handsome as ever with his plain T-shirt, jeans. He even wore a bomber jacket.

Huh. Mr. Top Gun.

Declan opened the front door, where the sign was still flipped to Closed. "Hey."

"Hey," she croaked out.

"Thanks for coming."

She couldn't think of a response, so just moved through the space in the doorway he'd created. He closed it behind them, locking the door and facing her again. "Do you mind joining me in the kitchen?"

"I guess not." Lily clutched her small cross-body purse to her side as she followed him through the newly painted door—it was now the same yellow color as the sign.

Wait. Hadn't she proposed using that color in her business plan?

As Lily entered the kitchen, she gasped. There was no longer any evidence of damage. Every surface sparkled and gleamed—even the brand new, high-end stove, yellow cabinets, and stainless steel prep stations. The only thing that remained of the old kitchen were the marble tables that had been used for generations by her family to make fudge.

"Wow." She ran her fingers over a table's cool surface. "How did you get this all done so quickly?" It was no secret that renovation projects on Jonathon Island could be difficult, what with getting materials over on the ferry and finding contractors ever since Joe Barrett's construction company no longer serviced the island.

Declan grabbed a file folder from one of the marble tables. "Liam hooked me up. He had some workers and materials that could be spared for a few days since some other project on the hotel was running behind. He also had some contacts to get the insurance adjuster out here in a matter of days."

"That's impressive." What would it be like to create in this kitchen? It felt invigorating just being here, pulsing with the nostalgia of tradition mixed with the freshness of the new. "And the sign?"

"Mia painted it for me."

"But . . . the name."

"Oh yeah." He scratched behind his ear. "I may have gotten a peek at your business plan a few weeks ago when you left it lying on the desk in our shared office."

Shared . . . just like it never would be again.

"Oh. Okay." Lily forced a smile. "Um, well, congrats. Everything looks great. Guess you can open up Monday, then. Unless you're leaving?" He'd mentioned once that he might hire his cousin Olive to run the shop when he left for Chicago, but that had been before . . .

Now she had no clue what his plans were.

"I am planning to leave, yes." He looked away, seemed to straighten as he blew out a breath. Then he faced her again. "But before I go, I wanted to say how sorry I am."

"For what?"

He huffed. "For a lot of things. But mostly that I didn't listen to you. That I didn't see things from your perspective. That I chose my family over you—again."

Now it was her turn to glance away, staring at the yellow and brown swirls in the granite countertop beside the sink.

He continued. "I want you to know that I really didn't have any idea about this, but after you left the night of the festival . . ." His voice broke.

Her gaze snapped back up to him. "What happened?"

"Isaac admitted that he *did* sabotage you. And not just with the pipes. With other things, including slipping some bad fudge into your sampler box for Kent Mercer."

"What?"

"I know. I'm so, so sorry. Almost as soon as I found out—though I'm ashamed to say it wasn't sooner—I went to the town council. Told them everything."

Her head spun. "And your family was okay with that?"

"No. They were furious."

Lily paced. He'd gone against his family's wishes? "So what does this mean, then? What did the council say?"

"Unfortunately, they didn't think there was enough evidence since Isaac only admitted it to me."

"Oh." She halted, slumping against the counter. For just a moment, she'd hoped . . .

"But, Lil." Declan moved closer, placing the folder on the counter in front of her. He flipped it open, pointed to the paper on top. "It doesn't matter. I'm giving it to you. Here's the lease agreement, sublet to you. And here are the keys, and a copy of my own business plan in case that will help you." His brow dipped as he flipped to the last document in the folder. "And the lease to my grandma's house, if you want it. It's yours by rights."

"Declan. No." She pulled the paper from the folder and placed it in his hands. "I told you. I'd never take it from her."

"Thank you, Lily." Swallowing hard, he looked away. "My family really doesn't deserve your mercy, not after they tried to cheat you."

All of the implications from their conversation—from what was happening right now—swirled in Lily's brain. "I'm assuming they're against this. Will that be a problem?"

He shook his head and flipped his attention back to hers, his gaze intense. "I double checked, but the contract was in my name only. Theirs isn't mentioned anywhere. So while they're not very happy with me right now, and they don't fully understand my reasons, they don't have a say." Picking up the folder, he held it out to her. "The shop is yours, as it always should have been."

Her mouth opened, closed. This was the last thing she'd expected when she'd arrived here this morning. Her family's fudge shop, safe. Their legacy, continuing. "Thank you, Declan. Really."

He smiled, but it didn't reach his eyes. "Well, I'll get out of your hair. I've got to get home and pack. I need to leave early in the morning, and my whole family is gathering tonight for dinner. So." His head tilted. "I really am sorry, Lily. But I know you're going to make this a huge success. And I wish you all the best."

His words burrowed into her heart, made a home there. "You're really leaving?" she whispered.

"Yes. But before I did, I wanted you to know that I heard you. That I . . ."

"Chose me."

He nodded. "And I'd do it again. I'm only sorry it's not enough. That I didn't do it right away. That I didn't see a world in which I could have my family's respect and your love. I'm not sure I'll ever really forgive myself for that."

Oh, Declan. She set the file folder on the counter and stepped toward him. "We both made mistakes, you know. I'm sorry too. I didn't mean what I said. You're more than just a Kelley. You're your own man, and who you are is someone I will root for always, no matter what you do."

He just stared at her, both of them frozen between the swirl of *what if*s. Then he snatched her hand, looking down at it engulfed in his. "Thank you, Lily. That means more than you'll ever know." Then he gave it a squeeze, dropped it, and started to back away.

"Declan," she blurted.

He froze.

"Um. I . . . that is." She glanced around. What was the thrill in doing all of this by herself? She didn't want to be a one-woman show. Didn't need to prove anything anymore.

And she didn't want to be alone. Didn't want to live without the man she loved.

"Would you ever consider . . ."

He stilled. "Consider what?"

"Just . . . not leaving?"

He smiled then, the kind of smile that lit up her entire body. Sheesh, she should call him Maverick with the trouble in his blue eye. As if . . .

Had he wanted her to ask?

Maybe, because, "And what would I do if I stayed?"

Two could play at this game. "I know you've got a big important job waiting for you in Chicago, but how do you feel about fudge?"

"Meh. It's okay."

"Worth sticking around for?"

"Maybe." Declan edged up to her. "But I'm not much of a fudge maker."

She closed the gap between them, her hand on his chest. "No, you're not. But I can probably find a position here."

"Like?"

"I don't know. Handyman? Plumber? Maybe throw in some accounting?"

His hands found her waist, drew her closer. "I don't know. It's not much of an offer. Throw in the fudge *maker*, and we might have a deal."

"I think we can negotiate terms."

"Oh, you're such a hard-nosed business person." He wound his hand behind her neck, ran his thumb down her cheek, leaving tendrils of heat in its wake.

"I know you have a big job in Chicago—"

"No," he said. "I don't. I mean, yes, I do, but . . ." All teasing vanished from his eyes. "I wanted it for the wrong reasons. And being away from here holds nothing for me." His eyes turned misty. "I've fallen in love again with Jonathon Island."

He lowered his mouth, but she put her hand up.

"What?" he asked.

"*Just* Jonathon Island?" Her voice had turned husky, the nearness of him, the strength of his arms around her— she'd lost all power in this negotiation.

"No, Lily." He pulled slightly away, smiled. "The fudge shop too."

"Declan!" She started to wrench out of his hold, smacking him. But she laughed.

Oh, it felt good, so good, to laugh with him.

Chuckling, he grabbed her again. "Okay, you win." He cupped her face. "I love you, Lil. I choose you. Always. Forever."

"You're hired—"

He kissed her. His lips solid against hers, his arms tight around her, sealed the deal.

And what a deal it was.

He finally lifted his head.

She patted his jacket. "I like it. I guess I'll have to call you Maverick now."

He nodded, grinning. "Whatever you say, boss." Then he kissed her again. And of course he tasted of fudge, and homecoming, and the happy ending she'd always known was waiting for her on Jonathon Island.

She'd just had to win the war to get it.

Epilogue

THE LAST TWO WEEKS HAD BEEN A dream.

Who knew that the thrill of taking over the business operations of a fudge shop would be on par with making multi-million-dollar mergers and acquisitions in the big city?

Though Lily had a lot to do with it.

Yes, working with the woman he loved—in a town that had nurtured and grown them both up—had given Declan a greater sense of purpose than ever.

But it wasn't enough.

Not until he made Lily his for good and gave her the desires of her heart.

He was starting to doubt the wisdom of pulling double shifts, though. Hammering out details in the fudge shop office all day, then sneaking down to the Quinn livery just south of Blueberry Hill Park in the evenings, working in secret alongside Cody to retrofit the Harts' old Volk-swagen van—the one that Lily's great-grandparents had brought with them to Jonathon Island more than seventy years ago when they'd first opened the fudge shop.

Vehicles may not be allowed on the island anymore, but this one would be parked on Main Street. At least, that was Declan's plan.

It could all blow up in his face.

It might not.

But there was a certain peace in giving the results to God.

Cody stepped back from the van-turned-food truck, a heat gun in his hand. "I think that'll do it." He started to wind up the gun's cord.

Declan studied Cody's application of the vinyl wrap he'd ordered. Not surprisingly, it was flawless. "Great job, man."

"All in a day's work." Squatting on the ground—which was littered with old bits of hay—Cody placed the heat gun back in his toolbox. "You think my sister has any idea?"

"I hope not. I've tried to keep it a surprise."

"I gotta admit. When you first suggested turning our family's old van into a food truck so Lily would have a place to sell her ice cream too, I thought you were crazy. But it's turned out well."

"I'm hoping it'll be a nice marriage of her love for fudge and ice cream."

"Marriage, huh?" Cody grinned as he snapped his tool-box shut. "Nice choice of words."

"Shut up." Declan gave him a friendly shove before his hand went to his pocket on instinct. For over a week now, he'd been carrying the ring in his pocket, unsure when he'd give it to her. For someone who liked to have everything planned, he sure was flying by the seat of his pants on this one.

But he wanted the moment when he asked Lily to be his wife to be perfect.

Or at least perfect for them.

The wooden door to the livery opened, bringing cracks of dusty light streaming in from Blueberry Boulevard. Mom and Nancy Hart stepped inside pushing a cart filled with ice cream containers. Now that was a sight he'd never thought he'd see—a Kelley and a Hart working together for a common purpose. His whole family might not be ready to come around just yet, but this was a good start.

"We've got the ice cream," Mom said, wiping her hands on the back of her jeans. "Is the van ready? The festivities are going to start soon."

Since the Main Street Festival had gone so well, Dani had decided at the last minute to do a Labor Day evening arts and crafts festival in the park, complete with fireworks later tonight. Lily was there setting up the fudge shop booth now, probably wondering where Declan was.

"It's as ready as it'll ever be." And there was nothing like cutting it so close. He pulled a phone from his pocket, dialed Asher's number, told him they were ready, then hung up. "All right, let's get the ice cream loaded in."

"Unfortunately, there are quite a few of Lily's recipes

that I don't know," Nancy said. "But I was able to sneak some copies of the ones she'd written down."

"I'm sure it'll be great," Mom said.

Nancy smiled at her tentatively. Mom smiled back.

Declan rubbed the spot over his heart, then set to work loading the ice cream containers inside the freezer drawer they'd custom fit for the truck. Finally, it was ready. Nancy and Cody slipped out and headed for the festival. Meanwhile, Asher arrived and started hitching up the horses to the van—a sanctioned way to get the vehicle from one place to the other.

"It looks great, honey." Mom patted his back. "She's going to love it."

"Yeah?" He slipped an arm around her shoulder. "Thanks, Mom. I just wish Dad . . ."

"Give him time. He's trying. Just this morning, he saw Randy Hart outside the fudge shop and didn't outright glare at him. That's real progress."

Groaning, Declan shook his head. "A little slow if you ask me."

"Nobody said change happened quickly. It takes longer than a few weeks for old habits to die. But Lily's willingness to give Grandma her house went a long way in healing old wounds." She paused. "Besides, I have a feeling once there's a wedding on the horizon, he'll get on board pretty quickly."

Declan's eyes widened "How did you know?"

"Oh, don't insult my intelligence." Mom tapped her nose. "I can smell these things."

"*These things* being gossip?"

"Now I'm really insulted," Mom teased. "All right, I'd better get to my booth. I'll see you over there?"

"Yep, we'll be there shortly."

Mom headed out, and then it was just Declan and Asher. The other man stayed mostly silent except when speaking in low murmurs to the horses. Finally, he turned. "Ready?"

Was he? Declan rubbed his hands together. "Ready as I'll ever be."

Declan opened up the livery doors and Asher whistled and flicked the reins from his place on the cart behind the horses. The horses trotted slowly out onto the road, pulling the food truck behind it. The yellow and purple glittery swirls of the words *Lily's Ice Cream* shone and sparkled.

After shutting the livery doors again, Declan jumped on board with Asher and they made their way slowly up the street toward the park, where a banner swept across the entrance welcoming visitors to the Jonathon Island Labor Day Celebration. The clip clop of the horses' hooves was soon drowned out by the din of voices and upbeat tunes of Coldplay resounding from speakers someone had set up.

Children squealed at the sight of the horses, which Asher expertly maneuvered onto the park's pathway. Declan hopped off, politely ushering people off the sidewalk so they could make their way toward the opening beside the fudge shop booth—the one Dani had arranged for in advance.

She appeared from the crowd, grinning at him. "Just a little more that way, around the curve, toward the playground. That's where you'll find her." Leaning closer, she grabbed Declan's arm. "It looks amazing. She's going to flip."

"In a good way, I hope."

"Definitely."

Asher and Declan slowly led the horses toward the end of the line of booths. They passed Mia's artwork booth, where she and Cody both flashed huge grins and thumbs-up. When gliding past Patrick's booth, Declan took in the delicious smells of burgers and nachos—and ignored his uncle's stare. Yet another family member who needed to come around.

Finally, the booth—and the woman—he'd been looking for came into view as they rounded a corner.

Dressed in that same yellow dress she'd worn to the wedding when he'd first started to fall in love with her again, Lily spoke to a mom and young daughter, handing them samples of fudge and laughing at something they'd said.

She was beautiful. Radiant.

As the mom and daughter skipped happily away, Lily glanced up, and even from here, he could hear her gasp. Then she was rounding the booth, sprinting toward him, meeting them halfway. She grabbed Declan's hand. "What is this?"

"It's a food truck."

Asher halted the horses right there in the middle of the path, in front of Jemma's glassblowing and Grace's maritime booths.

Declan led her around to the side of the truck. "See,

that part folds down into a counter, and then you just pop up the roof there, and voilà! Food truck."

"Wait." Her mouth flopped open. "Is this my family's old Volkswagen?"

"It is."

"How did you . . ." She turned to him, eyes filling with tears. "Lily's Ice Cream? This is mine?"

"It's yours, if you want it. I thought we'd park it on the west side of the fudge shop. We can bring it out for festivals like this too. A piece of history along with your new creations." He licked his lips. "Do you like it?"

"Declan, I love it!" She threw her arms around his shoulders and kissed him. Her lips tasted like chocolate and something exotic he couldn't quite identify. Probably some new ingredient for her fudge. "How did you do this?"

"With some help from both of our families."

Tears filled her eyes. "Really?"

"Yes, really."

"I didn't think . . . I mean, I'd hoped they'd . . ."

"I know." He kissed the tip of her nose, risking a glance back at Asher, who sat patiently waiting for them to finish their public display. "Come on. Let's get this set up. Then I can tell you more about something my mom said—a way to bring our families even more together." He pressed his fingertips against his pocket, feeling the outline of the ring there.

Yes, his plans were going to come to fruition one way or another. And the sooner, the better.

"I want to know. Tell me now."

He shook his head, laughing. "We've kept Asher wait-ing long enough."

Lily swooped her head to the side, looking over Declan's shoulder. "You don't mind, do you, Ash?"

The man grunted, pulling his ball cap lower. "Well . . ."

"Be right back, man. As for you." He looked at Lily. "Come here, then." Declan pulled her out of Asher's way, behind the trunk of a large tree, where they were alone—if alone meant an entire town watching and waiting around the corner.

Grinning, Lily slid her hands into his hair, leaving a blazing trail of heat up his back and a dizziness in his brain. "So what's this about your mom's idea for how to bring our families together?" Her eyebrows waggled.

"You're impossible, you know that?"

"Why, thank you." She pulsed her fingertips against his scalp. "Now tell me."

"So bossy." Declan slid his hands up her arms, lowered her hands back in front of her.

She booed his actions, making him chuckle.

"Calm down. I need you there for this next part." Fish-ing in his pocket, he drew out the ring and held it in his fist. "My mom's idea—which, I'll have you know, was my idea first—was for us to get married." Then he knelt and held the ring in his open palm.

Lily's eyes went from the ring to him, and they were big and bright and round. "Are you serious?"

He nodded.

With a reverence and awe, she picked up the one-carat amethyst—perfect for his non-traditional woman. Slipping it on her finger, she held it up and examined it, a huge smile overtaking her face. "Yes!" Then she knelt right there in front of him, tackling him until his back hit the tree. She kissed him with the same fervor she did everything else.

He laughed against her lips. "Yes, what? I didn't actually get a chance to ask you anything." Lowering himself to the ground, he pulled her into his lap.

"Oh. Right." She blinked up at him. "Well, go ahead."

"*So*, so bossy." Another kiss planted firmly on her lips. "Lily Ann Hart, I love you more than I love classic chocolate fudge."

She giggled. "And we know that's a lot."

"We do indeed. So would you bring all manner of chaos and joy into my life and become my wife?"

"Hmm. I need to think about it." She grinned and gave him a wink. "Just kidding. Of course I will. Under one condition."

"And what's that?" He leaned down, drew his fingers through her silky hair, and nipped at her lips.

"You finally admit that I was right about your fudge being boring."

Chuckling, he shook his head. "I guess if that's what it takes to finally end this feud, then I'll do it. For the good of our families."

"And for the good of us."

"Yes." He sobered. "Because I will choose the good of us first, always. I promise you that, Lil."

"I promise that too," she whispered.

Declan cupped Lily's face in his hands, his touch gentle and reverent. He gazed into her eyes, seeing his future reflected in their depths. Slowly, he leaned in, his lips meeting hers in a kiss that was soft and sweet and filled with assurance.

Lily's eyes fluttered closed as she melted into the kiss, her hands coming to rest on his chest. The world around them faded away as the kiss deepened, a tender exploration that was just the beginning of things to come.

Summer on Jonathon Island had never felt so perfectly delicious.

Thank You

Thank you so much for reading *Meet Me at the Fudge Shop*. We hope you enjoyed the story. If you did, would you be willing to do us a favor and leave a review? It doesn't have to be long—just a few words to help other readers know what they're getting. (But no spoilers! We don't want to wreck the fun!) Thank you again for reading!

We'd love to hear from you- not only about this story, but about any characters or stories you'd like to read in the future. Contact us at www.sunrisepublishing.com/contact.

Bonus Epilogue

Thank you for reading *Meet Me at the Fudge Shop*. We hope you loved this story. Find out what happens next for Lily and Declan with a Bonus Epilogue, a special gift, available only to our newsletter subscribers.

This Bonus Epilogue will not be released on any retailer platform, so scan the QR code to get your free gift. You acknowledge you are becoming a Sunrise Publishing, Lindsay Harrel, and Rachel D. Russell subscriber. Unsubscribe from any newsletter at any time.

Jonathon Island

Return to Jonathon Island in book 4
Meet Me on Blueberry Hill
by Lisa Jordan.

The last thing Sadie Hudson expected to find on her grandmother's doorstep was a second chance at love—or another chance at heartbreak.

Copywriter-by-day Sadie Hudson used to dream of songwriting. But that all changed when her sister died in a senseless tragedy five years ago. Now, Sadie returns to Jonathon Island to help her beloved grandma Henrietta recover from surgery. Because Sadie will do anything for family—even if it means returning to the one place her memories haunt her most.

But just as she begins to find peace in the island's tranquility, a fallen tree damages her grandmother's home, forcing her to accept help from Gran's gruff, mysterious neighbor. Despite the way he cares for Gran, Sadie can't shake the feeling that Asher is keeping secrets, and after her last relationship ended in lies and betrayal, she's determined not to be fooled by another man. But the more time she spends with Asher, the more she's drawn to him.

Asher Quinn has his own reasons for seeking solitude on Jonathon Island. Behind his hard work and generous spirit lies a past he longs to forget—one that could destroy any chance at the new life he's carefully constructed...especially when he discovers that he's the reason Sadie lost her sister.

Can two wounded souls find the courage to be honest with each other, or will the weight of their pasts destroy their chance at love before it truly begins?

One

ASHER QUINN JUST WANTED THE nightmares to stop.

Until he found redemption for the tragedies of his past, they would continue to haunt his sleep.

The sound of splintering wood, the creaking of timber, and a crash jerked him from the same dream that plagued him repeatedly for the past five years.

Sweat slicked his chest as he dragged a shaky hand over his weary face. He forced his ragged breathing to slow and stared into the darkness, trying to erase the images flickering through his head.

Impossible.

Nothing would remove the echoing screams or the sear of flames as he fought to escape his metal prison.

Thunder rumbled outside his bedroom window.

Lightning slashed, throwing brilliant light across the wooden floor.

The storm.

Triggers he didn't expect to turn his gut to mush.

But he didn't have time to wallow in the past. He needed to make sure Henrietta Hudson, his elderly neighbor recovering from hip replacement surgery, was safe.

He couldn't have more deaths on his conscience.

Not your fault.

How many times had his counselor said that?

Lies.

Someday, he'd believe him.

Maybe.

Until then, knowing he couldn't save them ate at his conscience.

He snatched an olive-colored T-shirt off the floor and jammed it over his head, his fingers scraping against the puckered skin along the left side of his neck.

Scars that served as a reminder.

He pulled on the tan cargo shorts he'd kicked off earlier, then shoved his feet in a pair of worn leather flip-flops.

Grabbing the flashlight kept by the door, he hurried down the stairs, through the house, and into the storm.

He raced to the stable to check on the few horses still on island. Scents of hay and warm animal flesh mingled with the steamy air fraught with storms that shook the island.

Jagged fingers of lightning sparked across the blackened sky, casting shadows over too many empty stalls.

Pegasus nickered.

He ran a hand over the Percheron's muzzle. "Hey, Gus. It's okay. The storm'll be over shortly."

Next to him, Ginger bumped his shoulder with her

nose. "Hey, sweet girl. This isn't your first storm. You'll be okay."

After giving each of them another pat, he plunged into the night air, dark as smoke, the light in his hand doing very little to shine a path through the storm. Rain pelted his skin as he sprinted across the yard. His feet slipped and he nearly face-planted in the soppy grass. He kicked off his flip-flops and raced barefoot to his older neighbor's front porch.

A long limb had smashed through the side railing of the white storybook cottage. He'd need to come back first thing in the morning to clear it and make sure there was no other damage.

Swiping water and hair off his face, he rang the doorbell. Barking sounded from inside the house. Georgie, Hetty's Lhasa Apso, scratched the other side of the front door as the porch light flashed on.

Squinting against the glare, Asher gripped the doorframe and let out a breath.

She was fine.

The door yanked open.

But Hetty wasn't standing in the doorway.

Asher took in the dark-haired woman a little younger than his thirty-three years and dressed in a gray tank top and navy running shorts that showed off long, shapely legs. Her long hair tangled around her face. She tried to push it out of her eyes as she scooped up the barking dog. "Georgie, that's enough." Then she squinted at him. "Yes? Can I help you?"

"Is Hetty okay?"

"Who?"

"Henrietta Hudson. She lives here. Is she okay?"

The woman cradled the dog against her chest. "Why do you want to know?"

He jerked a thumb over his shoulder. "I heard a tree come down, but it's too dark to see anything. I just wanted to be sure Hetty's okay."

"My grandmother's fine. She sleeps through anything. Doorbells too, apparently. I didn't realize it was storming until now."

"You've inherited that trait from your grandmother." He tried to crack a smile, but her steely look showed she didn't share his humor. He stepped back, hands up. "Sorry to disturb your sleep. Just wanted to make sure everyone was okay."

"Yes, we are. Thanks for checking." She shot him a sleepy smile, then started to close the door.

"Wait."

"What?"

"What's your name?"

"Sadie. Sadie Hudson."

"The copywriter. Your grandma's mentioned you."

"And you are?"

"Asher Quinn." He jerked a thumb over his shoulder. "I manage my aunt and uncle's ranch next door."

"Right, the reclusive neighbor. Gran mentioned you as well. Thanks for ensuring she was safe. That was kind of you, Asher." This time she closed the door and secured the deadbolt in place.

A moment later, the overhead yellow glow from the porch light went out, shuttering him in darkness again.

Taking a deep breath, he exhaled loudly then launched into the rain.

Back at his aunt and uncle's house, he padded up the stairs and to the large guest room that had become his over the past year. He flicked on the lights, then shivered against the fan in the window. He changed into dry clothes, then grabbed a towel out of the small bathroom and rubbed it over his head.

What he wouldn't give for a cold beer.

But he'd given up drinking eighteen months ago. The same night his aunt and uncle rescued him from the depths of his self-sabotage.

Only the nightmares resurrected the desire to hold the cold beverage in his hand, to feel the icy liquid slide down his throat. As he pounded back bottle after bottle, his troubles disappeared.

But only for a while.

Instead, he reached for his water bottle on the side table, then chugged until his parched throat was quenched.

He pressed his back against the windowsill and eyed the queen-size bed with its twisted sheets that spoke of his restlessness. Instead of crawling back under the covers where sleep would elude him, he dropped in the dark brown leather chair in the corner that gave a perfect view of the TV sitting on the electric fireplace. He set his water on the floor and reached for the remote.

Stretching his legs out on the matching ottoman, he stopped on a random channel and threw an arm over his eyes. Maybe he could fall back to sleep to the droning of some mindless show.

"In this episode of *Where Are They Now?*, what happened to the rock band Phoenix? After the fiery tour bus crash that claimed the lives of nearly everyone on board, including the band's famed lyricist, fans are wondering where Eli Noble, the lead singer who was the only one to escape, has disappear—"

Asher scrambled for the remote and shut off the TV. He tossed it on the ottoman, then strode across the room and grabbed his phone that was charging on the side table. As he sat on the edge of the bed, he thumbed through his contacts and tapped on a number.

"'Ello?" Corbin Gray's gravelly voice sounded in his ear.

"Hey, man. Sorry to call so late, and it's been a while, but you said . . ."

"Yeah, yeah, no worries. I'm here for you. What's going on?" His counselor's deep voice mellowed with sleep eased the band around Asher's chest. "Another nightmare?"

"Yeah." Asher dragged a hand over his face. "It's storming tonight. Maybe the thunder triggered it. I dunno. Woke up to a tree falling. Literally. It's too dark to find it right now."

"What was the nightmare?"

"Same one—the crash. I can't get anyone out. The screaming. The fire." Chills skittered across Asher's puckered skin. "I'm so tired of this."

"I'm sorry you're still experiencing them. What you're feeling is valid. Anxiety manifests itself through our dreams. Anything else stressing you right now? Where are you, by the way?"

Asher waved a hand around the room. "I'm still living in paradise, man. What do I have to stress about? My aunt and uncle's place on Jonathon Island is as far out of the spotlight as I can get. I'm managing their ranch while they're on their year-long RV tour. I'm caring for horses who are kinder than most people. So, nothing out of the ordinary."

"Right. Glad you're still there. I went to Jonathon Island as a kid. Before the hotel burned. We had the best pastries at this family-owned bakery."

"The Hudson Bakery. Hank and Henrietta Hudson ran it. Hank passed a few years ago. Hetty—Henrietta, I mean, retired after she lost her husband. Too hard to do on her own. She's my neighbor."

Asher thought back to Hetty's granddaughter, who didn't like her sleep disturbed by things like storms. Or fallen trees. Or concerned neighbors, apparently.

"The five-year anniversary is coming up."

Asher didn't need a calendar to remember the day burned into his memory. He grunted.

"Perhaps the approaching date is coming out through your dreams. How are you feeling about it?"

Asher dropped the phone on the table and stabbed the speaker button. He jumped to his feet and paced in front of the rain-splattered window. Lacing his fingers behind his neck, he wrestled with the words stuck in his throat. "How do you think I'm feeling about it? They're dead because of me. The choices I made."

"Asher, they're dead because of the accident. This isn't your fault."

"I should've said no when Chet and Dom pressured me to let them drive. They were over hours but insisted we drive through the night—and the storm—to get to the next venue on time. My bus, my fault. I couldn't save them."

"Have you read the police report your uncle gave you yet?"

"No." His eyes slid to the wooden dresser where the sealed envelope lay untouched in the top drawer.

"Maybe it's time. Then you can forgive yourself and begin healing."

Asher ran a hand over his jaw, his fingers scraping over the rough skin on the left side of his neck. "My burns are healed. I have the scars to prove it."

"I'm talking about spiritual healing."

"Yeah, well, I'm the last person God wants to hear from." An ache formed behind his burning eyes. "Listen, man. Thanks for picking up. I appreciate it. I'm going to try to see if I can crash for a little while before I need to feed the horses and muck out their stalls."

"You know where to find me, day or night."

"Thanks, man. Appreciate you." Asher ended the call and dropped back on the chair, face in his hands. He picked up the remote and found a decades-old comedy playing. He stretched out. The laugh track echoed in his head as he closed his eyes.

Now that the storm had lessened to a soft rain, maybe it would lull him to sleep.

If the nightmare didn't come back.

He needed to find a way to reconcile the past, to be redeemed from his mistakes.

Then he'd find healing.

Maybe.

Someday.

Sadie Hudson had one month to put her life back together.

If only the mistakes of the last year could've been washed away by last night's storm. Returning to Jonathon Island was supposed to give her the peace she'd been craving, but the consistent turmoil in her chest made her restless.

After her mother had come down with the flu and wasn't able to care for Gran as planned, Sadie sought refuge at her grandmother's cottage nearly a week ago to help care for her while she recovered from her recent hip surgery.

And caring for her meant giving her breakfast at a timely hour.

Smothering a yawn, Sadie dipped the remaining slice of homemade bread into the egg and milk mixture and then placed it on the heated cast-iron griddle on the middle burner of the stove.

Bubbles snapped and sizzled as the French toast cooked. She lifted a skillet off the adjacent burner and rolled the sausage links. While those finished cooking, she poured a small glass of orange juice and set it on the towel-lined tray next to Gran's steaming cup of English Breakfast tea.

Journey's "Don't Stop Believin'" came on the oldies station through Gran's Alexa that sat on the kitchen counter.

Sadie sang along with the eighties song as she moved through the cottage kitchen with white cabinets, gray countertops, and original hardwood floor.

She turned off the heat and plated the French toast and sausage. She added the food to the tray, then carried it out of the kitchen and down the small hall to Gran's first floor bedroom, humming the lyrics to the song now playing in her head.

Palming the tray, she tapped quietly, then opened the door. "Gran, you up?"

"Come in, honey. I was just spending some time with the Lord."

Sadie pushed the door open with her foot and headed into the room. Georgie, Gran's seven-year-old brown and white Lhasa apso, raced between her legs and bounded onto the bed.

"Georgie, get down. You're hurting Gran."

"Oh, he's fine." Gran wrapped her thin arms around the fluffy nuisance and gave him a hug. Then she moved her red leather Bible and matching journal off her lap and set them on her nightstand. She smiled at Sadie, her blue eyes reflecting the serenity Sadie always found comforting. She finger-combed her silver bangs away from her forehead. "What's all this?"

Sadie placed the tray on the bed in front of her. "I made French toast and sausage. I wasn't sure what kind of tea you wanted, but I found some English Breakfast in the cabinet next to the stove."

Gran pressed a hand against Sadie's cheek. "Thank you, love. It's perfect, but you didn't have to go to all this trouble for me."

Sadie laughed. "You're the one of the few people in the world that I'll do anything for."

"Same here, honey." Gran lifted her cup. "Did it rain last night, or was I imagining it? Thought I heard pounding, then Georgie barking."

"Yes, a pretty intense one. In fact, your neighbor came over and checked on you."

"Asher?" Gran smiled. "He's such a nice guy. Sorry the storm woke you."

Sadie waved away her words. "I couldn't sleep once the storm settled down, so I did some work until my alarm went off at six."

Gran exchanged her teacup for her fork and cut one of the sausage links in half. "Why are you setting an alarm? We're on island time, love."

"Island time or not, I need to stay on routine. I can't afford to become lazy. I have four weeks to figure out my future. I picked up remote copywriting work to pad my bank account until I can decide what I want to be when I grow up."

"Trust the Lord, love. He has a plan for you." Gran held out a hand and wiggled her fingers.

Easy for her to say. Gran's faith was rock solid.

Sadie reached for Gran's hand and gave it a gentle squeeze, then sat on the edge of the bed, careful not to upset Gran's tray. "To be honest, Gran, the thought of dealing with SEO, keywords, meta data, and content creation for the rest of my life digs a pit in my stomach."

"You used to love being a copywriter. You have such a lovely way with words."

Sadie released her grandmother's hand and dropped her chin to her chest. "Yeah, well, that was before the fiasco at Sternwood."

"Oh, honey. I'm so sorry you got caught up in that mess. Garrett was a cheating snake who had no business getting involved with you. He had all of us fooled."

"Especially his wife. When she stormed into the office and, in front of everyone, accused me of sleeping with her husband . . . well, I just wanted to die." Sadie's face heated as the memory from six months ago surfaced.

"Well, I'm glad you didn't. I know it hurt at the time, but you're moving through the pain, and you will be that much stronger for it."

"Strong enough not to give my heart away again."

"With the right man, you'll find it's easier than you think."

"Yeah, well, that's not going to happen. I learned my lesson."

Gran reached up and tucked a stray piece of hair behind Sadie's ear. "I heard you singing in the kitchen. It's been a while. I've missed it. Remember the concerts you and your sister used to do on the front porch for Gramps and me when you were little?"

"Lauren had the voice. I just gave her the words to sing." Her heart squeezed as more memories flooded her mind. Sadie blinked back the sudden rush of tears as she edged off the bed and moved toward the door. "I'll leave you to eat in peace. I'm going to tidy the kitchen before Dani and Lily arrive."

"Dani Sullivan and Lily Hart? They're coming here?"

"Yes, I ran into them at Martha's last night when I picked up dinner. They asked if we could get together today because Dani has an idea she wants to discuss, so I suggested breakfast here. You don't remember me mentioning it when I came back last night?"

Gran waved a hand as she picked up her fork. "Right, right. I remember now. These pain pills Doc has me on give me foggy thinking."

"You just had your hip replaced, Gran. Healing takes time. Isn't that what you just told me?" Sadie left the door open, then returned to the kitchen.

She wiped spilled milk off the counter, put the cobalt blue mixing bowl in the dishwasher, and slid a tray of French toast and sausage in the oven to stay warm. As she set the skillet in the sink of soapy water, she heard a nickering from somewhere close by.

She peered through the blue and white checked curtains and found a gray horse staring at her through Gran's open kitchen window. The skillet slipped from her hands and splashed into the water, soaking the front of her tank top.

"Uh, Gran." Sadie grabbed a dish towel as she backed away from the sink, then hurried down the hall. "There's a horse in the window."

Gran looked up from the devotional book in one hand,

her teacup in the other. She set it back on the tray. "A horse? Gray, dappled coat with a black muzzle?"

"I didn't get a great look, but that sounds about right."

"That's probably Gus. He's an escape artist who lives next door. He likes my apple trees. I'll give Asher a call to come and get him."

"Who?"

"Asher Quinn, Terry and Angie Quinn's nephew who's managing their ranch while they're RVing around the country."

"Right—the one who rang the doorbell at three this morning." The image of the soaked guy with dark hair, dark beard, and even darker eyes swam into focus. In her sleep-fogged brain, the details were a little fuzzy.

"He's always looking out for me." Gran patted the white top sheet with lavender flowers rumpled around her. "My phone's around here somewhere."

Sadie lifted the quilted lavender bedspread. The phone tumbled from the folds. She caught it and handed it to Gran.

"Thanks, love." Gran scrolled down her screen, found the number, and called. When he didn't answer, she left a message and set her phone on the tray. "Maybe you should take Gus back to the barn."

Stepping back, Sadie pressed a hand to her chest. "Me? I don't know anything about horses. And that thing was huge."

Gran waved away her words. "Aww, he's a gentle giant. Grab an apple from the kitchen, talk softly as you approach, then hold out your hand. Direct him across the lawn to the Quinn property."

She made it sound so simple. As if an apple was going to lure the horse home.

Gran raised her eyebrows and lifted her chin. "You may want to change first."

Sadie glanced at the wet, gray tank and navy running shorts she wore as pajamas. She blew out a breath and headed for the guest room down the hall, calling over her shoulder, "If I'm not back soon, you'll know that beast got the best of me."

Sadie exchanged the wet clothes for tan shorts and a red T-shirt. She pulled her hair into a ponytail and threaded it through a navy hat to help shade her eyes from the rising sun. Sliding on her sunglasses, she headed to the backyard.

The morning air chilled her arms as the wet grass soaked her flip-flops. Maybe she should've borrowed Gran's rain boots.

She rounded the side of the white cottage and stopped, a gasp whooshing from her lungs as her eyes widened.

A large tree sprawled across the patio. Splintered wood, shattered glass, broken pots, spilled dirt, and decapitated flowers littered the concrete. She followed the length of the tree and found the fractured base on the other side of the damaged split-rail fence that separated Gran's property from the Quinn ranch.

The gaping hole explained how the horse had escaped.

Sadie eyed the large animal grazing under the apple tree. Without any kind of rope, she had no clue how to get Gus back to his owners. And she'd forgotten to grab an apple out of Gran's fruit bowl. Sadie shielded her eyes and glanced at the large stone house next door.

Was it too early to knock and ask Asher to fetch the horse? It wasn't safe for the animal to be roaming free.

The sound of a chain saw whined across the yard. Okay, so someone *was* awake.

Sadie plodded through the wet grass, climbed over the fence, and headed for the neighbor's property.

She passed the dark stone house and headed down the dirt path that led to the large, white-washed building with a forest green metal roof. Scents of hay and fresh wood wafted in the morning air.

Chips of wood flew around a man bent at the waist as he sliced through the thick trunk of a different downed tree. Sawdust blanketed his cargo shorts, bare legs, and grimy work boots.

Apparently more than one tree suffered in last night's storm.

The man cut the power to the saw and straightened, pressing a hand to his lower back.

"Excuse me."

He turned. Dark sunglasses shielded his eyes, and a black ball cap covered his dark hair, shadowing his face. Stray wood chips clung to his dark beard. Faded, puckered scars ran down the left side of his neck and disappeared into the collar of his T-shirt. "Yeah?"

"Are you Asher?"

"Who wants to know?"

Feeling a sense of déjà vu, she cleared her throat and removed her sunglasses. Squinting against the morning rays shining toward her, she jerked a thumb toward Gran's house. "I'm Sadie, Henrietta's granddaughter. I believe we met early this morning when you checked on us during the storm."

"Right." He lifted two large pieces of wood and chucked them toward the growing pile next to the building.

Okay, then.

She took another step toward him. "Your horse is in Gran's backyard, and I need you to get it."

Straightening again, Asher turned and dragged the back of his wrist across his forehead, dislodging his hat. Then he reached for a half-full water bottle sitting on the ground and chugged the rest. As his head tipped back, she caught the lines and angles of his profile—straight nose, high cheekbones, and squared jaw covered in scruff. Something about him seemed familiar, but she couldn't place it.

Without a word, he headed into the large open door that led to the stable.

Sadie exhaled and followed him. "Well?"

"Well, what?" He pulled some sort of equipment off a hook near one of the empty stall doors.

"Are you going to get the horse?"

He held up his full hand. "Had to get his harness and lead rope."

"You could've mentioned that."

"I just did." He strode out of the stable.

She hurried after him. "Whatever. There's also a tree across Gran's back patio. It came from this property. You'll need to get it removed."

He started for the yard, then faced her. "Are you always this bossy?"

She swallowed the words blistering her tongue. "Would you please get your horse and remove the tree?"

He snapped a salute that would've made her father proud. "Ma'am, yes, ma'am."

Rolling her eyes, she jammed her sunglasses back on her face and headed back to Gran's.

Jerk.

What did Gran see in him?

Wasn't Sadie's problem. She didn't do mysterious. Since Asher had it practically tattooed on his skin, she planned to stay as far away as possible.

She'd been gullible once, and that was enough for a lifetime.

Trudging into the house, Sadie headed down the hall to her grandma's room. She heard talking and paused. Something in Gran's tone kept Sadie from returning to the kitchen and giving her privacy.

"Thank you, Mia. I'll have to think about it, then let you know what I decide." Gran let out a sigh.

Sadie knocked on the doorframe and stepped into the room. "Everything okay?"

Chin trembling, Gran fingered the quilt, then looked at Sadie with watery eyes. She waved a hand over the room. "The cottage needs some work if I'm going to stay here. Aging in place, I think your father called it during our phone conversation last week. My only option is to sell the bakery, so I contacted Mia Franklin. She called with the appraisal, but it's much lower than I expected. Maybe it's time to sell this place too and move into an apartment complex off island."

Sadie moved into the room and sat on the edge of the bed. "Gran, no. You love this place. It's been your home for decades. You can't leave the island. What would you do without your daily visits with Doris and Annabelle?"

"I don't want to leave, love." She waved a hand over her room. "The cottage needs a new roof, new windows . . . It's too much for one person, especially on a limited income. And the bakery's just sitting there. Seb Jonathon offered to buy it after Gramps passed away, but I couldn't part with it, sentimental fool that I was. With your father stationed in Hawaii, he's not going to want it." She shook her head. "I don't know what to do."

Sadie leaned forward and gathered her in her arms. "Don't make a rash decision based on how you're feeling right now. After Dani and Lily stop by, I'll call Mia and talk to her about the appraisal. We'll figure it out."

"Promise me one thing, love?"

"Anything, Gran."

"Don't tell your parents about me needing to sell the bakery. I'll tell them when I'm ready. Your dad's already questioning my decision to stay here. I don't want to give him more ammo to ship me off to a retirement home."

Sadie hated secrets, especially keeping things from her parents, but she also didn't want Gran to worry needlessly. "I won't say anything, Gran, but you know Dad would never do that. He's just concerned, especially after your recent fall. With them being in Hawaii, it's challenging for him to be here when you need him. I think that's what's bothering him more than anything—they aren't here for you."

Having lived around the world as an Air Force brat, Sadie always found security in her grandparents' home on Jonathon Island, and she'd do whatever she could to keep Gran in the cottage she loved so much. Even if it meant paying for the repairs herself.

But that meant taking on more SEO remote work until she could find a better job.

She'd do it for Gran. She'd been so supportive after Sadie's life had fallen apart and she'd spent the last six months treading water.

She'd figure it out.

Somehow.

Acknowledgments

Thank you for coming along on this super fun journey with the Harts and Kelleys—specifically, Lily and Declan—and the rest of the Jonathon Island clan. We hope you had as much fun reading as we did in writing this one.

There's just something about a second chance romance, isn't there? Something about high school sweethearts getting another go at things? It just grips our hearts and leaves us breathless. Add in a little enemies to more, and this one was a complete blast to write!

We hope you've been enjoying Jonathon Island and all it has to offer. If you haven't read the first two books in the series, make sure you go grab them right away. They give such a fun introduction to this charming town and these characters that feel like family.

Loving what you've read? We've got a LOT more Jonathon Island stories brewing, and we hope you stick around for the ride.

As for our thank you's, they wouldn't be complete without acknowledging several people who assisted in the editing of this story: Susan May Warren (of course!), Denise Harmer, Charity Henico, and Emma Hedges.

And for our amazing Sunrise production and marketing team (Rel, Sarah, Essie, Tari, and Katie)—thank you!! Things literally wouldn't get done without you, and we are so grateful.

To our fellow Jonathon Island authors—it has been so much to collaborate with you!

Thank you to all the bookstagrammers and book reviewers who share about our books. You get the word out in such a fun and encouraging way. We are constantly in awe of your brilliance and generosity.

To our readers—a simple thank you doesn't seem like enough, but it's what we have. Thank you.

And thanks to our families and friends who constantly support us as we daydream and write the stories in our hearts.

Finally, to God, the One who takes our failures and makes us whole in spite of them, thank you for loving us, for gifting us, and for providing the strength we needed to finish another story. We pray you use this offering to bless others.

Lindsay Harrel is a lifelong book nerd who lives in Arizona with her husband and kids. She's held a variety of professional jobs over the years, and now juggles school volunteering with being an author and editor. When she's not writing or keeping up with her children, Lindsay enjoys making a fool of herself at Zumba, curling up with anything by Jane Austen, and savoring sour candy one piece at a time.

Connect with her at www.LindsayHarrel.com.

Award-winning author **Rachel D. Russell** writes contemporary inspirational romance focused on forgiveness, redemption, and grace. She's a country girl living in the suburbs, whose resume includes presenting live-animal reptile programs, being a park ranger, a reserve police officer, and a stint in federal prison (where she worked, not lived). She makes wild attempts to balance writing under publisher deadlines with her full-time career with the federal government. When Rachel's not cantering her horse down the Oregon beaches, she's probably interrogating her husband on his own military and law enforcement experience to craft believable heroes in uniform. The rest of her time is spent enjoying her active family, including two college-age sons and three keyboard-hogging cats.

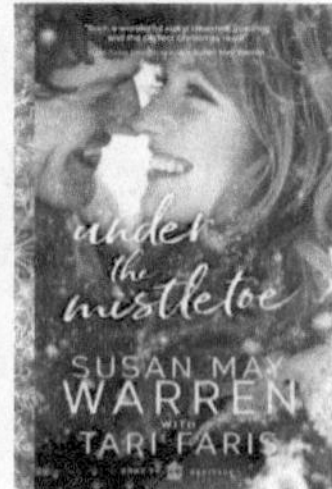

Home to Heritage

SUSAN MAY WARREN and **TARI FARIS**

with **Mandy Boerma** and **Andrea Michelle Wood**

We solve the problem of what we read next.　　Available on Amazon

**WHERE EVERY STORY IS A FRIEND,
AND EVERY CHAPTER IS A NEW JOURNEY...**

Subscribe to our newsletter for the latest news, weekly giveaways, exclusive author interviews, and more!

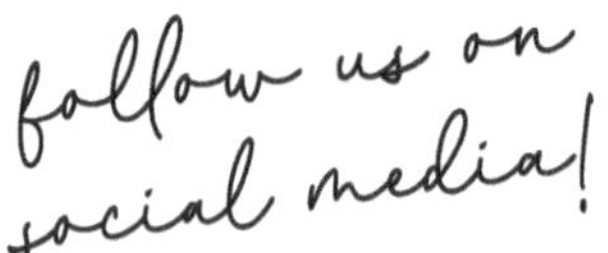

Shop paperbacks, ebooks, audiobooks, and more at
SUNRISEPUBLISHING.MYSHOPIFY.COM